As Amina sear_____ ____ ____ _____ what she was feeling, Troy reached for her hand, his own sneaking into her lap to clasp her fingers between his fingers. He pulled her hand to his lips and gently kissed the back of it. As he did a current of heat coursed from the center of her feminine spirit and spiraled throughout every nerve ending in her body. She felt her breath catch in her chest as she took a swift inhalation and held it. Tears suddenly pressed hot behind her eyelids.

"I really want to see you again," Troy said, his voice a muffled rasp rising from someplace deep in his chest.

She nodded, knowing that there was nothing and no one that would be able to keep her from seeing him again. "Just call me!" she said. "I definitely want to spend time with you."

He shook his head. "No. I want to know now when you will see me again."

Amina squeezed his fingers. "Whenever you want," she answered.

His head was still waving from side to side. "What I really want is for us not to let this night end. What I *want* is for you to stay with me and not go home. But I know I can't have what I *want*."

Also by Deborah Fletcher Mello

The Sweetest Thing

All I Want Is You
with Kayla Perrin

Published by Dafina Books

Craving Temptation

DEBORAH FLETCHER MELLO

Dafina
BOOKS

Kensington Publishing Corp.
www.kensingtonbooks.com

DAFINA BOOKS are published by

Kensington Publishing Corp.
119 West 40th Street
New York, NY 10018

All Kensington titles, imprints and distributed lines are
available at special quantity discounts for bulk purchases
for sales promotions, premiums, fund-raising, and educa-
tional or institutional use. Special book excerpts or cus-
tomized printings can also be created to fit specific needs.
For details, write or phone the office of the Kensington
Special Sales Manager, Attn.: Special Sales Department,
Kensington Publishing Corp., 119 West 40th Street, New
York, NY 10018. Phone: 1-800-221-2647.

Dafina and the Dafina logo Reg. U.S. Pat. & TM Off.

ISBN-13: 978-0-7582-9298-8
ISBN-10: 0-7582-9298-8
First Kensington Mass Market Edition: August 2014

eISBN-13: 978-0-7582-9299-5
eISBN-10: 0-7582-9299-6
First Kensington Electronic Edition: August 2014

10 9 8 7 6 5 4 3 2 1

Printed in the United States of America

*To MeeMi's sweet, sweet, baby,
Micaela Susie Mello.
Grandma loves you very much!*

Acknowledgments

Gratitude first, and foremost, to my Lord and Savior, for without his many blessings, none of this would be possible. I owe everything to a generous and loving God and I am grateful beyond measure.

There are times when telling a story I believe in comes with challenges. This one had many. Foremost was my desire to be true to a culture that many do not know and have no understanding of. It was a learning process for myself as well and a journey I feel privileged to have taken.

I have much love and appreciation for my dear friend, Amina Arnold, for allowing me into her world and for sharing her stories. Thank you for answering my questions and for trusting me to be true to the information you shared so readily.

To the family who continue to support and love me, please know that I value each and every one of you. And much appreciation to those friends who continue to motivate me to do what I do. I've got much love for you all!

Troy Elliott was not expecting the chaos that greeted him when he came through the doors of Just Desserts, the thriving Beale Street bakery that he co-owned with his brother, Quentin, and Quentin's new wife, Harper. But chaos reigned as Quentin and Harper stood staring into a massive hole that had been cut through the wall that bordered the building next door.

Troy moved to stand between them, staring where they stared. "Hey," he chimed cheerily. "What's going on?"

Quentin shook his head from side to side, tossing a nod toward Harper.

She responded excitedly. "They broke through the walls today! This expansion is going to be so perfect. The contractors promised me they'll be able to frame out this entrance by Wednesday, then we'll be able to take down this dust sheet and be right back to business."

"They still have some work to do in the new building. We won't be taking down the dust sheet. I can just hear the list of violations the health department would have for us if we did," Quentin stated. "We're losing money being closed, Harper!"

Harper rolled her eyes. "It's only two days, Quentin. Maybe three."

Troy laughed. "You know they say a renovation can kill a marriage. You two sure you want to do this so soon after saying your vows?"

Harper waved a dismissive hand at her brother-in-law. "This renovation won't challenge our marriage one bit," she said.

The two brothers locked gazes, Quentin's eyes stretched wide as he stared at his sibling. The two men suddenly burst out laughing.

"You two are not funny," Harper chided as she tossed a look at one brother and then the other. "I'm not talking to either one of you now." She pushed past the plastic wall sheet into the other space, gesturing for the building contractor's attention.

Quentin moved behind the bakery's large counter, toward the coffeepot. He poured a cup for himself and one for his brother. Troy crossed to the other side of the room, dropping down into a seat at the corner table.

"So what's on your agenda today?" Quentin asked, moving to take a seat across from his brother.

Troy took a sip of his morning brew. "I have to close out my last cases this morning. Then I have a meeting with my election committee."

"Mayor Elliott! That's going to be something. Pop would have been proud," Quentin said, referring to their mentor and surrogate parent. Pop had also been Harper's biological father.

The late Everett "Pop" Donovan had been the

brain trust behind the bakery, dedicating his life to his business and his two foster sons. His death a year earlier had taken all three of them by surprise and had cemented their familial bond in ways none of them could have anticipated. Both men enjoyed telling people how Quentin had married their sister, the reactions always priceless. It made for a good laugh-out-loud moment.

Troy couldn't have been happier for Quentin and Harper. The love the two shared was the sweetest thing. And with the two of them happy and content, both focused on the growth and success of their family business, it was now Troy's chance to do something he'd wanted for himself. To follow one of his dreams.

Running for political office was the next step to what had already been a successful legal career and Troy was excited for the new challenge. He saw putting in a bid for mayor of the city of Memphis as the beginning of a trek that would eventually lead him to a gubernatorial run or maybe even a senate seat in Washington. With no one and nothing to distract him, Troy imagined his political ambitions were limitless.

He smiled warmly. "Yeah," he said. "Pop would have been proud of both of us."

"What are you wearing?" Basil Salman asked, his gaze shooting from the top of his sister's head to the bottom of her low-heeled pumps.

Amina Salman cut an annoyed eye at her older brother. "I'm wearing clothes. What are you wearing?" she asked, her tone curt.

Basil's jaw tightened, his eyes narrowing. "Your attire is inappropriate, Amina. Father will not be happy."

Amina looked down to the conservative Ann Taylor suit that fit her petite frame nicely. She blew a deep sigh. She'd barely been in Memphis one month and her family's criticisms were already starting.

Her younger sister, Rasheeda, giggled softly. The girl was covered from head to toe in a traditional Islamic niqab, befitting their strict Muslim upbringing. No one ever criticized what Rasheeda wore. Amina shook her head, unable to see her sister's smile beneath the veil that covered her face. She turned back to eye her brother.

"I appreciate the fashion advice, Basil, but after earning two college degrees and procuring my law license in three states, I think I'm more than qualified to pick out my own wardrobe."

Basil skewed his mouth to give her a terse retort when their father, Nasser Salman, entered the room. All three of his children stopped speaking as he slowly crossed the room to take a seat behind his oak-toned desk. He looked from one to the other, his gaze pausing on Amina.

"Daughter, we have had this conversation before. I cannot control what you do in your mother's home, but you will respect my rules in my house."

Amina took a deep breath. "Yes, Father."

"So what are your plans today?"

"I've rented space to house your campaign headquarters. I need to pick up the keys and make sure all the utilities are turned on. By tomorrow I want to have most of the computers and equipment in place.

The phones will all be connected by the end of the week."

Nasser nodded as he leaned forward, resting his chin on his hands. "I'm glad that you agreed to come run my campaign, Amina. It's good to have all my children here working with me."

Amina smiled. "So am I, Father." She tossed a quick look to her brother and sister. There was a hint of hostility in her brother's hazel eyes, a smile shining in her sister's. She turned back to her father. "I actually need to get going. We need to have a press conference next week to announce your candidacy so I want to contact the local newspaper and the television stations to get that scheduled. I have a lot of work to do."

As she headed to the door Basil called after her. "You should change clothes before you leave, Amina."

Turning back around, she gave her brother a wide smile. "Whatever you say, Basil," she answered as she met her father's stern stare. As the door closed behind her that smile dropped to a deep frown. "In another lifetime maybe," she muttered under her breath as she exited the home and headed to her car.

Maneuvering her way toward downtown Memphis, Amina shook her head from side to side. Working for her father was going to be a bigger challenge than she'd fathomed, she thought. Despite her proven track record with grassroots fundraising and success as a political game changer in Atlanta, running her father's mayoral campaign was starting to feel like she'd bitten off more than she could chew.

Her mother had warned her and Amina had chosen not to listen. It had been some sixteen years since her parents' divorce. Amina had been twelve years old when she'd packed her belongings and gone with the matriarch. In Atlanta her mother had chosen to leave their Muslim faith behind, returning to her Baptist roots. Between summers with her father and the school year with her mom, Amina had been raised in both religions and was only now finding any level of comfort with her own faith and beliefs. Amina was slowly realizing that battling her father's political agenda was not going to be the only fight she would have on her hands as she wrestled with his strict values and her own moral code.

She blew a deep sigh. It was starting to feel like a chocolate doughnut kind of moment, she thought. *Maybe even two!* She suddenly smiled, a bright lift to her face as her full lips bent upward. Paused at a stoplight, she thought back to the Beale Street bakery she and her sister had found on one of their recent jaunts. There'd been a wedding reception taking place and the bakery storefront had been closed. The bride and groom had been beautiful as they'd danced together inside.

There'd been a very nice-looking man who'd spoken to them as they stood outside watching, kindly inviting them inside to share the wedding cake. He'd had the most inviting eyes and the most welcoming smile. Amina had wanted to take him up on his invitation but Rasheeda's pulling on her arm to leave had killed the mood. He'd invited them to come back the next day and had her father's plans not interfered, she would have. That had been three weeks ago and she still hadn't found her way back.

Amina pointed her car in the direction of Beale Street and Just Desserts, that chocolate doughnut calling her name loudly. As she did, she found herself hoping that she might run into that handsome stranger one more time.

"I'm sorry, but the bakery's closed for the next few days," Harper said, her gaze resting on the young woman who'd found her way inside. Under her breath she cursed whichever brother had neglected to lock the door when he'd left.

"Oh, darn!" Amina responded. "I was really hoping to get a doughnut."

Harper moved from where she stood to the other woman's side. "We're just doing some renovations but we hope to be open again by the end of the week."

Amina smiled as she extended her hand. "My name's Amina. Amina Salman. I just moved to Memphis a few weeks ago and people keep telling me about your bakery. Every time I've come though you've been closed!"

Harper winced ever so slightly. "Ouch, that's not good! I appreciate that you keep coming back though," she said with a warm smile. She shook Amina's extended hand. "I'm Harper. Harper Elliott. Welcome to Memphis!"

"Thank you. It's taking some getting used to."

"Where did you come from?"

"I grew up in Atlanta."

Harper nodded. "I'm originally from Louisiana. I moved here one year ago so I know exactly what you mean."

Amina smiled brightly. "I guess I'll try back next week."

Harper held up an index finger. "Give me a quick minute," she said as she turned and rushed to the back of the bakery. She returned minutes later with a cellophane bag in hand. "We don't have any dough-nuts but I dug into my personal stash of chocolate cookies. I don't share these with just anybody but I can't have you walk out empty-handed. Especially since this wasn't the first time we were closed on you!"

"Thank you," Amina said with a warm chuckle as she took a quick peek into the bag. "You have just made my entire day. I have a weakness for anything chocolate!"

Harper laughed with her. "Actually my motives are purely selfish. I know once you taste those cookies you'll definitely come back and I'm looking forward to becoming really good friends."

Amina nodded. "We already are," she said as she headed toward the door and waved good-bye.

Trailing after her, Harper waved back, her gaze following the woman as she moved back to her car. As he moved from behind the counter Troy called her name.

"Is everything okay?" he questioned, moving to stare where she stared.

Harper nodded. "It is," she said as she watched Amina pull out of the parking space into traffic. She waved one last time.

"Who was that?" he asked, not recognizing the vehicle.

"My new friend," Harper answered. "And she's very pretty!"

Troy cut an eye at her. "You're telling me this why?"

Harper shrugged her narrow shoulders. "You never seem to notice any of the pretty women who come into the bakery."

Troy laughed. "I notice them, Harper. I choose to

ignore them. I don't have time for a woman in my life right now."

Harper cut her eyes back at him, a sly smile on her face. "Whatever you say, Big Brother."

Troy was still laughing. "I mean it, Harper! So please don't try to play matchmaker with me and your new friend. I am not interested."

Harper moved back to her seat at the table. "Don't be interested," she said nonchalantly. "You're probably not her type anyway. I get the impression she has very discerning tastes when it comes to men."

"And how would you know that?"

Harper laughed. "She has a weakness for chocolate."

2

Harper eased herself down the stairs into the commercial kitchen. The smell of cinnamon and vanilla assaulted her nostrils. Quentin was putting the final touches on a wedding cake, the elegant six-tier confection certain to be a showstopper at the wedding of Westley and Denise Woody. He lifted his gaze as she leaned against the stainless-steel counter, resting on her elbows as she stared in his direction.

"It's beautiful!" she exclaimed.

Quentin's gaze danced over her curvaceous frame. She was wearing one of his dress shirts, the garment closed with one button. Simple leather flip-flops adorned her manicured toes. Her hair was pulled back into a loose ponytail and her natural complexion glowed. "It pales in comparison to how beautiful you are, gorgeous!"

Harper smiled. "You are such a silver-tongued devil. You make a girl blush."

Quentin laughed. "Why are you still awake, baby?"

"I was missing you. The bed's cold."

"I guess I need to do something about that," Quentin said as he lifted the cake from the counter and transferred it to a metal moving cart.

He rolled the cake into the cooler for keeping. When it was safely tucked away he dropped his work utensils into the commercial dishwasher. He washed his hands and reached for a dish towel. With one last check of the yeast rolls rising on the countertops and all the timers he turned toward his wife, a sly smile on his face.

"What are you wearing under that shirt?" he asked as he leaned back against the freezer door, his arms crossed over his chest.

Harper gave him a sultry look with the hint of a smile as she toyed with the one button on her shirt. Undoing it slowly the shirt opened just a smidgen, the barest hint of warm mocha skin peeking through.

Quentin smiled widely, a wave of heat shifting through his groin. Harper grabbed the front of the shirt with both hands and flashed him a quick look at her goodies. Beneath the shirt she wore nothing. Her nipples stood at attention and she sported a perfectly manicured landing strip between her legs.

Quentin lifted his eyes back to her face as Harper bit down against her bottom lip, beckoning him to her with a sultry, come hither look. As he moved in her direction Harper turned and began her own slow stroll toward the back stairwell. Quentin was right on her heels.

Harper was midway up the steps when Quentin eased an arm around her waist, causing her shirt to rise up on her body. He pulled her back against himself as he leaned to place one kiss on her right cheek and another on her left. Harper giggled as he followed each kiss with a gentle slap. She turned in his arms as he moved to stand on the riser beside her, dropping his mouth to hers. The kiss had her dizzy with wanting, everything about her new husband teasing her senses.

Quentin moved her against the wall, lifting her up as her legs wrapped tightly around his waist. His rising member was hard, the length of him tapping eagerly at the door to her most private place. He purred, the guttural moan rising from someplace deep in his chest.

Their kisses were fervent as their hands danced a slow drag across each other's bodies, fingers tap-dancing over warm skin. Harper whispered sweet nothings and dirty somethings into her man's ear. His eagerness rising with a vengeance, Quentin chuckled softly. Their intimate moment was suddenly interrupted when Troy swung the lower-level door open. The couple turned abruptly to stare at him just as he caught sight of them on the stairwell.

With his eyes wide Troy quickly slammed the door closed between them. He stood on the other side, the moment awkward as he fought not to laugh out loud.

"Sorry!" he said, calling out to his family. "But you two might want to consider getting a hotel room!"

The door swung open as Quentin moved back into the kitchen, his clothes readjusted. His cheeks were heated, a crimson red tint coloring his complexion. Troy could hear Harper's loud giggling fading off in the distance.

"Sorry about that," Quentin said. "We got a little carried away."

Troy shrugged. "Don't apologize to me. If you and your wife like it, I love it."

The two men stood staring at each other, then both

burst out laughing. As the moment passed Quentin waved a dismissive hand in Troy's direction. "What brings you here this time of night?"

"I couldn't sleep so I thought I'd come do the books for next month."

"I'd think you would be exhausted with the schedule you've been keeping."

"So would I," Troy said, his shoulders jutting toward the ceiling.

Quentin shook his head. "You need a woman, Big Brother!"

Troy laughed. "Not really."

"You might want to try it. I sleep well every night!"

"I'm sure you do." Troy shook his head as he moved back in the direction of the office. "Do me a favor when you go back up, please, and toss down those folders I left on the corner table in the living room."

"You can go get them."

Troy shook his head. "I might see something I don't want to see. I'm already scarred."

Quentin laughed. "Good night, Troy!"

"You're going to bed?"

"I'm going to go finish what my wife started."

Troy chuckled with his brother. "I swear I'll never be able to look at my little sister the same way ever again!"

They were finally able to reopen the bakery on Saturday morning and the space was filled to capacity. The thick aroma of rich, dark coffee and decadent treats greeted each visitor. Both Quentin and Harper were elated as they carried orders from behind the counter into the new expansion, serving the long line of customers looking for their infamous breakfast croissants and pastries. Friends, family, and tourists had come to share in their excitement.

Troy had been moving from table to table, reacquainting himself with old friends and introducing himself to anyone who didn't know anything about him. He was excited to announce his candidacy for mayor; more than ready to address the issues affecting their community.

Alice Moore, surrogate mother to Troy and Quentin, was extolling Troy's many virtues to a gathering of senior citizens who were all enjoying their morning meal together. "That boy's as good as gold!" Miss Alice chimed as she wrapped a thick arm around his waist and pulled him to her.

Troy dropped his own arm around her wide shoulders and hugged her back as he leaned against the seat she sat in. "Well, thank you, Miss Alice. I appreciate that," he said, his brilliant smile a mile wide.

Miss Alice tapped him on his backside. "Troy will do a wonderful job as mayor. Yes, he will!"

The gray-haired faction seated beside her all nodded their agreement, everyone extending Troy their best wishes. From the newly renovated space, Michael Chamberlain gestured for Troy's attention.

"Miss Alice, ladies, if you'll excuse me, please. Business calls," Troy said as he tossed them a wink of his eye.

Like a gaggle of hens the women giggled with amusement. "Good as gold!" Miss Alice repeated as Troy moved in the other man's direction.

Michael Chamberlain was seated at the family's corner table with its view of the door and window. A plate of freshly baked cinnamon rolls, still warm from the oven, sat on the table in front of him. The two men had a long history together, best friends since their freshman year at Craigmont High School when they had copied each other's answers on a science exam. Both had passed the test with better than average grades, drawing the attention of the instructor. With neither willing to admit their indiscretion, a second test with each on opposite sides of the room had been demanded. Despite passing the exam a second time, a fistfight had ensued on the bus ride home, followed by a lecture from Pop once they'd reached their destination. They'd been best buddies ever since.

With the exception of Michael's two-year trek through Europe right after college and the past year in Chicago where he'd worked as a state prosecutor, he had always called Memphis his home. He'd been eager to come back as Troy's campaign manager when the job had been offered and Troy appreciated the skill set he knew his friend Mike would bring to the table.

"These are good!" Michael chimed excitedly as Troy took the seat beside him. He licked the sugary residue from his fingers.

Reaching for one of the pastries, Troy took a large bite. "They are very good," he said.

Mike tapped at the notepad at his elbow. "Good job with the press. You looked almost presidential when you announced your mayoral run."

Troy laughed as he took a second bite. "Almost?"

His friend shrugged. "Almost. You're not quite there yet. We need to work on your wardrobe. You're not trying to make the cover of *GQ* magazine."

Troy smiled, his head waving from side to side.

"I don't know what you're talking about because I look good. You know I look good."

Mike rolled his eyes. "Trust me, bro. We just need to tone down the silk suits a tad and definitely get rid of that prep-school-graduate thing you have going on. I'm thinking something a little more country. Maybe find you a plaid blazer or two."

"Who wears plaid these days?" Harper asked as she suddenly appeared at Troy's elbow. "No one wears plaid anymore."

Troy laughed.

"Help a friend out, Harper," Mike chimed. "I was trying to ugly him up a bit. You women know about having that one unattractive friend that makes the rest of you look good, right? I'm trying to make Troy that friend."

Harper shook her head. "I don't know what you're talking about, Mike. That must be a guy thing because all of my friends are hot."

Mike shifted forward in his chair, his blond locks falling over his ocean blue eyes. "Don't you want to hook me up with one of your friends, Harper?"

"Oh, hell no!" Quentin chimed, suddenly joining the conversation. "Harper likes her friends."

"Yes, I do," Harper said in agreement.

"I'm a good guy," Mike said, his fingers lightly tapping against his chest. "In fact, I'm a great guy! Tell her, Troy."

Troy laughed. "When you're not wearing those ugly plaid jackets!"

Mike pretended to pout as he threw his hands up in frustration. "I like my plaid jackets," he said as everyone at the table laughed heartily.

The casual banter continued as the crowd in the

room began to thin out. Troy saw the woman first. She was easing her way through the intersection, mindful of the traffic that was ripping up and down Beale Street. His eyes widened as he thought back to their first encounter the night of Harper and Quentin's wedding. She'd actually come back and he felt a wide grin suddenly paint his face with excitement.

The door opening and then closing drew everyone's attention as the young woman made her way inside. She barely tossed a quick glance around the room as she moved straight to the counter, her eyes dancing back and forth over the assortment of pastries. Harper started to move from her seat when Troy stalled her.

"I've got this," he said as he jumped to his feet, a wide grin filling his face.

Harper tossed Quentin a curious look as their brother moved in the young woman's direction, his footsteps eager. They all turned to stare as he made his way to the woman's side, greeting her warmly.

"So, you came back," Troy chimed, catching her off guard.

Startled, Amina jumped, turning her gaze to meet his. Her mouth lifted into a bright smile, the gesture hidden behind the veil that covered her face. He was still as beautiful as she remembered. As he towered above her, her gaze swept from the top of his closely cropped, dark brown haircut down to the tips of his leather loafers and back. He was tall, standing somewhere in the vicinity of six feet plus a few inches. Khaki slacks and a white polo shirt adorned his solid frame. His complexion was a classic caramel, rich and smooth like melted candy. With his chiseled features, hint of a beard, smoldering chestnut-colored eyes, and full, plush lips, the man was incredibly attractive.

"Well, hello! How are you?" Amina chimed happily.

Troy's head bobbed eagerly against his thick neck. Her gaze was warm and inviting and still as stunning as that first time he'd seen it. Her eyes were wide, sitting against a complexion of pale honey. Their color was a light hazel with a hint of green and they shimmered, reflecting the midday light that brightened the room. He could feel the smile hidden behind the veil she wore. "I'm really well. It's good to see you again."

"I actually came back a few days ago but you were closed for renovations. I had a nice conversation with Harper, though."

"You met Harper?"

She smiled again. "I did. And she was very sweet. She turned me on to those really great chocolate cookies with the caramel filling and sea salt. I had to come back for some."

Troy nodded. "We can take care of that," he said, still staring intently.

There was an awkward pause. "My name's Amina, by the way," she said, extending her hand to shake his.

Troy winced ever so slightly. "Where are my manners? I'm Troy. Troy Elliott."

"It's nice to meet you, Troy."

He smiled, a sheepish look across his face. "It's nice to meet you, too, Amina." Suddenly feeling out of sorts Troy moved behind the counter. "So, what can I get you?"

"Chocolate cookies?" Amina said with a slight giggle.

Troy's head bobbed quickly. "Right. Chocolate cookies." He suddenly looked completely lost.

Harper suddenly came to the rescue, moving behind the counter to join him. "Hi, how can I help . . . ?" she started, recognition suddenly washing over her face. "Amina?"

"Hey, Harper!" Amina answered.

Harper smiled. "Girl, I almost didn't recognize you!" she exclaimed.

Amina nodded. "I know. It's my fashionable attire," she said as her gaze swept down the length of her robes.

Harper laughed. "I've seen women wearing the headscarf but why the veil?"

"My father insists on it. I would much rather just wear the hijab."

"Hijab? That's just the head wrap?"

Amina nodded. "I'm wearing the niqab," she said, explaining the difference. "It includes the veil to cover a woman's face."

"I've heard of the term hijab before. I don't think I've ever heard the other word."

"Unless you're wearing it you might not know the difference. Most people just lump it all under the hijab label. It's just easier that way." She shrugged her shoulders slightly.

"Did you just come back from mosque," Harper said, leaning against the counter. "It's mosque, right?"

Amina nodded. "Yes, it's mosque. But no. I had to attend a program at the Memphis Islamic Center on

Humphreys Road. My father insisted I participate," Amina said, her eyes rolling skyward.

Harper smiled. "Sounds like a story there."

"I'll share it with you one day," Amina responded.

"How about Tuesday?" Harper questioned. "We can do lunch?"

Amina nodded. "I would really like that," she answered.

Troy looked from one to the other, his head shifting from side to side as if he were watching a tennis match. He was surprised with the level of comfort the two women shared; the duo engaged as if they were age-old friends. Harper shot him a quick look.

"The chocolate cookies are back in the kitchen, Troy," she said, a wry smile pulling at her mouth.

He shot both women a quick look and nodded. "I'll go get those," he said, an index finger pointing toward the back as he disappeared through the swinging doors.

Harper and Amina burst out laughing.

"He's so cute!" Amina exclaimed, her voice dropping to a low whisper.

Harper nodded, whispering back. "He's a great guy. You're the first woman I know who's ever had him tongue-tied," she said with a low giggle.

Amina's eyes widened with joy. "I hope that's a good thing," she said softly.

The two women fell silent as Troy suddenly made his way back, an empty confection box in his hand. "I didn't ask how many you wanted," he said, looking from Amina to Harper and back.

Both women laughed again, the lilt of it warming the room.

Troy rolled his eyes skyward, his own grin blooming

full and wide. "Okay, I am officially embarrassed. I'm not usually this awkward," he said, his eyes meeting Amina's stare.

"Yes, he is," Harper said as she pulled the cardboard box from his hands. "How many cookies would you like, Amina?"

"I'll actually take two dozen if you have them," she answered.

Harper nodded her head as she pushed past Troy into the back kitchen area.

Troy could feel his anxiety level rising. He took a deep breath and held it. "So how long have you known Harper?" he asked, reaching for conversation.

"We just met the other day, remember?" Amina answered. Amusement shimmered in her light eyes.

The man's head bobbed against his broad shoulders, his eyes skating back and forth. From the corner table Quentin and Michael were each giving him a thumbs-up. He felt a rush of heat pierce his cheeks, color flooding his caramel complexion. He was grateful Amina had her back to them, his embarrassment already acute.

Harper suddenly returned with Amina's box of cookies, the white box sealed with the Just Desserts sticker. She and Troy were still staring at each other as Harper rang up the transaction and passed Amina her change.

"It was very nice to meet you, Troy," Amina said sweetly. "Harper, I'll see you on Tuesday."

"Great," Harper responded. "Let's meet here at eleven-thirty."

"Can we do one o'clock instead?" Amina questioned. "I have an appointment that might run over and I wouldn't want to rush or be late."

"I can definitely do one o'clock," Harper answered.

In agreement, the two women nodded as Amina shifted her eyes back to Troy. "It was very nice to see you again, Troy!" Everything about her body language confirmed the statement.

He grinned. "It was nice to see you, too, Amina," Troy said.

As she turned and headed for the bakery door, Quentin and Michael both came to their feet and applauded, cheering Troy on from the peanut gallery.

Laughing, Amina tossed Troy one last look as she waved good-bye. Her seductive stare hardened every muscle in his body. It was only after the bakery was behind her, Amina reaching her Toyota Corolla that she saw the oversize poster in the window. Troy Elliott's smiling image was looking back at her, his campaign slogan printed in bold letters: TROY ELLIOTT FOR MAYOR—WHEN ALL ELSE HAS FAILED YOU!

3

Troy stepped into a hot shower, tilting his head beneath the spray of water. He savored the sensation of wetness that rained over his face, down his broad chest, to the ceramic tiles beneath his bare feet. With both hands pressed against the shower wall he relaxed into the stinging pulsation that massaged his shoulders and back, the heated moisture feeling near perfect.

His day had been long and tedious. Laying out the game plan for his campaign was time consuming. Between planning his calendar for appearances, the telephone calls for sponsorships, and everything else necessary to kick off his campaign, he was exhausted. And exhilarated. Because support was quickly coming from people and places he had only hoped for.

He took a deep breath and then a second. He imagined that until the election he'd have little time for anything that didn't revolve around the campaign. Under normal circumstances that wouldn't have bothered him but for the first time it gave him reason to rethink what he wanted. Because for the first time he couldn't get a woman out of his mind, thoughts of Amina consuming him.

Since their encounter on Saturday, Troy hadn't been able to stop himself from thinking about her. He was curious to know more about her. There was something intriguing about the woman and it had little to do with his being unable to see her face or the wardrobe that hid her body from view. There had been something in her stare that had warmed his spirit and he liked what he saw when she'd looked at him.

Troy couldn't help but think about the old English proverb about the eyes being the window to the soul. Having only had Amina's eyes to look into had been engaging. She was spirited as evidenced by the fire in the pale orbs. And affable, her deep gaze filled with kindness and compassion. But there was something else about her eyes. Something intoxicating and sensual that fired his nerve endings with excitement.

Troy was mildly disturbed by his body's reaction to the nearness of her. Saturday had been a first for him, anxiety sweeping over him as her eyes had teased and taunted his sensibilities. He'd been nervous and tongue-tied, every ounce of rational thought melting beneath her gaze. And excited, her presence igniting a wave of heat through his groin as his muscles had hardened with the look she'd given him. Troy's composure had been lost and no other woman in his life had ever affected him like that. Amina had him feeling some kind of way and he found it both intriguing and disconcerting.

Blowing a deep sigh Troy reached for his washcloth and the bar of soap that rested below the showerhead. As he lathered his body, his hands gliding over his muscles, the scent of patchouli and vanilla teased his nostrils. He couldn't help but smile, the organic cleanser representing yet another change in the family home since Harper's arrival. Her feminine presence had completely transformed the all-male aura the home had once exuded.

Troy hadn't planned to stay over but his last meeting with his friend Mike had lasted longer than any of them had planned. Both Harper and Quentin had insisted he stay since both knew his day would be starting early. Troy had resisted at first, thinking nothing of making the thirty-minute drive to his Oak Ridge home. And then he remembered that the next day was Tuesday and Amina was coming back on Tuesday. He didn't want to risk missing another encounter with the beautiful woman. Troy was suddenly grinning from ear to ear at the prospect of seeing her again.

Stepping out of the shower Troy wrapped a large white towel around his solid frame, swiping at the moisture against his skin. As he stared at his reflection in the mirror he couldn't help but wonder if Amina had given him a second thought since he'd made a bumbling fool of himself. His head waved gently from side to side as he imagined the thoughts that had to have run through her mind. Hopefully he'd be able to redeem himself when he saw her next, he mused. Hopefully seeing her again might be eventful for them both.

Amina whispered her last prayer of the day, then crawled into the twin bed in her sister's room. Rasheeda was already snoring softly on the other side of the small space, the deep inhalation and exhalation of her breath muffled beneath the covers. It had been a long day and the next was going to be even longer as they officially announced her father's run for the mayoral office. She was looking forward to that moment being over, when she could steal away to have lunch with her new friend Harper and maybe see Troy Elliott one more time.

Amina smiled as she pulled the covers around her thin frame, a light chill running up her spine. She'd been thinking about Troy since their last meeting at the bakery, anxious to know more about him. She was also curious to know more about his run for mayor, to discover how his platform was different from or similar to her father's. She hated to acknowledge that her attraction to the beautiful man was suddenly a conflict of interest that could easily prove to be problematic.

She pinched herself, her head waving from side to side against the down pillows. She had no business being interested in any man. That wasn't why she'd come to Memphis and it definitely didn't fit into the plans her father suddenly seemed to have for her future. She rolled onto her back, pulling an arm up and over her head. As she stared toward the ceiling, Amina's mind raced, conflicted by the mountain of emotion flooding her spirit.

She was surprised that Troy Elliott had managed to capture her attention and hold it. There was something about the good-looking man that had her excited to know more. That interest went against the grain of everything she prescribed to. But the man's presence was magnanimous and when he walked into a room he captivated everyone's attention. Such an ability would make him a formidable opponent. It also teased her feminine spirit, striking heat deep in her center. That heat radiated into every nerve ending and left her in a thick sweat. Amina couldn't remember any man ever making her feel that way.

Since graduation from law school she'd been focused solely on her career and her ability to effect positive change in the community. A relationship had never been on the agenda. But since meeting Troy she was suddenly fantasizing about a relationship, pondering the mechanics of sharing her life with a man. She must have fallen and bumped her skull, she mused, a smile pulling at her mouth.

Amina heaved a deep sigh. Even if she wanted a relationship, her father would never approve of her being with a man who was not Muslim, and her mother would be adamant that she *not* marry a Muslim man. Amina knew she'd be caught smack-dab between a rock and a hard place. The more she thought about it, she fathomed that it would be better if she abandoned all carnal thoughts she suddenly found herself having. Nothing good could ever come from her giving any credence to such a thing. But minutes later she was still tossing from side to side, unable to get thoughts of Troy out of her head.

"I think it's love at first sight," Harper mused, a wide smile filling her face. She looked from her husband to his brother and back, the two men standing in deep conversation as Quentin tested a new bread recipe.

Troy rolled his eyes skyward. "No one said anything about love, Harper," he stated.

Quentin shook his head. "Why are you eavesdropping on our conversation?" he questioned, his eyebrows lifted as he met his wife's stare.

"You two are standing in the middle of the kitchen and expect that no one is listening to your conversation? Really?" Harper tossed a look to the other employees in the room.

Everyone around them laughed heartily. The two brothers cut an eye at each other as Harper continued.

"If you want to have a conversation about a woman and not have anyone hear you then you might want to talk in a more private place," she said matter-of-factly.

Troy nodded. "Point taken," he said with a soft chuckle. He should have known better than to mention his interest in Amina to his brother while they were in the bakery. Harper had been nowhere in sight when he'd come down the back staircase but her eagle ears hadn't missed a word. Having a woman in the space was still causing some adjustments between the two men.

"But she's cute, isn't she?" Harper chimed. "And you like her, right?"

Quentin laughed. "I can't help you, Big Brother!"

Troy laughed with him. "Thanks!" He turned his attention back to Harper. "Why wouldn't I like her, Harper? Amina seems like a very nice girl."

"Well, then you should come say hello," Harper replied. "She's in the front." Harper reached to give her husband a kiss. "I'll be back in a few hours, honey!"

Quentin kissed her back. "Have fun! I love you!"

Harper grinned as she turned an about-face. "Ah, love! You should try it, Troy," she said, tossing her brother-in-law a wide smile as she moved back toward the door and disappeared from view. Troy and Quentin both laughed again.

Following on her heels Troy hesitated for a brief

second. Taking a deep breath he tossed Quentin a quick glance over his shoulder before moving into the other room.

Amina and Harper were standing in the center of the room when Troy made his way inside the store-front. He came to an abrupt halt as Amina turned toward him, a bright smile on her face. The sight of her took his breath away, air catching deep in his broad chest.

Her bright eyes shimmered against her crystal complexion. She was smaller than he'd realized, her petite stature making her appear almost fragile. She wore a tailored navy dress with pearl buttons running the length of the bodice and pumps with just a hint of heel giving her some height. She had a wisp of a waist and just enough curve to her body to quicken a man's pulse. Natural auburn curls cascaded past her shoulders, the reddish brown tones complementing her warm coloration. With her hazel eyes radiating vivaciously, she was absolutely stunning.

The two women giggling brought Troy back to his senses. He shook his head, his eyes blinking rapidly as he moved to where they stood.

"Good afternoon, Troy!" Amina chimed warmly.

He cleared his throat, finding his voice. "Amina, how are you?"

Her smile was full and wide. "I'm really well. It's good to see you again."

"It's good to see you again, too," he responded. "Wow!" he exclaimed, the word flying past his full lips before he could catch it.

Amina's smile widened.

Harper laughed heartily. "Well, Amina and I are off to lunch. Would you like to join us?" she asked. She waved an index finger in his direction, gesturing for Troy's attention.

He struggled to take his eyes off Amina and meet Harper's intense gaze. "Oh . . . well . . . I . . ." he suddenly stuttered, unable to think coherently.

The two women shot each other a look and giggled.

Troy took a deep breath, heat coloring his cheeks a deep red. "I can't. I wish I could but I have a meeting with Mike," he said, words returning to him.

"Maybe next time?" Amina said, the comment coming as a question.

Troy nodded. "I would like that. I would like that a lot."

She grinned warmly. "So would I. A lot!"

Harper shook her head. "You two can arrange that when we get back. Bye, Troy!" she said as she ushered Amina toward the door.

"Good-bye!" he said, lifting his hand in an easy wave.

Tossing him one last look as they made their way out of the bakery Amina waved back, everything about her making Troy wish he could follow behind them. He heaved a deep sigh and then a second as he watched the two women get into Amina's car and disappear into traffic.

Quentin moved to his side, two cups of coffee in hand. "Harper might have a point," he said when his brother turned to give him a look.

"What do you mean?" Troy questioned.

"It might be love at first sight!"

Troy shook his head. "I don't know about love, but it's definitely something. The woman's got me tongue-tied and sweating. I'm usually a lot more together than that around women. She's ruining my image."

Quentin laughed as he passed one of the mugs to

Troy. The two men moved into the new space and took a seat. Both paused to admire the décor. Harper had duplicated the design from the original interior, continuing the warm celadon green color on the walls and the chocolate-tinted concrete on the floors. Just a handful of tables decorated the space, affording them the ease of manipulating the seating as each event dictated. Eventually there would be a separate catering kitchen in the back, that area still under construction.

Two flat-screen televisions sat high in opposite corners. Both Quentin and Troy had been opposed to the additions but eventually agreed once Harper had pitched the decorative framed cases that could easily hide them from view. They had quickly become a popular attraction for the clientele; morning customers starting their day with the early news and the after-school crowd enjoying cartoons. The televisions were still playing although the space was empty, the midday crowd having thinned out considerably.

The brothers were enjoying their coffees when something on the television screen caught Troy's eye. "Hey," he exclaimed, sitting forward in his seat. "Do you have the remote? Turn that up," he said.

Quentin shifted in his seat to stare where Troy pointed. He reached for the remote and increased the volume. The local television station was broadcasting the afternoon news. The newscaster had noted a forthcoming story, the byline announcing someone's bid for mayor. Days earlier they had all watched the same announcement play out about Troy. When the channel returned from its commercial break, the newscaster played back an early morning press conference.

Town councilman Nasser Salman had announced his candidacy with his family standing by his side.

Troy and Quentin turned to stare at each other at the same time. Neither had missed the beautiful woman who'd stepped up to introduce herself as Salman's campaign manager. The camera loved everything about his daughter Amina.

4

Amina and Harper were laughing gleefully, the abundant chortle drawing the attention of everyone around them. Amina swiped at a tear that had dripped past her thick lashes, rolling its way over her full cheeks. She suddenly tossed a quick glance down to the watch on her thin wrist.

"I had no idea it was so late!" Amina exclaimed, her eyes widening.

Harper looked at her own wristwatch. "Me neither. I'm sure my husband is wondering what happened to me."

"He won't be upset with you, will he?" Amina asked, concern washing over her expression.

"No, of course not. If he needed me he would have called," Harper answered.

Amina nodded. She didn't bother to comment on the twelve missed calls registered on her iPhone. "My father is probably having a fit right about now, wondering where I am."

"You didn't tell him where you were going?"

Amina shook her head from side to side. "He

probably would have forbidden me to come. If not him, then definitely my brother."

Harper rolled her eyes skyward. "I wish I did have a brother who would try to tell me what I could and couldn't do," she said facetiously. "Ours would not be a harmonious home!"

"I know that's right!" Amina said, nodding her agreement. I don't know how my sister, Rasheeda, does it. My brother, Basil, tells her to jump and she'll ask how high. He really intimidates her and I hate that she won't stand up to him."

"Has he always been that way?" Harper asked, curious to know more. She reached for her glass of white wine and took a sip.

Harper shrugged. "Probably. We were just kids when our parents divorced. Basil was twelve. I was ten and Rasheeda wasn't quite six years old. Basil and Rasheeda stayed with our father who had custody of us. But I wanted to be with my mother. After a month of me acting out and throwing horrific tantrums my father gladly let me go. I tried to get Rasheeda to come with me but she was too afraid. She's always been Daddy's baby. So my mother raised me in Atlanta and my brother and sister stayed here in Memphis."

"That's so sad."

"I used to come visit but everything was always a problem. My clothes, my hair, everything! So I stopped and my father would never let them come stay with us in Atlanta. We missed out on a lot of time with each other over the years. That's why I agreed to come to Memphis and work for my father. I was hoping it would help us all to rebuild our relationships."

Harper nodded her understanding. "I grew up

estranged from my father too. He died before I had the chance to know him. I came to Memphis for his funeral and that's when I met Quentin and Troy. My father raised them. You're lucky that your family is still here and you have this opportunity. I hate when people tell me what a great man my father was and I know I'll never have the chance to experience that for myself."

Amina smiled. "I agree, which is why I am trying very hard not to let Basil or my father's ways get to me. Both are very conservative and they still think women should be seen and not heard. I think my father's hiring me for his campaign is his way of trying to meet me in the middle. That's why I agree to wear the niqab and attend mosque when he asks."

"So you don't practice Islam anymore?"

Amina shook her head. "I'm not a faithful follower. There's much about the religion I don't know or understand but because I love my father I've been willing to learn."

Harper nodded. "Quentin and Troy are steadfast Baptists. I don't think either has missed a Sunday service since I moved here. I'm not so good about that kind of thing. But I have a lot of faith and I respect what they believe and what they practice."

"Exactly. My mother shied away from religion so I didn't grow up in the church either. But because of my situation I minored in religious studies in school. I've read the Bible and now I'm studying the Quran. In all honesty though I'm probably more Buddhist in my thinking than anything else. I won't be telling my father that though. Not anytime soon anyway," Amina said with a soft chuckle.

Harper laughed with her.

Amina changed the subject, a light sparkling in her eye. "So, tell me, is Troy dating anyone?"

Harper shook her head from side to side. "No one. I've tried to fix him up a few times but nothing has ever worked out. He makes it very hard for a woman to get close to him."

"I really wanted to get to know him better but I guess that might not happen now," Amina said, blowing a deep sigh.

Harper laughed. "You two working on opposing campaigns might be a problem," she said, still surprised with the news Amina had shared earlier. She leaned forward in her seat. "But then, you never know what you might be able to make happen if you put your mind to it."

"I really hope so!" Amina gushed with a bright smile. "I really do!"

Troy and Michael were seated in a corner talking strategy when the two women returned from their afternoon jaunt. Both men fell silent, staring intently as Amina trailed behind Harper into the bakery.

Quentin greeted both women warmly as he moved from behind the counter to wrap his wife in a hug. "How was your lunch?" he asked.

"We had a great time," Harper answered, kissing him easily.

"We really did," Amina echoed. She extended her arm. "Hi. You must be Quentin. I'm Amina."

Quentin shook her extended hand. "It's nice to officially meet you, Amina. And welcome to Memphis!"

"You have a wonderful business here," she said. "I'm officially addicted to those chocolate cookies!"

Quentin laughed. "Thank you. I appreciate that! We'll need to make sure we always have some stashed away for you. I have to hide them though. Harper gets a little greedy every now and then."

Harper punched him playfully in the arm. "I do not!"

Quentin hugged her tightly a second time, leaning to kiss her forehead. "Okay, baby. Whatever you say."

"I don't!" Harper exclaimed as she rolled her eyes skyward.

Amina laughed. The newlyweds were endearing, their very public displays of affection warming her spirit. They seemed perfect for each other and she couldn't help but be a little jealous. Amina found herself wondering what it might be like to be in love with a man who complemented her personality like Quentin seemed to complement Harper's. A man who thought nothing of showing his affection. As she stood watching her new friends with their easy caresses and light touches, she found herself imagining a man's hand pressed against her own waist, his lips grazing her brow, his fingers dancing across her bare skin. She was suddenly embarrassed to have given such thoughts any consideration and her face flushed warm with color.

She took a deep inhalation of air and then a second, fighting to stall her wayward imagination. Diverting her attention elsewhere she stole a quick glance around the space. She couldn't stop herself from hoping that she might catch a glimpse of Quentin's brother.

Across the way Troy was still staring at her, his intense gaze causing her breath to catch deep in her chest as their gazes connected. Her face lifted brightly,

her smile stretching from ear to ear. She was tempted
to ease herself to his side when she was suddenly bom-
barded by his campaign manager.

Mike's hand was damp and clammy as he shook
hers eagerly. "I'm Mike Chamberlain, Ms. Salman.
Troy Elliott's campaign manager."

"It's a pleasure to meet you, Mr. Chamberlain," she
said politely. "Your reputation precedes you."

Mike's head bobbed eagerly against his thick neck.
"So, you've heard of me! That's good to hear," he said
as he brushed the back of his fingers against the
breast panel of his plaid jacket. "I'm pretty good at
what I do, if I can say so myself!"

Amina gave him one of her sweetest smiles. "From
what I know you've worked on some twenty campaigns and won two of them. Is that right?"

There was a moment of pause as Mike's eyes blinked
rapidly. "My numbers are much better than that," he
finally sputtered. "I've worked on eighteen winning
campaigns!"

Amina laughed, knowing full well that she had
purposely inverted his win results. "I'm sure they are,"
she said.

Mike pulled at his jacket, buttoning it closed
around his beer belly. "I hope you're not planning to
get *too* comfortable in our little camp here. We can't
have a whole lot of fraternizing going on between our
two teams," he said as he shot Harper a look. "We
wouldn't want any secrets spilled."

Amina chuckled softly. "They say politics makes for
strange bedfellows, Mr. Chamberlain. You never know
what might happen."

He paused for a brief moment as he reflected on
her comment. Then he spoke. "Well, I do hope that

we can pit our candidates against each other in a debate at some point. Give the people a good show."

"You mean provide an opportunity for the constituents here in Memphis to make a side-by-side comparison of both candidates so that they can make an informed decision and vote objectively?"

The man hesitated for a brief moment. "Okay, that works, too," Mike said. There was a feigned look of confusion on his face. He shot his best friend a glance and winked an eye.

Moving behind the man Troy laughed. "Don't let him fool you, Amina. He really is good at his job," he teased, brushing his good friend aside. "But it does make me question if he's as good as you are, since it would seem you know more about his résumé than he knows about yours."

Amina smiled. "He isn't," she said matter-of-factly.

Mike tossed up his hands. "I take offense at that," he said, looking from one to the other. When neither bothered to give him a glance he eased his way over to where Quentin and Harper were watching with interest, taking his own front-row seat.

Troy met her gaze, clearly fascinated by her self-assurance. He nodded his head slowly, his eyes still locked tightly with hers. "You're a highly organized political professional with exceptional research, writing, and analytical skills. You have multiple years of public service experience, working with government, nonprofits, and political candidates. You have a proven capacity to handle confidential and time-sensitive documents and materials; the ability to multitask and adapt to changing work priorities and environments; and you're adept at communications with people from diverse cultural backgrounds and age groups."

"Someone's been doing his homework."

Troy grinned and shrugged his shoulders. "You were a political reporting specialist with Nielsen, Crosby, and Gross in Atlanta. You worked as a field manager for three high-profile senators and ran the campaigns of four governors and one other mayor. Plus, you hold some seriously impressive fund-raising records, as well as being licensed to practice law in three states. Those are some very successful accomplishments for someone so young, which indicates you're a high-achiever with a strong work ethic."

Amina nodded. "Anything else?"

"Your favorite color is lavender, daylilies are your favorite flower, and your favorite food is anything Italian. You enjoy quiet walks on the beach, soft jazz in front of a fireplace, Shakespearean sonnets, and you collect fine art, preferably figurative work. You also enjoy reading mysteries."

Amina's eyes narrowed ever so slightly.

"If I didn't know better, Troy Elliott, I'd think you might be a bit of a stalker."

Troy laughed. "Why would you think that?"

"Googling my Match.com profile is a wee bit excessive, don't you think?"

He shrugged his broad shoulders. "I need to know what I'm up against. It was necessary to access everything I could on my competition."

Amina's smile widened. "I'm not your competition. My father is. I hope you were as thorough researching him."

"I was," Quentin said, his gaze still dancing with hers.

A ripple of sexual tension suddenly vibrated through her body. She took a deep breath and held it for a quick moment before blowing the air past her thin lips. With her cell phone suddenly vibrating in her pocket, Amina bit down against her bottom lip, her confident expression shifting to a bevy of nerves.

Troy found himself wondering what her lips might feel like against his. He imagined they'd be sweet and soft like sugared silk gliding across his mouth. Heat rained in a southern direction and he felt his muscles harden. He took a deep breath and held it, hoping to stall the rising sensations.

"Well, I need to be going," Amina suddenly said, fighting her own growing emotions. "It was good to see you again, Troy."

Troy nodded. "The pleasure was all mine."

Amina turned and headed for the exit, waving her good-byes toward the Elliott family. Troy called after her.

She turned and eyed him curiously. "Yes?"

"How's that dating site working for you?"

Amina laughed, the warmth of it shooting a current of electricity up Troy's spine. "It's not," she answered.

Troy nodded. "Good, because I would really like to take you to dinner."

5

Amina's brother was still ranting at her. He'd been ranting since she'd come through the front door, had ranted through dinner, and he was still raging. He'd gone through the alphabet, his discourse covering everything from her attitude to her zealous disregard for everything he valued. She rolled her eyes for the umpteenth time and blew a loud sigh.

"That's enough, Basil," their father finally said, blowing his own loud sigh.

"But, Father . . ."

"Enough I said!" Nasser had raised his voice for the first time. His chocolate complexion furrowed with frown lines. As children they'd thought he looked like a black Patrick Stewart, the actor from *Star Trek*. His youthful appearance belied his age but he suddenly looked tired. His hair was snow white, a stark contrast to his skin tone and his eyes were bright. He lifted those eyes to Amina. "Daughter, the next time, just remember to check in with one of us so that we do not worry about you. I do understand that things happen. Perhaps we should get you one of those phone chargers for your car so that the next time your battery dies you can recharge it easily."

Amina nodded. "I'll pick one up tomorrow. And, I apologize again, Father. I didn't mean to worry you."

Nasser nodded. "I see that you scheduled an early morning meeting with the campaign staff tomorrow so I am going to turn in for the night. Good night, children," he said as he kissed Amina's cheek and then Rasheeda's. He wrapped Basil in a warm embrace. "Rest well, Son," he said as he exited the room.

As the door closed behind him, Amina tossed her brother a look, her eyes narrowed, her jaw tight. The expression on her face dared him to say one more word. Rasheeda interceded.

"I'm sorry that your phone died, Amina. If you want me to pick that charger up for you I will."

Amina tossed her sister a quick look. She took a deep breath and blew it out slowly. "Thank you, Rasheeda. I really appreciate that."

Basil stomped toward the door. He turned abruptly, his anger still raging. "You don't fool me, Amina," he snapped. "I will not let your bad behavior embarrass this family."

"Shut up, Basil," Amina snapped back. "Shut up and mind your own business and not mine. You are not the boss of me!"

If looks could kill, Amina imagined she would have been standing dead in her low-heeled pumps from the look her brother was giving her. Hostility rained from his pale eyes and in that brief moment Amina couldn't imagine them ever having a healthy relationship. Tears suddenly burned hot behind her eyelashes.

Basil muttered something under his breath and

Amina knew the words were nothing but ugly. He pointed a finger toward her, shaking it vehemently as he suddenly moved too quickly in her direction. Rasheeda jumped to her feet, moving between the two of them, her hands raised as if in surrender.

She shook her head. "Stop, Basil! Father would not like this!" Rasheeda exclaimed. Her voice was a loud whisper as she repeated herself, urging him to calm down.

Basil looked from Rasheeda to Amina, his eyes skating back and forth from one to the other. "School your sister," he finally spat. "She better learn her place and she better learn it quick."

Amina bristled. "If there's something you think I need to learn, Big Brother, then educate me yourself. Rasheeda doesn't need to run interference between us."

He stepped toward her a second time, Rasheeda pushing against him with both palms.

"You can act like a fool if you want, Basil, but you don't scare me," Amina said, both hands falling to her lean hips in defiance.

Still glaring, Basil hesitated for a brief moment before finally taking a step back. He shook his head from side to side. Turning back toward the door, he paused in the entranceway. "You need to be scared," he said emphatically.

Amina's two hands clenched into tight fists, her gaze narrowed. "You should be, too, Big Brother. You should be, too!"

The door slammed harshly behind their brother. His footsteps vibrated across the hardwood floors toward the front door. When Amina heard it slam as well she let go of the breath she'd been holding. She dropped down onto the leather sofa, her body shaking from the adrenaline.

Rasheeda was still standing, her head waving. "You should not taunt him, Amina," she said, turning to face her sister.

"He shouldn't be such a bully," Amina responded. She shifted forward in her seat. "Why do you let him treat you like that, Rasheeda?"

"He's really not so bad."

"Yes, he is. He has no right to talk to either of us that way. I'm going to speak to Father about him."

"Please, leave it alone, Amina. You don't understand him and you really have no right to come into our lives now and cause trouble."

"I wasn't trying to cause trouble, Rasheeda."

Rasheeda shrugged. "Just do what you're asked, please. Work on Father's campaign and let Basil be the man Father wants him to be. Had Mother raised you properly we wouldn't be having any of these problems."

Amina bristled. "Don't you dare talk about her like that! Those are Father's words and he has no right to bash her. Our mother raised me well and she's been proud of all of my accomplishments. Had you made any effort to have a relationship with her you'd know that."

The two women stood staring at each other, a wave of emotion billowing between them. Eventually Rasheeda turned and headed toward the door. "It's time for our evening prayers," she said, tossing a quick glance over her shoulder. "You do still pray?"

Amina's head waved ever so slightly. "Don't be a bitch, Rasheeda," she said softly. "I really don't need that from you."

Without saying another word Rasheeda turned and made her exit. Minutes passed before Amina made any effort to move. Her tears had finally fallen, raining down her face. She hated that her nearly perfect day was ending on such a sour note.

She'd been excited when she'd finally made her way home. Troy Elliott had invited her to dinner and they'd made tentative plans for the following week. Amina had hoped to share her excitement with her sister but within minutes of coming through the front door Basil had begun to berate her and her father had allowed it.

She hated that she'd told a little white lie about her cell phone battery having died—that being the reason she'd not returned any of their calls. And she disliked not being able to tell her family where she'd been. But she knew telling the truth would have opened a whole other can of issues between them. Keeping secrets from them was surely not the kind of relationship she wanted to have with her father or her siblings. But they weren't making things easy and she didn't want her father to be disappointed with her.

Amina swiped at the tears that dampened her cheeks. Blowing a deep sigh she knew that her next move wasn't going to sit well with any of her relatives either. But prayer was going to have to wait. She needed someone to talk to and since she couldn't talk with her sister, a long-distance call to her mother was definitely necessary.

Amina was still pouring over paperwork when her cell phone rang. The chime was unexpected and her focus was so deep that it startled her. She jumped, the papers piled on the bedspread before her falling into disarray. The device chimed a second time and her sister shifted in the other bed, lifting her head to stare at her.

Amina and her mother had finished their conversation hours earlier so she couldn't begin to imagine who would be calling her at such a late hour. She disrupted her paperwork even more as she reached across to the nightstand, hurrying to silence the noise. Pulling the phone into her hand, she didn't recognize the number that blinked for her attention.

"Hello?"

"Amina, hello! It's Troy Elliott." His voice was pure molasses; thick, rich, and sweet, the seductive cadence coming as a complete surprise.

"Troy, hi!"

"I know it's late. I hope I'm not calling at a bad time," the man intoned.

She shook her head, oblivious to his not being able to see her. "No, not at all," she said, her own voice a loud whisper. "Can you hold on for a second?"

"Sure."

Amina eased her body off the bed. She tossed Rasheeda a slight smile, the girl staring at her through glazed eyes. Moving into the connected bathroom Amina closed and locked the door. A night light illuminated the space. She pulled the shower curtain aside and stepped into the porcelain tub, settling herself comfortably in the corner.

She took a deep breath and then a second as she pulled her phone back to her ear. "Sorry about that.

I share a room with my sister and I didn't want to wake her."

"It's not a problem. I understand completely."

"How did you get my number?" she asked, remembering that she'd not given it to him.

"I bribed Harper for it. I hope you don't mind."

Amina could feel herself smiling, a wide grin spread across her face. "Bribed?"

"My sister-in-law has a wicked shoe obsession. I'm told my money is going to buy her a great new pair."

Amina laughed. "That's too funny!" She could sense Troy smiling on the other end.

"You weren't in bed or anything were you?" Troy questioned.

"No. I was just sorting through some paperwork."

"Burning the midnight oil. I'm impressed."

"You should be," she said. "I'm not planning on losing this election."

Troy laughed. "Neither am I."

"That might be a problem for us," Amina said.

"Not if we don't let it be."

There was a pregnant pause as Amina considered his words. "You never told me why you called," she finally said, breaking the silence.

Troy hesitated for a brief moment before he answered. "To be honest, I just wanted to hear your voice," he replied.

Amina gasped, his frankness surprising her. She didn't know how to respond and so she said nothing. The silence was awkward for a second time.

He called her name. "Amina?"

"I'm still here."

"I didn't mean to be so forward. I just . . . well . . ." Troy stammered, suddenly at a loss for words.

She took a deep inhalation of air, blowing it out slowly. "I'm glad you called," Amina whispered.

Troy blew his own breath into the receiver, a weight feeling like it had been lifted off his shoulders. "You had me worried for a moment," he said.

Amina laughed. "You don't do this often, do you, Mr. Elliott?"

"I really haven't done something like this ever," Troy answered.

"I find that very hard to believe."

"Why?"

"I just imagine that you have a ton of women vying for your attention."

Troy laughed. "Well, you can be assured that you are the only woman who *has* my attention."

"Why?"

"You know why."

"No," she said emphatically. "I don't."

Troy took another deep breath and held it, seeming to choose his words carefully. "Because there is something special about you, Amina Salman. I saw it in your eyes. That's why."

She felt a rush of heat course through the pit of her stomach as butterflies took flight. No man had ever made her feel the way she was suddenly feeling about Troy Elliott. She took a deep breath and held it.

Amina wasn't necessarily naive when it came to the ways of men. She'd been dating since high school, some good and some not so good guys. Her mother had been supportive of most of her choices. A select few hadn't given either of the women any warm and fuzzy feelings. Too many lunches and dinners had never amounted to much of anything, not one teasing her sensibilities the way Troy was suddenly teasing her.

Amina could only imagine what her father would have to say, especially since her twenty-one about-to-be twenty-two-year-old sister had yet to enjoy any man's company.

Two hours later she and Troy were still talking, banter flowing easily between them. When Rasheeda knocked on the bathroom door, the harsh rap jarred Amina back to the moment. She depressed the mute button on her cell phone.

"I won't be much longer, Rasheeda!" she said.

"Hurry up! I have to go," the girl whined.

"I promise, I'll be right out," Amina repeated. She resumed her conversation. "Troy, I hate to end this but it's late," Amina said.

"I understand," Troy said. "I appreciate your not hanging up on me sooner."

Amina smiled into the receiver. "You have a good night, Troy."

"Can I call you again tomorrow?" Troy asked, "Or maybe you can stop by the bakery for a cookie?"

Her smile widened. "Definitely call me again," she said, her voice a loud whisper.

"Good night, Amina," Troy whispered back.

"Sweet dreams, Troy!"

Amina and her father were already at odds over his political stance. He'd come out of the gate being critical of the current mayor and Amina wholeheartedly disagreed with that approach. They'd been butting heads most of the morning about him publicly voicing negative opinions about his opponents.

"Father, you would be better served to present a positive front about your platform. Focus on the changes you would make if elected, not what your opponents are doing wrong."

Basil chimed in with his two cents. "Father should point out their shortcomings. He needs to let people know that he would do things differently. He wouldn't award contracts to his friends. He wouldn't underfund the schools or the police department and the incumbent has done all those things and more. You've heard the rumors about his other dealings."

Amina blew a deep sigh. "It's only been *alleged* that the current mayor has done those things, Basil, which is why Father doesn't need to risk making them issues without definitive proof. Father's campaign needs to be about the strengths he brings to the table that will benefit the citizens of Memphis. We do not want to run a negative campaign."

Basil shrugged his shoulders, his eyes rolling skyward. "I don't agree."

"You don't have to," Amina responded. She looked toward her father, waiting for him to respond.

Nasser looked from one offspring to the other. "I am personally offended, Amina, by the mayor's actions. He's cut services for our youth and the elderly while giving incentive packages to a number of corporate interests. I agree with Basil. I think voters need to be reminded of that and I think I can point those shortcomings out and show how I'll govern differently at the same time."

Amina wished she could smack the smirk off Basil's face, his grin wide and full. She blew another deep sigh, feeling that her father taking such a position was a mistake and would not serve his campaign well. She told him so.

Nasser nodded. "I appreciate your opinion, Amina, but that's the direction I plan to go in."

"I still don't agree that attacking the current mayor is a good thing. And what about the other candidates and their positions? Do you plan to attack them, too?" Amina questioned.

Basil interjected a second time. "What other candidates? The mayor is Father's only true competition and only because he already has the job."

Amina rolled her eyes. "Basil, that kind of arrogance will not get Father elected. There is a very worthy list of candidates all vying for this position and you cannot take that for granted. He's going to have to beat out a field of twenty-five people who have declared their candidacy, including Mark Prentiss, who's the Shelby County public defender, and attorney Troy Elliott, who has an impeccable public reputation."

"His reputation is not that impeccable," Basil chimed.

Amina bristled ever so slightly. "Do you know him?"

"Who, the public defender?"

"No, Troy Elliott."

Basil shrugged. "Not really but I'm sure if we dig deep enough we can easily find some dirt on him to knock him out of the running. Like I said, Father has no true competition."

Amina threw her hands up in frustration. She turned to her father. "May I speak with you privately, please?"

Nasser nodded, waving a dismissive hand at Basil. Her brother hesitated for a brief second before turning an about-face and moving to the other side of the room.

Amina reiterated her concerns one last time.

Nasser smiled, pressing a warm palm against his daughter's face. "You need to trust in me, Daughter. I will keep everything you've said in mind but I must follow my instincts."

"There's something else, Father," Amina started, pausing for a brief moment. "And I know you'll think it's inappropriate for me to be bringing this to you."

"What bothers you, Amina?"

"Basil. I am offended by some of his behavior. He mistreats Rasheeda. He tries to bully me. Basil is a tyrant and that kind of behavior is not only oppressive, it's barbaric. He's verbally and emotionally abusive to us both and it's not right."

"I disagree, Amina. Your brother is only asserting his position as a man. Rasheeda understands that. And as a Muslim woman you need to be more accepting of your role as a woman."

"My role?" Amina questioned, her eyes wide.

Nasser nodded. "As the prophet Mohammed has said, men have authority over women because Allah has made the one superior to the other, and because they spend their wealth to maintain them."

"And that justifies him treating us badly? Because I don't see Basil paying any of my bills."

"Good women are obedient, Amina. Your mother would not accept that and she has not taught you that. Now you come home to us and want to criticize our ways and our beliefs and your brother is offended by that."

"I have never criticized any of your beliefs, Father. Never!"

"But you mock us, Amina. Look at how you're dressed. You know how I feel about the attire you wear and you still don't heed my words, or your brother's."

Her father quoted his beloved prophet a second time. "Women should guard their unseen parts because Allah has guarded them."

Amina looked down to the business suit she wore. Her silk blouse was buttoned to the neck, the collar a large bow tied neatly beneath her chin. The skirt fell below her knees with a matching blazer in a dark shade of gray. The heel on her shoe was barely an inch high, the simple leather pump as nondescript as she could find. She'd be willing to argue that her unseen parts were very well guarded. She couldn't fathom how her father would deem her clothing modest and appropriate only when she was wearing a hijab and veil. She looked back up and met his stare.

"Your brother is offended when you do not heed Allah's teachings."

Amina took a deep breath. "Are you offended, Father?"

Nasser smiled. "I hope that in time you will change your ways, Daughter. I am confident that we will help you to know and understand where your mother failed you."

Before Amina could respond Basil called out to their father, gesturing for his attention and just like that Nasser dismissed her. She watched as the two men stood huddled in conversation. She suddenly imagined that if things were bad before they were only going to get worse.

6

"You cannot go to dinner with that woman," Mike admonished as he maneuvered his car through downtown Memphis. He cut an eye toward Troy, then returned his gaze to the road.

"Why not?" Troy questioned, cutting an eye back at his friend.

"She's working for your opponent. Her father wants to be mayor, too. Isn't that reason enough?"

Troy shook his head. "No."

"She's a distraction and your being distracted could very well cost you the election. How about that?"

Troy had to ponder his friend's comment. Amina was a distraction, he thought, but a very pleasant one. Since that first call, he'd called her every night, his day feeling incomplete until he heard her voice. Their conversations lasted into the wee hours of the morning as they were slowly getting to know each other. Troy liked talking to her and he imagined that spending time with her would be even sweeter. He had no interest in heeding his friend's concerns.

He chuckled. "You're worried about nothing. It's just dinner."

Mike cut another eye at him and shook his head.

"Change the subject," Troy countered. "Because I have no intentions of changing my mind or canceling my date."

"The fundraiser went exceptionally well," Mike said, referring to the lunch event they'd just left. "Those women were just clamoring to support you. You might not get that kind of support if you're chasing after one woman."

Troy blew a loud sigh. "Leave it alone, Mike. I mean it."

"I'm just saying. If you're going to sport that *GQ* thing you have going on we might as well work it to our advantage. You can be a political superstar and instead of the babes tossing their panties at you they can toss their checkbooks and credit cards. A pair of panties here and there would be okay, too."

Troy laughed. "On the serious, what do you know about Nasser Salman? Is he a contender?"

"He's pulled together an impressive campaign team. Amina is like the cherry on top of some very sweet cake. The woman has mad skills. If I could have I would have run for mayor and hired her for myself."

"So you're saying she's better than you are?"

"Hell, yes!" Mike chimed.

Both men laughed as Mike continued. "Hey, you know I'm good and you know I'll work my butt off for you but she's so good she scares me. The woman is hardcore. She has the credentials, a stellar reputation, and she's cute as hell! The only thing she's lacking is my killer personality and great sense of humor."

Troy smiled, knowing that he could personally

attest to Amina's having both a winning personality and a great sense of humor. He nodded. "Okay, so Mr. Salman has an edge on us. We'll use that to our advantage. Amina will keep us both on our toes."

Mike cut an eye at him. "Brother, it's not your toes I'm worried about!"

When Amina entered the bakery, Harper and her husband were seated at a table with another couple. Harper cradled an infant in her arms as the four adults cooed over the small bundle.

Nervous anxiety spilled past her veil, furrowing Amina's brow and her friend noticed it instantly.

"Amina, hey! What's wrong?" Harper intoned as she moved quickly to her feet and made her way to Amina's side.

Amina waved a nervous hand. "I didn't mean to interrupt," she said as she smiled down at the baby still in Harper's arms.

"You're not," Harper answered. "Not at all."

"Who's this little cutie?" Amina asked.

"This is our goddaughter, Joanna," she said as she snuggled the baby closer to her chest.

Amina smiled again. "She's beautiful."

The handsome man seated at Quentin's side chimed excitedly. "That's my little princess," he said. "She looks just like her mother!"

Amina extended her hand in introduction. "Amina Salman," she said, "and little Joanna looks a lot like her father, too, I think!"

"Yes, she does!" Dwayne laughed. "Nice to meet you, Amina. I'm Dwayne Porter and this is my wife, Rachel."

"Dwayne and Rachel grew up with Quentin and Troy," Harper explained. "They've been friends since forever."

"You just made my husband's whole day!" Rachel said as she laughed with them. Her gaze skated from the top of Amina's veiled head down to the length of hem that skirted against the floor as she surveyed the woman's appearance. "It's nice to meet you, Amina," she said as she appraised her. "I followed your lawsuit against the State of Georgia for student rights. Congratulations! It set some serious precedents that many states are now adopting. That was very nice work."

"Thank you," Amina smiled. "Are you an attorney, too?"

Rachel nodded. "I am. I have a private practice here in Memphis. We specialize in corporate litigation. On occasion some criminal. We were thinking of acquiring a new partner a few years ago and your brother, Basil, had given me your name. I did some research and was very impressed."

Quentin interjected. "Troy and Rachel are also legal partners," he said.

Amina's eyes widened. "Oh," she said, her voice dropping ever so slightly, surprised that her brother would have thought to recommend her for anything.

Dwayne suddenly made the connection. "You're related to Basil Salman?" he questioned.

Amina nodded. "Yes. He's my brother."

Rachel shook her head at her husband. "Didn't I just say that?"

Quentin nodded. "You know your man is a little slow."

Dwayne tossed a look around the table, his eyebrows raised. "So that would make Nasser Salman, who's campaigning against Troy for mayor, your father?"

Amina nodded. "Yes, he is."

"Amina is her father's campaign manager," Harper added.

"Please don't hold that against me," Amina said, making them all laugh. "So how do you know my family?" she asked, looking from Dwayne to Rachel and back.

"Your brother and I did some business together a while back," Dwayne answered. "Rachel was the attorney on the deal."

"What business was that?" Amina questioned. She eyed him curiously.

"I own a large food-services company and your brother brokered the sale of a small business I acquired."

In the back of her mind Amina recalled her father's excitement over Basil's accomplishment. "You own Home Grown Foods?"

Dwayne smiled. "I do and at the time we were looking to expand into the halal market. Your brother was instrumental in helping us acquire the right partners."

Quentin looked confused. "Halal? What's that?"

"In Arabic, the word *halal* means 'permitted or lawful.' Halal foods are foods that are allowed under Islamic dietary guidelines," Amina answered.

"Interesting," Quentin said.

"It actually is," Dwayne added. "According to the guidelines gathered from the Quran, there are a number of foods that Muslim followers cannot consume. It's not just about pork or pork by-products. I wanted a product line aimed at that market and I wanted to make sure we got it right."

"That was very socially conscious of you," Amina said.

Rachel shook her head. "I wish. With my husband it is always about the money. Don't let him fool you."

Dwayne shrugged. "I won't lie. My bottom line is very important to me."

Amina gave him a slight smile as she nodded her head slightly.

"Didn't Basil and Troy go to high school together?" Rachel suddenly questioned.

Quentin shook his head. "I don't think so."

"No," Dwayne added. "I think Basil went to Melrose High. You all went to Melrose, right?"

Amina shrugged. "I actually went to school in Atlanta."

"Speaking of Troy," Harper said, a puzzled expression crossing her face. "Don't you two have a dinner date tonight?"

Amina took a deep breath as an awkward silence suddenly filled the space. Her eyes shifted around the table, everyone staring in her direction. Her voice dropped an octave as she met Harper's stare. "I do," Amina answered, biting down against her bottom lip, her anxiety rising a second time. "I actually need a big favor," she said.

Harper nodded. She passed Baby Joanna back to her mother's arms. "Anything," she said as she excused herself from the group and guided Amina back across the room, through the double doors and into the kitchen.

Once they were out of everyone's earshot Amina blew a calming breath past her thin lips. Harper eyed her curiously, waiting for her to speak.

"Do you think I can change my clothes here?" Amina finally asked. "I can't go home to change so I told Troy I'd meet him here. My father would have a fit if he found out."

Harper laughed. "That's not a problem at all."

Amina looked skeptical. "I'll have to change again when our date is over. I promise it won't be too late though," she said.

Harper nodded. "Don't you worry about that. Come on," she said, gesturing for Amina to follow her to the back stairwell that led to the private living space above the bakery.

The second floor boasted a family room, a kitchen with a breakfast nook, and a mudroom. There was also a third floor with a master bedroom and bathroom, a guest suite, a home office, and a deck that sat atop a garage and looked out over a garden. The calming green color from the bakery below flowed throughout the space.

"This is very nice," Amina said as Harper showed her around upstairs.

"This is where my father and the boys used to live," Harper said. "When I moved in Quentin was camping out here periodically. Once we got married it didn't make much sense for us to move, especially with the schedule Quentin has to keep with the bakery.

"Troy has a beautiful home of his own across town," Harper added, answering the question Amina had hesitated to ask.

The woman smiled. "I really appreciate this. You'd think I was sixteen and not twenty-six the way I'm sneaking around," she said with a loud sigh.

"Have you thought about getting your own place?" Harper questioned. "Quentin actually owns a town house not far from here that we're thinking about selling. There's a tenant there now but her lease is up at the end of the month and she'll be leaving so it'll be available if you need something fairly soon."

Amina nodded. "I've thought about it but my father was so adamant about my moving into the family home with them. I didn't think about it at the time but it's really an issue of control with him. And appearances. Especially now that he's running for office."

Harper nodded. "The things we do for a parent's approval," she said.

The two women paused in the doorway of the guest room. "Make yourself at home," Harper said. "If you need anything just let me know."

Amina smiled. "Thank you. I can't begin to tell you how much I appreciate this."

Harper leaned and gave her a quick hug. "That's what friends are for."

Behind the closed door Amina dropped down against the corner of the queen-size bed. She took a deep breath and then a second, holding them both until she couldn't hold them any longer.

Her nerves were frazzled and she couldn't begin to explain to anyone how she was feeling. She had known girls in high school who would come to school and change out of their parent-approved clothing into garments that were usually too short or too tight for any parent to approve. Her mother had allowed her much freedom in her choices and Amina had never felt the need to do such a thing. Now, here she was, hiding from her father, knowing that he would never approve of her dating, let alone approve of her wardrobe choice for a date. Had she not overheard some of the young women in the mosque whispering about sneaking out of their hijabs without their father's or husband's knowledge, she would never have given the idea any consideration. She shook her head at the absurdity.

Taking a quick glance at her wristwatch, Amina blew a deep sigh. She needed to change and get back downstairs to meet Troy. She hated the secrecy but she would have hated not being able to spend time with Troy more.

Troy was surprised to find his family in the front of the bakery. The shop had closed an hour earlier but they were still there with the lights on. Quentin gave him an easy wave as he made his way inside.

"Hey, what's up?" Troy said as he greeted the two couples. He leaned to kiss Rachel's cheek first and then Harper's. He shook Dwayne's hand, leaning to coo at the sleeping baby resting on the man's shoulder.

Dwayne nodded. "It's all good," he said as he kissed his daughter's forehead.

"She is too sweet," Troy said, rubbing a palm against the infant's back. "How are you two enjoying parenthood?"

Rachel smiled. "It's amazing. Our little munchkin is just too perfect," she exclaimed.

Troy nodded. "Well, you look great. Motherhood becomes you."

Troy tossed a quick look out the bakery window, his eyes skating across the landscape. The gesture did not go unnoticed.

Quentin winked an eye at his friends. "So what brings you here this time of the night?" he asked. "And you're all dressed up!"

Everyone turned to admire his silk suit. It was a deep navy blue and he'd paired it with a pale pink dress shirt and navy-striped necktie. His shoes were highly polished and he sported a fresh shave and haircut.

Troy shrugged. "I'm meeting a friend for dinner," he said, staring out the window a second time.

"Anyone we know?" Harper asked, a sly smile on her face.

Troy tossed her a look. "Mind your business, Harper, not mine."

"I was just asking. You look kind of nervous."

He tossed her another look, his eyes rolling.

"How's the campaign going?" Rachel asked, seeming to change the subject.

"We're on track," Troy said. "I have a great team, everyone's working really hard, and things are moving along nicely."

"Good to hear," Dwayne chimed. "In fact, Rachel and I were talking and we would like to host a fundraising event for you. Toss our support behind you."

Troy nodded. "Thank you. That would really be great."

"I have to know who you're having dinner with first," Rachel said, her eyes narrowed as she crossed her arms over her chest.

Harper and Quentin laughed.

"Why is that your business?" Troy asked.

"Because we're family and I'm nosy."

Troy shook his head, not bothering to respond. His gaze moved back to the street outside.

Movement over Troy's left shoulder caught Quentin's eye. He gestured ever so slightly with his head, a wide smile filling his face. Harper's eyes followed where he stared, her own smile lifting brightly.

"So," Harper said. "What time is Amina supposed to be here?"

Troy blew a deep sigh. "Don't start, Harper."

Rachel laughed. "So Troy's having dinner with Amina?"

Harper nodded. "That's what I'm told."

"Amina is a stunning woman," Quentin said. "Beautiful and smart."

"So, she's not like the other women he used to date," Dwayne said, mischief shimmering in his eyes.

"Then why is she going to dinner with Troy?" Rachel teased.

"Because he's buying," Amina said, moving from the doorway toward them.

Troy turned in surprise, his eyes widening at the sight of her.

"Plus, he's kind of cute," she added, joy painted across her face as she locked gazes with the handsome man.

Dwayne and Rachel turned in their seats. Neither could hide the surprise on their faces, both in awe of Amina's change.

"Hot damn!" Dwayne murmured under his breath.

His wife gave him a swift punch to his shoulder.

Amina had changed out of her hijab and veil into a formfitting black dress and three-inch designer heels. The fit and flare design had an off-the-shoulder bodice, delicate ruching accents, and a hemline that stopped just above her knee. She was waif thin with just enough hip and dip that it fit her petite frame perfectly. Her curls were flowing past her shoulders, the natural styling of the reddish-brown strands framing her delicate face.

Stunning didn't begin to describe her, Troy thought. The woman was absolutely mesmerizing. He grinned, heat radiating from every pore on his body. He tossed his family a quick look. "You all think you're funny," he said as they burst out laughing.

7

The restaurant and wine bar was the epitome of fine dining. Amina instantly loved everything about the place. Service started with the valet parking and was unending as their waiter ensured everything about the experience was met with approval.

Troy had requested a corner table and the spot was quiet and intimate. The restaurant's ambiance was sultry and romantic, easily a favorite for anniversaries, engagements, or special date nights. Fresh flowers and candlelight graced the table and the lull of soft music was beguiling. Neither Amina nor Troy could remember the last time either has been so completely enamored.

Troy had ordered for them both, starting their meals with an appetizer of lobster ravioli. Salads followed; watermelon, mint, and red onion tossed with a light balsamic vinaigrette. By the time the entrée was served, a seafood-stuffed flounder served on a bed of spring vegetables with a miso lemon brown butter, Amina couldn't imagine the evening being more perfect.

The conversation between them had been as easy as breathing. Both felt completely relaxed, each other's company feeling like home. They'd laughed with each other and had laughed at each other, the wealth of it like a warm blanket laid over their shoulders. As the waiter delivered their desserts, a decadent Memphis Belle pie filled with Georgia pecans and rich dark chocolate, neither could imagine the evening ever ending.

Troy leaned back in his seat. "I couldn't eat another bite," he said.

Amina pulled the last forkful of her pie into her mouth. She nodded in agreement. "You? I'm about to bust," she said, washing down that last bite with a swig of lemon tea.

"Is that why you're still chewing?" Troy teased.

Amina laughed. "Yep! I have no intentions of leaving one crumb on my plate."

Troy laughed with her. He leaned forward in his seat, pulling his elbows against the table as he dropped his chin into his hands. His gaze washed over her, as he tried to record every line and dimple of her profile. Amina was all charm, her demeanor as polished as her looks. He couldn't remember ever having had a better date and he said so. "I have had a great time, Amina. I don't want it to end."

She was thoroughly elated and it shimmered in her bright eyes. She nodded in agreement. "I feel the same way. I feel so comfortable with you, Troy."

Troy found himself staring. Her complexion was flawlessly smooth and her features were perfectly sculpted. Her narrow face was complemented by her sultry eyes with their unique color, high cheekbones, and lips that begged to be kissed. His gaze focused on her mouth, the curve of her slight smile and the hint of pink tongue causing a rush of heat to sweep across his groin. Her smile was the sweetest, the beauty of it engaging. Her teeth were pearl white and there was a hint of a dimple in each of her cheeks. Amina met the stare he was giving her and he felt his heart skip one beat and then a second. He was staring so intently he barely heard the waiter calling his name.

He was still staring as the young man named Steven laid the tab on the table, asking if there was anything else that he could do for them. When neither responded he backed away from the table, leaving them to their moment.

Troy couldn't resist reaching out to brush a stray hair from her eyes, his finger lightly tracing her profile. "You are so beautiful," he whispered, his words like a gentle flutter against her ears.

"Thank you," Amina whispered back. A hint of color flushed her cheeks.

"Why do you hide yourself?" he asked.

"You mean with the veil?" she questioned.

He nodded. "I've known Muslim women who wear the headscarf that covers their heads and chest but they don't conceal their faces. Why do you conceal your face?"

"We're taught that we should not display our beauty except to our husbands, fathers, and sons. In Islam, the major school of thought is that our clothing should not be formfitting and the hijab should be worn as a symbol of our modesty and morality. What part of the Muslim world you're raised in dictates what that actually entails. My parents spent some time in the Middle East when they were first married and my father subscribed to the practice that all of a woman's body should be hidden, including her face."

"And your mother agreed with this?"

"My father's rigidness and his being unwilling to compromise is why they divorced."

"But you're okay with it?"

Amina smiled. "I'll be honest. It's been hard. My mother raised me and she left the faith after they separated. I'd never really worn the hijab until I moved back with my father. It's taking some getting used to."

Troy nodded. "So, it would be correct of me to assume that your father would not approve of what you're wearing right now?"

His hand fell against her knee and his fingers lightly skated the edge of her hem line. His touch was heated and Amina jumped ever so slightly before allowing herself to ease into the sensation. She took a deep breath to stall the quiver of energy shooting through her.

"He would be mortified! In fact," Amina said, "I have to change back into my hijab before I can go home. Harper let me get dressed at the bakery and she said that I can change once we get back."

Troy clenched his hand into a tight fist and pulled it back onto the table. "So, you did this just for me?"

Amina shrugged, her voice dropping an octave. "I wanted us both to be comfortable and I wanted to look nice for you."

There was a moment of pause as Troy pondered her comment. His head bobbed slowly up and down. His smile returned to his face. "I can understand why your father would want to keep you hidden away. I might want to keep my wife and daughter in a tent, too. Other men don't need to be drooling over you!"

Amina laughed, her head waving gently from side to side. "Are you drooling, Mr. Elliott?"

Troy grinned as he pretended to swipe his mouth with the back of his hand. "Like a baby!" he gushed. "I'll need a bib if this keeps up!"

"You're funny."

He leaned in closer to her, his face mere inches from hers. "I like to hear you laugh. You have a beautiful laugh."

Amina took a deep breath, her cheeks flushed with color. Her gaze danced in sync with his and she felt as if her temperature had spiked. She suddenly sat back in her seat, stealing a quick glance at her watch. Her eyes widened. "I didn't realize it's so late."

Troy looked at his own watch. "It's not late. It's not even eleven o'clock yet."

"I know, but I really need to be heading home. My father will be looking for me."

Troy nodded but disappointment painted his expression.

"I'm sorry," Amina apologized. "I'm having a great time and I really don't want to leave but I'm conflicted right now. I don't want to disappoint my father. I'm trying to follow his rules *and* do what makes me happy, but it's hard to find a happy medium."

"I understand. I know how much your relationship with your father means to you. And I wouldn't want to do anything to interfere in that. When my pop was alive his approval was important to me, too."

Amina smiled. "I wish I'd had an opportunity to meet your father. From everything I've heard he was a remarkable man."

Troy nodded. "He was. Quentin and I owe everything we have to him. He made it possible for us to have the lives we have now. I really miss him," he said as he dropped into a moment of reflection.

Amina drew her palm across his forearm, the gesture light and easy. She blew a low sigh. "I really like your family. Harper and your brother have been really sweet. And I liked Rachel and her husband, too. She seems very nice."

He chuckled softly. "There is nothing nice about Rachel. Don't turn your back on her. She is a shark through and through! That's why I practice law with the woman!"

"I'll keep that in mind," she said.

Troy nodded. "So tell me more about your family. Your mother raised you, right?"

Her smile was bright. "She did. I adore my mother. She's very much a free spirit. I look at her and then at my father and I can't imagine the two of them together."

"So it was just the two of you growing up? Just you and your mom?"

"Not at all. My mother comes from a big family. I have uncles and aunts and cousins. They give new meaning to it taking a village to raise a child."

"I can see that. Quentin and I used to joke that we had a dozen mothers. Every woman who had her eye on Pop mothered us!" he said with a hearty laugh.

Amina laughed with him as they fell into a moment of pause. "Thank you," she finally said, her smile seeming even brighter.

"For what?"

"For showing me a wonderful time. For your

friendship. For understanding. I really appreciate that."

Troy leaned back, his eyes appraising her. "I really like you, Amina. I like you more than you realize and I want you to have more from me than just friendship."

Amina's eyes were wide, her expression stunned as Troy dropped his credit card onto the table and gestured for the waiter to come retrieve the check. Minutes later they were back in his car, heading through town toward Beale Street. When they reached the bakery, Troy pulled his car around to the driveway in the back of the building. An awkward silence billowed between them as he shut down the engine. At the back door, a light was still on, Harper having promised to open the door for Amina no matter what time she returned. Neither moved, both hating that their time together was coming to a quick end.

Amina's hands were clenched tightly together in her lap, her palms beginning to perspire. The radio was playing softly, someone's love song singing the sweetest melody. She could feel her heart beating in her chest, the intensity of it like a drum line in full swing. Beside her Troy's breathing had become heavy, a deep, low pant that seemed to further ignite her nerves.

As Amina searched for words to express what she was feeling, Troy reached for her hand, his own sneaking into her lap to clasp her fingers between his fingers. He pulled her hand to his lips and gently kissed the back of it. As he did a current of heat coursed from the center of her feminine spirit and spiraled throughout every nerve ending in her body. She felt her breath catch in her chest as she took a swift inhalation and held it. Tears suddenly pressed hot behind her eyelids.

"I really want to see you again," Troy said, his voice a muffled rasp rising from someplace deep in his chest.

She nodded, knowing that there was nothing and no one that would be able to keep her from seeing him again. "Just call me!" she said. "I definitely want to spend time with you."

He shook his head. "No. I want to know now when you will see me again."

Amina squeezed his fingers. "Whenever you want," she answered.

His head was still waving from side to side. "What I really want is for us not to let this night end. What I *want* is for you to stay with me and not go home. But I know I can't have what I *want*."

Amina lifted her gaze to his, the intensity of his stare consuming. It took her breath away and despite her best efforts a tear rolled past her lashes. Before she could utter another word, Troy leaned his torso over the center console and captured her mouth beneath his own. A current of electricity shot through them both as flesh touched flesh. His lips were eager and searching as they skated easily over hers. No man had ever kissed her with so much passion, the intensity of it sweeping every one of her sensibilities from her. She was suddenly hungry for him as she parted her lips, her tongue seeking his. He tangled his fingers in the back of her hair as he pulled her closer. There was something magical about the dance they were doing, their tongues twisting and turning in perfect sync. Amina couldn't imagine the moment being sweeter.

* * *

Her father was sitting in his study when Amina entered the family home. The house was quiet, nothing at all stirring. She had barely gotten the front door closed behind her when he called her name, his tone commanding her to join him. Amina took a deep breath, blowing it past her lips before moving into the room.

"Father, you're still up," she said, fighting to keep her tone casual.

Nasser was sitting in an upholstered wingback chair, the piece like a throne around him. His legs and hands were crossed. He'd been reading and as she'd entered the room he'd set his book aside and had pulled his reading glasses from his face. He nodded, gesturing with his head for her to take a seat.

"My daughter is out running around until all hours of the night and you would expect me to be able to rest?"

"I'm sorry, Father. I didn't mean for you to worry."

"But I do, Amina. What kind of father would I be if I did not worry about my children?"

Amina blew a deep sigh. "I understand but . . ." she started before he interrupted, stalling her comment.

"You don't understand, Amina, and I do not believe you are trying to understand. I know that your life was very different when you were living with your mother and I know this is a big change for you but I expect you to do better. There will be obedience in my home and I will not be disrespected."

"But, Father, I didn't—"

Nasser cut her off a second time. He shook his head as he continued. "I believe that I have given you far too much responsibility with my campaign. My expectations are too great, especially since there is much you still need to be learning about Islam and our beliefs and values. I've asked Basil to step in as co-campaign manager to assist you."

Amina bristled. "But I don't need Basil's help! I am perfectly capable of running this campaign, Father."

Her father nodded. "No, you don't. You are very capable. But I do think you need you brother's support. This position has demands on your time that would be better served by a man. A woman should not be keeping such late hours. For certain situations it is more appropriate for Basil to step in and support you."

The man paused to take a breath, leaning forward in his seat as he did. "You need to trust me on this. A father does know best and this is for the best. I expect that you will try to spend more time with your sister. You can both be great influences on each other. It's time you started thinking about marriage and a family of your own; preparing yourself to be a good wife. Rasheeda can help you with that."

"And what can I help Rasheeda with?" Amina asked, her tone slightly sarcastic as she met his stern gaze with one of her own.

Nasser's jaw tightened. He took his own breath and held it before speaking. "Rasheeda has been sheltered here with me and your brother for far too long. I think you can help her blossom; to realize her full potential. You can help her realize some of her dreams; to become as accomplished as you've become."

Amina dropped her gaze to the floor as she nodded.

Nasser smiled. "I am not your enemy, Daughter. I only want the very best for you. I hope you know that."

"I do, Father."

Rising from his seat Nasser moved to Amina's side. He gripped her face between his two palms and gently kissed her forehead. "We're having family dinner tomorrow. Please, be punctual. Company will be joining us."

Amina nodded once again. "Yes, Father."

He kissed her one last time then moved toward the door. "Good night, Amina. Sleep well, child."

"Good night, Father."

Upstairs, Rasheeda was sitting up, a paperback book nestled against her lap. When Amina entered the room, the girl jumped, not expecting that anyone would have caught her awake when she should have been asleep. She shoved the book in her hand beneath the pillows, pulling the covers up to her chin.

"It's just me," Amina said. "I didn't mean to scare you."

Rasheeda shrugged. "I wasn't scared."

Her sister smiled. She moved to Rasheeda's side and pulled the paperback from its hiding spot. A pretty couple in a seductive pose graced the cover. The book's titillating title indicated it was an erotic romance. She tossed Rasheeda a smile. "I haven't read this one. Is it good?"

Rasheeda took the book from Amina's hand and pushed it back between the covers. "You read romances?"

Amina nodded. "I do."

She moved back to her side of the room and searched through a backpack on the table. She pulled her electronic book reader from an inside flap. Crossing back across the room she dropped down onto the bed beside Rasheeda and passed the device to her sister.

"I probably have a few hundred titles loaded on this thing. I have them sorted by sensuality level. Some are really sweet and then there are some that are really heated. Those are in the folder labeled with the five Xs," she said.

Rasheeda pressed the power button as she tossed Amina a quick look. "It's asking for a password," she said, dropping her gaze back to the device.

Amina shared the six-digit code that allowed access. "Keep it to yourself, please. If you push the power button again the screen will go black and you'll have to enter the password again to turn it back on. It keeps people from accidentally seeing what you're reading."

"And I can borrow it?" Rasheeda asked.

"You can have it," Amina responded.

Neither woman said another word as Rasheeda flipped through the device's contents, a full smile pulling at her mouth. Amina stripped out of her clothes and stepped into her nightgown. She dropped down against her own bed, closing her eyes as she thought back to her day.

Her lips still burned hot from the kiss she and Troy had shared. She could still taste him and as she licked her lips she found herself wishing their night had never ended. Troy had made her happier than she could ever remember being. He liked her and had wanted her and he hadn't been afraid to tell her so. Troy had been open and honest and had no qualms about opening himself up to her.

Rasheeda's alto voice broke through the quiet. "Did Father ask where you were so late?"

Sitting up, Amina met her sister's curious stare. She shook her head. "No."

"He probably knew you would lie."

Amina shrugged. "Then again he might have known that I would have told him the truth."

Rasheeda pondered the response for a moment then laughed. Her gaiety made Amina smile. "Did you have a nice time with your friend?" Rasheeda asked when she'd regained her composure.

"I did. I had a really great time."

"Don't let Father or Basil find out," Rasheeda said.

"I won't tell if you don't."

Rasheeda smiled back. She waved her romance novel in Amina's direction. "I'll keep your secret if you keep mine."

The two sisters laughed, understanding sweeping between them. From the nightstand Amina's cell phone chimed, the unit vibrating harshly against the hardwood. Amina grabbed it, silencing it as quickly as she could.

Rasheeda jumped from the bed.

"What's wrong?" Amina asked, her voice dropping to a loud whisper.

"I need to pee before you lock yourself in the bathroom!"

Amina laughed. "Hurry up!" she said.

8

Troy only had time for one quick cup of coffee and a pecan Danish. He had taken a seat at the corner table and was previewing his schedule on his iPad when Quentin made his way over and took a chair by his brother's side.

"Good morning."

Quentin nodded. "How are you doing this morning?"

Troy shrugged. "I didn't sleep well."

"Company in the bed will do that to a man."

Troy chuckled. "I wish that had been my problem."

Quentin took a sip of coffee from his own cup. "How'd your date go? You two were back fairly early, weren't you?"

Troy nodded. "Amina is living with her daddy," he said, his tone sarcastic.

Quentin laughed. "We remember those days, don't we? Pop was a stickler about the hours we came in and went out in his house. Even after we were grown."

"That's why we both purchased our own homes, remember that?"

His brother nodded. "So, why didn't you get enough sleep?"

Troy shrugged, not having the words to tell Quentin everything he might have wanted to share with him. He was grateful when one of the staff suddenly called for Quentin's help back in the kitchen.

Troy thought back to the previous night. Dinner had been amazing. He couldn't remember ever having that much fun on any date. But then Troy had never done a lot of dating. There had been a few women who'd briefly captured his attention but no one who'd been able to hold it for any length of time. There was something about Amina though that had his full attention on lock.

He hadn't known what to expect when their evening had started. But he had never expected that he'd be wanting Amina as badly as he found himself wanting the woman. His desire for her had been consuming, simmering on a low burn until he found himself so heated that he felt like he would combust from the inside out. Leaving her had been the hardest thing he'd ever had to do.

That first kiss had been monumental. She'd been too sweet and he had felt an addiction for her rising with a vengeance. She'd left him weak, and wanting, and none of it made an ounce of sense to him.

He'd kissed her one last time before she'd knocked on the back door for his sister-in-law's attention. When Harper had answered he'd wished both women a good night and had gone on his way. He'd been afraid to follow her inside. Troy knew that if he had stepped into the home behind her he would never have been able to let her go. That knowledge disturbed him more than he was willing to admit. He blew a deep sigh.

It had taken him almost two hours to regain a semblance of control over his emotions and his body. He had resisted calling her but dialed her number, his want like an addiction causing him to need to hear her voice one more time. Frustration had tainted the conversation. Amina had been frustrated as she'd told him about her conversation with her father. They'd talked into the early morning hours and Troy had wanted nothing more than to wrap her in his arms to take her hurt away. He had wanted to protect her, to assure her that he would make everything well. All he could think of was having her with him, by his side, and then he'd felt selfish for even having had those thoughts. It disturbed him because Troy had never been a selfish man, but wanting Amina had him thinking of very little else.

Shaking the thoughts from his head Troy tossed back the last drops of caffeine in his cup and stood up. He had a full schedule ahead of him and couldn't afford to be late to his first meeting. He also had to be focused and after the sleepless night he'd had, he was finding that harder and harder to do.

Amina had been at the campaign headquarters for most of the morning by the time her brother found his way there. Her father and Rasheeda were attending a benefit lunch and Amina welcomed the opportunity to talk with her brother alone.

"Glad you could join us," she said flippantly.

"I'm a busy man, little girl. What's the problem?"

She shook her head unable to mask her annoyance. "First, don't call me little girl. Ever! And what were you busy doing? What is more important right now than this election?"

Basil narrowed his gaze. "Who are you to question a man's business?"

She met the stare he was giving her, her own eyes the thinnest of slits. "Don't test me, Basil. You will lose this fight. I promise you. Now, we have a job to do and I fully expect you to hold up your end of that responsibility. This has nothing to do with your manhood or me being a woman. Nothing at all."

Basil crossed his arms over his chest. He leaned back against the wall and stared at her. "I'm going to let your insolence pass this time but only because I'm in a very good mood. Now, exactly what is it that I missed?"

Amina gave him a harsh stare before bothering to respond. "Have you read this morning's newspaper?"

"No, should I have?"

"The *Memphis Daily News* shows Father behind in the polls. They also gave their endorsement to Troy Elliott. Mr. Elliott also got an official endorsement from the governor, the lieutenant governor, the Memphis Education Association, and the Memphis Urban League."

"That's not good."

"No, Basil. That's not good. Not if Father hopes to win."

"So what do we do now?"

"I've arranged for Father to speak at the Students for Change event next week. Father really needs to appeal to the young voters."

Basil nodded. "I also think we should set up a debate or two with Father and the other candidates. Put him front and center in the public eye."

"I don't know if that's a good idea. Not yet."

"Well, I disagree. So make it happen." Basil turned to leave. He was halfway across the room before he suddenly turned back around to face her. "Hey, I need some legal work from you."

Amina took a deep breath. "What kind of legal work?"

"I did business with a man named Dwayne Porter a while back and—"

"Dwayne Porter?" The color drained from Amina's face and she felt her eye begin to twitch.

"Yeah, he's a local businessman and . . . what's wrong with you? You look like you just saw a ghost!"

Amina shook her head. "Nothing. Go on," she said, gesturing with her hand.

Basil tossed her a curious look. "Anyway, rumor had it that Porter was trying to acquire some property down on Beale Street last year. There's an eatery or something there now. But something changed his mind. I did a little digging and it seems the city is about to make some ordinance changes that will make that property worth three times its current value."

"Has this ordinance been voted on already?"

Basil smiled. "Let's just say that once Father gets into office it'll be on the table for consideration."

"And you know this how?"

"Let's just say I have an inside track."

"What kind of inside track?"

"I have a friend in the city planning office. She tells me things."

Amina shook her head. "What are you up to, Basil?"

"I want that property from the corner of Beale Street, down Front Street all the way to Peabody Place. Once Father's in office and the ordinance passes I'm going to be a very rich man."

"Your goals are lofty, Basil, but really? If the owner isn't willing to sell, how do you propose to acquire that property?"

He tossed her a wink of his eye. "I already hold the titles to a good portion of land in that area. I just need that final piece of the pie." Basil stole a quick glance toward the clock. "I have to run. We'll discuss it more at dinner."

As her brother walked away Amina shook her head. If she hadn't been sure before, she was definitely certain of it now. Basil had completely lost his chauvinistic mind.

Amina glanced quickly at the clock on the wall. Minutes ago she'd been early and now Troy was running late. Stealing away to Germantown to meet him had involved a little white lie to her father and a thirty-minute drive away from prying eyes. It was as far as their limited time would allow.

Amina couldn't stop thinking that her agreeing to meet Troy was a mistake. She knew that she was playing with fire and she was suddenly afraid that she might get burned if things didn't work out. But she liked him. She liked him a lot even if it did mean stealing away to spend time with him.

As he made his way into Java Café, moving to the back table where she sat, every one of her concerns was washed away by his smile. Troy stole his own quick

86   *Deborah Fletcher Mello*

glance around the room before he leaned to kiss her cheek, his lips warm and gentle against her skin.

"I missed you," Troy said as he settled himself against the seat next to her.

She beamed. "I missed you, too!"

"How's your day going?"

"Busy. How about yours?"

"Busier." Troy took a deep breath, then blew it out slowly. He gestured for the waiter and when the young man moved to their side, he ordered two cups of coffee and two chocolate chip scones.

When the young man had served their order and was out of earshot, Amina said, "I was surprised to get your text."

Troy nodded as he swallowed the first bite of his pastry. "I was surprised I sent it. But I wanted to see you." His eyes brushed hers for a brief moment before he lowered his gaze to the table. He suddenly didn't have the words to tell her that talking to her in the late-night hours was no longer enough for him. That he was desperate to lay eyes on her, if only for a brief moment. "I just *needed* to see you," he finally said, lifting his gaze back to hers.

A moment of understanding seemed to pass between them, volumes spoken without one word being uttered. Amina smiled. She extended her hand to brush crumbs from his top lip, her fingers lingering against his cheek for a second longer than necessary.

"We have exactly thirty minutes," Amina said as she tossed a second glance toward that clock. "I have to make it home on time."

Troy nodded. "Fine and the only subject we cannot talk about is the campaign. Agreed?"

"Agreed. So tell me something I don't know about you, Mr. Elliott."

Troy smiled. "Something you don't know . . ." He pondered her question briefly. "I think I've told you everything about myself."

"I'm sure there's something. Think harder."

He took a breath and another bite of his snack. "I have a passion for airplanes. I love everything to do with aeronautics. In another life I would have been a pilot."

"Why not this life?"

"Because I'm afraid of heights."

Amina laughed. "Really? I can't imagine you being afraid of anything."

"So, what would your career choice have been in another life?"

"I'd have been a high-fashion model. I'd also be twelve inches taller."

Troy nodded. "I could see you walking the catwalk."

She giggled ever so slightly. "But I love being an attorney and I especially enjoy the work I've done in Atlanta to help the community. Eventually I hope to do more of that here."

"I eventually hope to make a senate run. I'm hoping you'll be available to run that campaign."

"What about your buddy Mike?"

"I love Mike but even he says you're the best."

"He's being kind."

"Tell me about your brother and sister. I'd like to meet them someday."

"I'm having a really hard time connecting with the two of them. Basil is just mean-spirited and ill-tempered. And Rasheeda . . . well, she's her father's daughter. It's hard to get past that but we're working on it."

"Keep trying. Family is important. I don't know where I would be if I didn't have Quentin and Harper."

Troy reached across the table for her hand, his fingers entwining with hers. Touching her felt good, warm and tender. Amina pulled his hand to her lips and kissed his fingers, her touch endearing. He slid his palm along her jawline, resting it against her cheek. He met the look she was giving him, joy shimmering in her stare. Her smile was wide and in that moment he would have given anything to have lingered beneath it forever.

Not only was she on time for family dinner but Amina was early enough to give her sister a hand with the evening's meal. The two women were actually having a good time together and Amina vowed to make more of an effort to spend time with the young woman.

They were sharing a laugh when the front bell rang and they heard Basil open the door to greet their company. Nasser's voice rang out warmly, the man's exuberant greeting moving the two women to toss each other a curious look.

"Who's eating with us?" Amina questioned.

Rasheeda shrugged her narrow shoulders. "I don't know. Father just said to set three extra places."

"I'm going to go see and say hello," Amina said.

Rasheeda shook her head. "You should wait until Father calls for us. Trust me. We'll have a better evening that way."

"Don't all these rules get on your nerves?" Amina

asked as she shook salt and pepper into the mixed vegetables.

Rasheeda smiled, the faintest lift to her mouth. She didn't bother to answer.

Amina shook her head. "Well, I know they get on my nerves," she said.

Rasheeda laughed as she moved to her sister's side. She passed her a stack of china plates. "It really isn't so bad, Amina. Now go set the dinner table, please."

Amina gave Rasheeda a look, then both women burst out laughing. Minutes later the table was set and the platters were filled with food, ready to be served. Rasheeda seemed happy with the presentation so Amina was happy too. As if on cue, Nasser peeked into the room.

"Amina, there is someone I want you to meet," he said, gesturing for her to follow behind him.

Just as Amina reached the door Rasheeda called her name. The young woman gestured with her hand, passing her palm and fingers in front of her face. "Your veil," Rasheeda whispered loudly, her eyes wide.

Amina shook her head and blew a deep sigh. "My *last* nerve!" she said as she lifted the covering back across her face.

As she entered the living room, an older couple and a younger man were standing in the center. There was no mistaking the familiarity between them, the son a spitting image of his father. Of average height both men had significant potbellies that made them look pregnant; one more so than the other. The younger man wore an expensive silk suit but it was ill-fitting, the single button looking like it was about to pop. A bright white dress shirt and red bowtie complemented the rest of his outfit. The father was similarly adorned and the matriarch was dressed in a traditional hijab. All three greeted Amina with wide smiles and warm brown eyes that shimmered against black coffee complexions. Her father made the introductions.

"Daughter, allow me to introduce you to Mr. and Mrs. Fayed and their son Kareem.

Mrs. Fayed stepped toward her, placing two hands on Amina's shoulders. "It is an honor for us to finally meet you, Amina. Your father has always spoken very highly of you."

Amina nodded. "Thank you. It's very nice to meet you all as well."

Kareem Fayed had a pleasant face and generous smile and he greeted Amina as if they were long-lost friends. "Amina, it's good to see you," he said, reaching for both of her hands.

He was tall and lean, his dark complexion complemented by a dark brown Hugh Jackman haircut. He gripped her fingers just a touch too tightly, the gesture making Amina feel slightly uncomfortable. She tried to pull her hands from his without showing her uneasiness, her own smile waning substantially. Mr. Fayed had not bothered to speak, still standing there and appraising her. She nodded in his direction, lowering her eyes to show him respect as her father moved to her side.

Nasser wrapped an arm around her shoulders. "I have been friends with the Fayed family since before you children were born. I regret that you and Kareem didn't grow up together like he and Basil did so that you two could have gotten to know each other sooner." He gestured for them all to take a seat.

Hearing his name Basil eagerly joined the conversation. "Kareem and I have been friends since forever. We are more like brothers than anything else. And my brother here is a real estate broker. He and I have done much business together," he said.

"I actually own a very successful real estate investment firm," Kareem clarified.

"Kareem is also one of the founding members of our young men's group at the mosque," her father added as he listed a host of Kareem's other accomplishments.

Amina suddenly felt as if she were observing some ritual she had no understanding of. She looked to her brother who seemed oblivious to her confusion. Mrs. Fayed chuckled softly, seeming to read Amina's mind.

"You must excuse the men, Amina. They have no decorum when it comes to a woman's destiny," she said, her tone teasing.

"I'm not sure I understand," Amina responded.

Mrs. Fayed gave her another wide smile. "When you were just a baby your father and my husband negotiated a marriage commitment between you and my son. Of course, now that you two are adults you both have complete say whether or not to honor that commitment but I'm confident that once you and my son spend time together and get to know one another that you will think we made a wise choice for you both."

Her eyes wide, Amina shot her father a look, then rested her eyes on Kareem, who was staring at her intently. His grin was a mile wide. "I know that I am ready to honor that commitment as soon as you are comfortable with doing so, Amina," he said. "I look forward to making you my wife."

9

Harper was laughing so hard that tears were streaming down her face. She and Amina sat Indian-style in the center of the queen-size bed in Harper's guest bedroom. They'd been talking since Amina had shown up hours earlier, neither woman in any hurry.

"So you've been engaged since you were an infant!" Harper exclaimed excitedly.

Amina shook her head vehemently. "Is that not crazy? I know that arranged marriages are perfectly acceptable in some cultures but it's the twenty-first century. Did my father really think I'd marry some guy he picked out for me twenty-plus years ago?"

Harper nodded, her laugh dropping to a loud giggle. "I really want to see Troy's face when you tell him! You have to let me be there."

Amina rolled her eyes skyward. "I have no intentions of telling Troy this. He'll think my entire family is crazy."

"Oh, you're going to tell him. I just want to be a fly on the wall when you do!"

Amina's head waved from side to side. "It's just too much, Harper! What do I do?"

"Well, did you say yes?"

"Of course not! In fact, I didn't say much of anything at all. My sister said I looked shell-shocked."

"What did your father say?"

"What he always says. That I should trust his judgment. That he knows best. That a good Muslim woman is an obedient woman. Then he said he approved of that man and I spending time together to get to know one another as long as Basil is there to chaperone."

"How sweet! He wants to protect your virtue!"

"He wants to ruin my life!" Amina exclaimed. She fell face forward, dropping her forehead against the mattress.

The two women were still giggling when they heard a door slam harshly followed by Troy's booming voice calling for his brother. As the man moved through the home Amina's eyes widened.

"He's early!"

"Actually, I think you're late," Harper said, taking a glance at her wristwatch.

Troy suddenly came to an abrupt stop in the doorway, spying the two women. He looked from one to the other. "Hi. What are you two up to?"

Harper shrugged. "Girl talk. What are you doing here?" she asked as she unfolded her body to a standing position, her feet planted firmly on the hardwood floor.

"I needed to ask Quentin a question before I picked up my date for dinner," he said as he winked an eye in Amina's direction.

Amina's bright smile widened with excitement.

"Well, your brother is sound asleep. He was up all

night and all day baking. He only lay down an hour or so ago. And, as you saw, I was gossiping with your date."

"About something juicy, I hope."

"We were talking about you."

Troy's mouth lifted into a slight smile. "I suddenly imagine that if I'd had you for a little sister sooner, I'd have strangled you by now."

Harper laughed. "I love you, too, Big Brother!" She reached up to kiss his cheek. "Do you want me to wake Quentin?" she asked as she moved toward the door.

Troy shook his head no. "Let him sleep. I'll catch up with him later," he said.

Harper smiled. "I have some work to finish up," she said. Her hand rested on the doorknob. "Why don't I give you two some privacy."

Making her exit, Harper tossed Amina a wink of her eye, then closed the bedroom door behind herself. As her footsteps faded down the hallway Troy turned his gaze toward the beautiful woman. As he looked into her eyes he felt something surge through his spirit that he couldn't quite name. It was as if an electrical current was running through him and the pleasant feeling was like nothing he'd ever experienced before. A nervous flutter rippled between them.

"Hi," she whispered, her voice dropping low.

"Hi," Troy responded as he eased himself closer to the bed. He stood staring at her for a brief moment before he lifted one knee and then the other onto the bed top.

He crawled slowly toward where she was still sitting. As he reached her, Amina extended her arms and wrapped them around his neck. She pulled him close as he dropped his mouth against hers and kissed her hungrily.

His lips grazed hers lightly at first then with more vigor. He sucked on her bottom lip and then her top, his tongue teasing the flesh across her mouth. When he eased an arm around her waist and dropped his body weight against hers, she opened her mouth and welcomed him in, his tongue dancing alongside hers.

So lost in the moment, Amina was oblivious to Troy's having eased himself between her legs, his pelvis joined nicely to hers. They lingered in the sheer beauty of the connection until Troy suddenly pulled himself from her, lifting his body back onto his feet. He was panting heavily and an erection had lengthened in his pants. The weight of it pressed tight against the front of his trousers. He turned his back to her and sat down on the bed.

Her own breathing was raspy as Amina gasped for air. Still lying back, she drew her knees to her chest and rolled onto her side, then pulled her arms up over her head. Troy's touch had ignited something deep in her core, something she knew only he could quench. His touch had felt too good and she fathomed that something that good couldn't possibly be right for either of them. She blew a deep sigh.

Troy drew a large palm across her back, his hand coming to rest against her hip. "I'm sorry. I didn't mean . . ." he started. There was a moment of hesitation before he suddenly shook his head vehemently. "No, I'm not sorry. I wanted that. I *want* you. I'm not going to apologize for how I feel about being with you, Amina."

Amina took a deep breath and blew another sigh

past her lips. She rolled back against him, her eyes lifting as they connected with his. "What's happening with us, Troy?" she said as she fell into the look he was giving her. "This just feels too . . . well . . ." She stammered, searching for the right words to express what she was feeling. When she couldn't find one she looked to him for help.

"It feels amazing," Troy finally answered. "I feel complete when I'm with you, Amina, and when you're not there I feel like something important is missing. I feel lost. Every night when we talk all I want to do is pull you through that damn phone and wrap myself around you. I think you must be a witch or something because you definitely have me under your spell."

Amina laughed. "That's exactly how I feel about you."

He met the look she was giving him, his eyes locking with hers as he sighed, warm breath blowing past his full lips. Troy lay back against the mattress and eased his body alongside hers. He curled himself against her backside as Amina snuggled her hips and buttocks against the rise of nature in his pants. With her softness nestled nicely against his hardened muscles he wrapped an arm around her waist and pulled her even closer. He snuggled his face against her hair and pressed a damp kiss to the back of her neck. Amina purred softly and the lilt of it was like music to his ears.

"So what do we do about this?" Troy asked.

Amina shrugged, gently beating her head against the mattress. "I don't know," she finally responded. "I really don't know. But I do think we may need to slow things down."

"Why?"

Amina wiggled her buttocks against him, his hardened member rolling against her backside. "That's why," she whispered ever so slightly.

"Does that make you uncomfortable? You know it only happens because you excite me, Amina."

"And you excite me too, but . . ." She hesitated.

She and Troy had already had a conversation about her convictions. He understood that she wasn't ready to take their relationship to the next level. The moments they'd spent alone had gotten heated beyond measure and Amina had needed to stall the desire that consumed her. Being with Troy, his hands painting heat across her bare flesh, had made her reconsider her beliefs, her body wanting to give in to the desire he so easily elicited from her. She appreciated that Troy never pushed her for more because if he had she knew she would have given in. She had wanted him that badly. She still wanted him, unable to think of little else. Troy echoed the sentiment.

"I want you, Amina. I'm not going to hide that. Not from you. But you have to want me just as much and the time has to be right for both of us," he said as he snuggled her closer to his body.

He continued. "Sex is an expression of love and one without the other is incomplete. When we do make love, Amina, you'll know how much I love you and I'll know that you love me back."

Tears sprung to her eyes. "I don't want you to be disappointed," she said. "I don't have the experience some women have."

"I don't care about other women and what they have. I care about you."

Amina could feel herself blushing. Heat warmed her cheeks.

An hour later Troy was still holding on to her, the

couple chatting easily. He'd taken the news of her arranged marriage well, finding it as humorous as Harper had. Amina wanted to find it funny as well, but knowing her father she understood that the patriarch was quite serious about her eventually marrying Kareem Fayed.

"That's not going to happen," Troy said.

"It's definitely not what I want," Amina said, trying to ignore the fingers that were gently teasing the flesh beneath her blouse, her stomach muscles quivering beneath his touch.

"No. I mean it, Amina. You are not marrying him or anyone else. I won't let that happen. I will go to your father myself first."

She giggled. "And what would you say to my father?"

A pregnant pause swelled full between them. Both fell into the quiet of it as Troy pondered her comment. In the distance they could suddenly hear Quentin and Harper in conversation, the couple laughing in another room. Troy kissed the back of Amina's neck one last time, then lifted himself from the bed. Extending his hand he pulled her to her feet beside him, his arms wrapping around her torso. He stared down into her eyes, a warm smile filling his face. And then he answered.

"I would tell your father that I love you. That I love you more than anything else in this world."

Amina was grateful that neither her father nor her brother was up to scold her when she finally found her way home. It was almost three o'clock in the morning and she knew any confrontation with her family would have ruined what had been the most perfect evening. She eased her way to the room she shared with her sister and, once inside, the door closed behind her, she released the breath she'd been holding. Rasheeda shook her head, her newly acquired electronic reader resting in her lap.

Amina pulled her index finger to her lips. "Shhh," she whispered.

Rasheeda whispered back. "Don't shush me. I'm not saying anything."

"Did Father say anything?"

Rasheeda shook her head. "He fell asleep early. And Basil's not home. I doubt we'll see Basil before tomorrow. Father doesn't even know you're sneaking into the house."

Amina blew a sigh of relief. "Thank goodness for something," she said as she changed out of her clothes.

"Did you have fun?"

"I always have fun with Troy."

"Troy?"

"My friend."

"Not the Troy who's running for mayor against Father?"

Amina nodded. "That Troy."

Rasheeda shook her head, a wide grin filling her face. "You're kidding me, right?"

"Nope!"

"I've seen his pictures. That man is really cute!"

Amina smiled. "I really like him, Rasheeda. And he likes me. In fact . . ." she paused. "He loves me."

"Do you love him?"

Reflecting on her sister's question, Amina nodded. Loving Troy was all she could think about since the words had come out of the man's mouth, him professing his feelings. She'd been stunned by his admission, then something had come over her, emotion so intense that it moved her to tears.

They'd gone to dinner with his brother and Harper. The meal had been easy and comfortable, the laughter abundant, and Amina had refused to interrupt their good time to rush home for curfew. She knew the decision would not be taken lightly and in that moment she hadn't cared. She was spending time with the man who loved her, the man she loved back, and nothing else mattered.

When they'd finally gotten back to the bakery, Quentin had lured them into the kitchen to taste a new dessert. The upside-down apple pie came with a candied walnut crust, and he had served it with warm caramel sauce and cinnamon ice cream. She and Troy had shared a single bowl and he'd fed her from his spoon. The moment was seductive and when Troy had led her upstairs to change back into the clothes she'd arrived in, he'd spent another hour kissing the sugar from her lips as both had fought the desire to take their intimacy further.

Her head was still bobbing against her shoulders. "I do love him. I love him so much!" she said as she met her sister's stare.

Rasheeda gave her a warm smile. "I want that some day!" she said. "My own personal romance story!" She gestured with the reader in her hand.

"What do I do?" Amina said as she threw her body back against her own bed. "You know Father will never approve of me and Troy being together."

"Does it matter?"

Amina tossed her sister a quick glance. "It does

matter. I love Father. I want to make him happy. I want him to be proud of the choices I make. Just like you do. Maybe even more because Mother didn't raise me the way he would have liked. I just don't want him to be disappointed in me."

"Then you're going to have to marry Kareem," Rasheeda said teasingly.

Amina rolled her eyes in annoyance. She pulled the covers up and over her body, turning until she was facing the wall. She hated to consider that Rasheeda was right, instead dropping into reflection as memories of her evening played through her mind.

Rasheeda resumed her reading, every now and again tossing her sister a quick glance. When she came to the end of her chapter she shut down the device and flicked off the nightlight that was shining above her head. Pulling her own covers around herself she blew a deep sigh. "Amina, are you asleep?" she asked, her voice a soft whisper in the early morning air.

"No. I can't sleep."

"Can I ask you something?"

"Of course. You can ask me anything."

"Are you still a virgin? I mean, have you been with a man that way?"

Amina smiled as she rolled to face her sister. "I've kissed some boys but yes, I'm still a virgin. I've never been intimate with any man."

"Oh. I just thought . . . maybe . . . well . . . since you lived with Mother . . ."

"Muslim parents are not the only parents who preach no sex before marriage, Rasheeda. That was the one thing Mother and Father both agreed on. But Mother always said that I should wait for the right man; the man I knew I wanted to spend the rest of my life with. Then it would be the most beautiful experience I would ever have. She also said the right man would not only be willing to wait for me but that he would be willing to marry me first."

"Father says we should wait just because he says so and he'll tell us who the right man is for us."

Amina chuckled ever so softly. "So have you? Have you waited, Rasheeda?"

The young woman shrugged. She didn't bother to answer, instead dropping her head back against her pillow. A minute later she sat back up and leaned forward, allowing her body to slide off the bed to the carpeted floor. Sitting upright Amina peered down at her as she finally spoke.

"One of the mothers at the mosque told us that our husbands will educate us in the matters of sex; that they will teach us their likes and dislikes. She also said that our sexual needs are different from a man's. That a good wife should be an active partner and not a passive recipient to keep her husband from the many temptations that will be outside the home. She said anything that adds pleasure to the marital bed is permissible and commendable. Except anal. Anal is forbidden and a man who enters his wife through her back passage is cursed. And a good wife should always be available to please him and not give him an excuse to make a choice between her and the hellfire."

"Do you believe all that?" Amina asked.

"I read a lot of romance stories. I sometimes think the more a woman knows the more a woman won't need to know. I can't help but wonder if a man might find that woman more desirable."

Amina nodded. "I wonder that sometimes myself," she said softly.

Rasheeda smiled. "Do you think Troy is the right man?"

Amina didn't have to consider the question at all. "I have no doubts."

Rasheeda blew a deep sigh. "I'm really happy for you, Amina. I really am."

Amina lay awake for some time, staring into the darkness. After crawling back into her bed Rasheeda had eased into a deep sleep and was snoring softly. Amina found her sister's breathing comforting, the lull of it soothing to her spirit. They were growing closer and that made her happy. Their earlier conversation had been one-sided, Rasheeda asking about her. But Amina was curious about her sister's dreams, wondering what things Rasheeda wanted for herself. She was hopeful that would be a conversation they'd be able to have soon.

The Clay Pit restaurant was named for the tandoori oven in which many of the restaurant's Indian specialties and breads were baked. The menu included samplings of tandoori beef native to Pakistan, as well as an assortment of curries, vegetarian dishes, and the cuisines of Greece and the Middle East represented by dishes of hummus and baba ghanoush to spanako-pita and moussaka. The common thread throughout all the diverse offerings was that the food was all halal. Basil had been raving about it since informing Amina of their dinner plans with Kareem Fayed.

For the first hour her brother had done nothing but

rave about all things Kareem, reading the man's résumé as if he were the who's who of accomplishments.

"So, tell me more about your work with the young men's group," Amina said, finally able to interject a question into the conversation.

Kareem leaned forward on his elbows, clasping his hands in front of him. He was as eager to talk about himself as Basil was. "I find it extremely rewarding," he said. "We have too many young men who are losing their way and it warms my spirit to guide them back onto the right path. I was just telling Basil today about a young brother who is challenged with issues of his sexuality. We've spent a lot of time in prayer and he's coming around."

"How is he coming around?"

"He understands that family is important and marriage is an institution and provides the proper context for raising families."

"So rather than accepting him as he is, you're telling him he needs to conform to the ideals others have of who he should be?"

"We do not break family ties in Islam, Amina. His parents would tolerate him but they would never be accepting of his behavior or his relationships if he chose to follow that behavior."

"Is this young man not an observant Muslim?"

"He is. He strictly follows Islamic practices, prays five times a day, fasts during Ramadan, and he gives charitably. He's even made the pilgrimage to Mecca, which is why we want him to understand that his behavior is unacceptable."

"But his sexuality and his faith are two meaningful aspects of his identity so why can't he balance both in his life?"

Kareem smiled, looking at her as if she didn't have a clue. "We don't encourage anything that is considered sinful, Amina, but we wholeheartedly support our brethren."

"So your message is that you will hate the sin but love the sinner?"

Kareem reached out and patted the back of her hand. "We focus on traditional family values and our young men's group is focused on helping our young men define that. You might want to do some work with our young women once you yourself are comfortable with the faith. I imagine you might have much to offer them."

Amina was thankful that he could not see the expression on her face. She dropped her gaze to the table, hoping that her dislike for him didn't show in her eyes. She blew a deep sigh as Basil jumped back into the conversation.

"Amina is licensed to practice law in three states," he said. "Georgia, Tennessee, and Florida."

Kareem gave her a bright smile. "Impressive. Where did you go to school, Amina?"

"The University of Pennsylvania's Wharton School. I earned both my undergraduate degree and my master's degree in business economics with a concentration on public policy. Then I earned my Juris Doctor from Duke University's law school."

"Impressive!" Kareem chimed. "You've done so much in such a short period of time."

"Not really," Amina responded. "I graduated high school early. I was seventeen when I was accepted to college."

"And you worked while you went to school, too! My, my, my!" Kareem said, his tone slightly patronizing.

Amina smiled. "Thank you. I will eventually get my doctorate in ethics and legal studies."

Kareem's eyebrows lifted ever so slightly. "So you're hoping to go back to school?"

Her head waved from side to side. "I'm not hoping at all. I definitely plan to go back."

She didn't miss the look Kareem and her brother exchanged. Basil rolled his eyes, annoyance like bad makeup across his face.

"What, Basil?"

"Amina, one would think that you would want to focus on being a good wife and mother. I know that is what Father is hoping for you. He is anxious to be a grandfather."

"Then why don't you have some kids for him?" she snapped.

Kareem chuckled. "You have spirit, Amina. I like that. I'm sure you'll be a wonderful wife and an even better mother to our children. It will be important for our daughters to see their mother have goals and ambition."

It was on the tip of her tongue to tell the man that she didn't really care what he liked but she bit back the retort instead.

As the two men fell into conversation Amina couldn't help but think that her being there had been a huge mistake. She hated that she'd allowed Basil and her father to bully her into meeting Kareem Fayed for dinner. She didn't like Kareem and there wasn't much that she was interested in knowing about him. The man was as egotistical and as chauvinistic as her brother. He also seemed convinced that a union between them was a done deal and that she should resolve herself to being a dutiful wife. He was in for a huge disappointment and didn't even know it.

Pushing the last of her dinner aside Amina came to her feet. "I hate to eat and run but I promised Father I'd be home early," she said, spinning the truth in her favor. "Thank you for dinner, Kareem."

Basil nodded.

Kareem came to his feet. "It was a pleasure, Amina. May I walk you to your car?"

She shook her head. "That won't be necessary. You and Basil stay and enjoy your dessert."

The man looked like a Cheshire cat, his smile wide and full. "I look forward to us doing this again soon," he said.

Amina nodded, not bothering to fake a smile beneath her veil. "Good night, Kareem."

10

The two sisters were walking together arm in arm. Their giggling was infectious as Amina mimicked Kareem and Rasheeda did her best imitation of Basil. Since that first dinner, Kareem had become a fixture in their family home and an appendage at campaign headquarters. Where Kareem led, Basil followed, the two men like two narrow-minded peas-in-a-pod. Amina was thankful that the duo was so focused on their own interests that Kareem had no interest in her.

"Kareem makes my skin crawl," Amina said out loud.

The two women paused curbside, looking in both directions before crossing the street. Their evening strolls together had become a staple in their daily schedules and both were thoroughly enjoying the time they shared.

"So what do you plan to do?" Rasheeda asked.

"At some point I'm going to have to tell him and Father that I have no intention of marrying him."

"Telling Kareem won't be your problem. Father doesn't want you to tell him anything. He just wants you to listen and obey."

Amina blew a deep sigh. "So, has Father picked a man out for you yet?"

Rasheeda nodded, her eyes lifting with the smile beneath her veil. "Yes."

There was a moment of pause as Amina eyed her sister curiously. "Well?"

"Well, what?"

"Who is he? What's he like?"

Rasheeda laughed. "His name is Todd Bashir and he's away at medical school."

"Where's he going to school?"

"He's at Johns Hopkins in Maryland."

"A doctor! And you like him? You're really thinking about marrying him?"

Rasheeda shrugged, something in her gaze moving Amina to smile. Rasheeda chuckled and Amina laughed with her.

"I can't wait to meet him," Amina said.

Their conversation continued as the two women hurried down the block. As they neared Beale Street and the bakery Amina's stride slowed significantly.

"What's wrong?" Rasheeda questioned.

Amina shook her head. "Nothing."

But Rasheeda sensed it was something. A crowd was gathered inside the bakery and there were people lined up outside the door trying to gain admittance. From where they stood they could hear the sound of music vibrating through the windows. She tossed Amina a look, their two gazes meeting evenly. "So much for cookies," she said.

They'd crossed the street and were both standing off to the side to peer in through the window. Amina took a quick step behind her sister when she saw the Elliott family gathered in their usual corner table.

Harper was sitting with their friends Rachel and Dwayne and an elderly woman that Amina didn't recognize. The trio were staring toward the stage and the band. Shifting her gaze Amina was surprised to see Quentin playing saxophone, the alto timbre sending the sweetest sounds through the space. A wide smile pulled at her lips. She clutched her sister's arm as they stood staring with the rest of the crowd, completely mesmerized by the show that was unfolding.

She caught a glimpse of Troy out of the corner of her eye. He was moving toward his family, an attractive young woman by his side. She was as tall as him and model thin. She had a voluptuous bustline and a curvaceous backside. She wore an expensive designer dress that fit her enviable figure perfectly and the short length of her hair, a vibrant red, accentuated her face nicely. The two stopped short in the middle of the room as the woman spun her body around toward Troy, the two beginning to dance together. His dance partner pressed her body tight to his, wrapping her arms around him in a seductive embrace. Troy's hands rested against the line of her waist and he was laughing heartily at something she'd whispered in his ear.

Amina felt her breath leave her body like air seeping from a punctured balloon. She suddenly didn't know what to think, jealousy sweeping over her with a vengeance. She gasped, the grip she had on Rasheeda's arm tightening.

"What?" Rasheeda suddenly questioned, her head snapping in Amina's direction. "What's wrong?"

Her sister shook her head. Amina's eyes were wide as she struggled to look everywhere except in Troy's direction. "We need to go," she said as she turned abruptly and rushed back across the street.

After throwing one last look through the bakery window Rasheeda rushed after her sister, calling out her name.

Movement out the window caught Troy's attention and he was surprised to see the two women in their hijabs running across the street. He bolted toward the door, leaving his dance partner standing with her mouth open but by the time he could push past the crowd to the sidewalk outside both women were gone, disappearing into the darkness.

It was the third time her cell phone had rung, and, once again, Amina refused to answer it. Rasheeda stared at her, and Amina tossed her a look.

"What?"

"So you're not speaking to him now?"

"I'm angry."

"I get that but how does he know you're mad at him if you don't answer your phone and tell him why you're upset?"

Amina eyed her sister with annoyance.

"I was just asking," Rasheeda said, her nonchalant tone irritating Amina even more.

She took a deep breath and blew it out slowly. The ringing stopped and she was tempted to turn off the device when it began to ring again.

"Answer the phone, Amina!"

"Why should I?"

"Because I want to know who that girl was that he was dancing with."

"Then you answer it."

Rasheeda tossed back her covers, moving as if she were getting out of her bed. Amina snatched the phone from its resting spot, depressing the ringer. The women stared at each other, Rasheeda's eyebrows raised questioningly and Amina's gaze narrowed. Rasheeda's face lifted into a bright smile, moving her sister to laugh, her head waving eagerly.

She blew a deep sigh. "Hello?"

"Hello," Troy said, a sigh of relief blowing into the receiver.

"Who was that woman you were dancing with tonight?" The question was abrupt, her terse tone surprising them all.

Troy laughed. "Which one?"

"You danced with more than one?"

"I danced with quite a few. I would have danced with you too if you hadn't run away."

"I didn't run away."

"It looked like you were running away to me."

There was a moment of pause before Amina spoke. "I suddenly feel like I'm fifteen and I caught my boyfriend kissing a cheerleader."

Troy laughed. "Now that I didn't do. I didn't *kiss* anyone."

"I don't know that."

"Yes, you do."

"How would I know that?"

"Because you trust me and you know I would never do anything with any other woman to disrespect you. As long as I'm kissing you I will not be kissing any other women."

"Do I really?"

"You should know it, Amina. You should know it and you should trust me," Troy said matter-of-factly.

Amina reflected on his words briefly. "I told my sister she was making something out of nothing. That girl really wasn't that cute."

In the background Rasheeda giggled, clearly amused.

Troy laughed again. "Oh, she was cute. But make no mistake, my girl puts her cute to shame. My girl is extraordinarily beautiful. The most beautiful woman I know."

Amina finally laughed with him. "I told Rasheeda that, too!"

"What are you doing?" Troy asked.

"I was headed to bed."

"Come back to the bakery."

Amina's eyes widened. "It's late. I can't come back to the bakery."

"It's not late. And you could come if you wanted to come."

"My father would have a fit."

"Don't tell him. Just come."

She met the look her sister was giving her. Rasheeda had leaned forward in her seat, her eager expression moving Amina to smile.

"And what are you going to do if I do come?"

"I'm going to dance with you. And then I'm going to kiss you. It will be my only kiss tonight."

"You're crazy, Troy Elliott!"

"Crazy about you. So, are you coming?"

Amina could feel her heartbeat racing. "I'm on my way," she said, her voice dropping to a loud whisper.

Thirty minutes later Amina stood outside the door of Just Desserts as Troy unlocked and opened it for her. As she stepped inside he leaned to kiss her cheek before locking the door back behind her. Amina met the intense stare he was giving her with her own, everything about the moment overwhelming.

From someplace upstairs Amina could hear Quentin playing his saxophone. The sounds were sweet and teasing and sexier than she could have ever imagined. Troy said nothing as he entwined his fingers between hers and led her to the center of the newly renovated space. He eased an arm around her waist and pulled her to him, his body nestling easily against hers. Amina wrapped her arms around his neck and shoulders as Troy dropped his cheek against hers. His skin was heated and she gasped as it sent a rush of current throughout every nerve ending. A shiver coursed up the length of her spine. As the music danced in the air around them they did an easy slow drag, their bodies gliding from side to side against each other.

They danced until there was a sudden lull, the music ending abruptly. Troy continued to hold tight to her, the duo moving to a beat that only they could hear. And then he kissed her, his mouth dancing easily atop hers. It took her breath away and as his lips claimed hers, his tongue two-stepping with her tongue, Amina felt like the luckiest girl in the whole wide world.

An hour later Amina crept back into the family home, easing her way back to the room she shared with her sister. Rasheeda was sleeping soundly as Amina locked herself in the bathroom, on the phone with Troy.

Trying to make amends for her behavior earlier, Amina really felt bad about how she'd behaved. Contrition echoed in her voice as she told him so, whispering her apology so as not to wake her sister. Understanding why she'd reacted so emotionally had been a learning experience for them both. Her going to him without giving it a second thought had told them both something as well.

For the first time Amina fully realized just how intense the depth of her emotions could be. Her connection to Troy was like a lifeline. It allowed her to breathe. It was necessary and nurturing and everything about it felt amazing. When Amina felt that lifeline threatened, something inside of her snapped. And for the first time she had to learn how to temper her sensitivities.

Troy had been encouraging, everything out of his mouth meant to reassure her. His response had endeared him even more to her and if he asked again, no one and nothing could keep her from him.

Mike Chamberlain tossed up his hands in frustration. "Where have you been?" he asked, clearly perturbed. "You missed the meeting with the finance team last night."

Contrition painted Troy's expression. He gave his friend an apologetic nod. "Sorry about that. My last meeting ran over."

"What last meeting? I didn't see any meeting on your calendar."

"It was a last-minute appointment," Troy answered, the little white lie falling before he could catch it.

Mike eyed him curiously. "You were with that woman, weren't you?"

A wide grin spread across Troy's face. "What woman? I don't know who you're talking about."

"Oh, yes, you do. You know exactly who I'm talking about. That sexy little thing with the tent dresses and come-hither eyes. The one who looks like the flying nun by day and a supermodel by night."

Troy's gaze narrowed ever so slightly. "Watch how you talk about my girl, please."

"Now that we're on the same page, that girl."

Troy shrugged, changing the subject. "How'd the finance meeting go?"

Mike hesitated, the two men staring each other down. "All's good," he finally answered. "Donations are at an all-time high. People are really throwing their support behind you."

"That's good, right?"

"Which brings me back to that woman."

Troy rolled his eyes. "Don't start, Mike."

His friend held up his hands. "I'm not starting anything. I'm saying what I have to say and then I'm not going to say anything else about it."

Troy took a deep breath, then gestured for Mike to continue.

"You're the most honest man I know, Troy. Even as kids you never lied about anything. Ever! Now I see you sneaking around, avoiding the truth, trying to be with this woman and keep it secret and it worries me. And not just because of the election. Troy Elliott hiding how he feels and sneaking around to be with a woman he clearly cares about isn't you, brother. If Quentin had done it or I was doing it, you'd have something to say. You'd be the voice of reason. So that's what I'm trying to do. This can't continue and go well. It can't. And if it blows up on you I'm afraid that it's going to hurt you and Amina more than it will ever hurt your election chances."

Troy heaved a deep sigh as he and his friend locked gazes. He nodded his head slowly. "So what do you suggest I do?" Troy questioned. "This is an unusual situation and these are unusual circumstances."

Mike nodded. "I told you when you first came to me about running that you were going to face some challenges. You knew it wasn't going to be easy."

Troy took a deep breath. "And you also told me that no matter where this election took me that I needed to always stand by my convictions and do what I knew was right."

"Exactly! Be the man I know you to be."

"So where does that leave me and Amina? Because I'm not going to give her up."

"No one says you have to give her up."

The two men talked for a few more minutes before Mike went his way, leaving Troy to his own thoughts. He loved Amina. Even after witnessing Quentin's relationship with Harper bloom, he hadn't imagined himself loving any woman as intensely. But he loved Amina that much, and more, everything about the woman making him feel whole. The essence of his spirit was connected to Amina and he had no doubts that connection was eternal, no one and nothing able to change that. He wanted nothing but the best for her. He needed to protect and care for her. He trusted that she had his best interest at heart the way he had hers. They would grow old together and every aspect of their lives would be connected until death parted them.

Mike had been right. Under normal circumstances Troy knew he would never have hidden his love for Amina from anyone, wanting to shout his intentions to the world. And although their circumstances were anything but normal, he knew it didn't make what they were doing right.

* * *

Harper and Quentin were upstairs in their living quarters when Troy poked his head in to say hello. The couple were snuggled close together on the living room sofa, the television playing quietly in the background.

"Hey, what's up?" Troy chimed as he knocked loudly, announcing his arrival.

"Not much," Quentin answered as he waved his brother into the room.

"What are you up to?" Harper asked. "Is Amina coming?"

Troy shook his head. "No. I had some work to do. I needed to catch up on the supply orders before you ran out of flour and sugar."

Harper laughed. "He ran out last week. I already did the order."

"Did you really run out?"

Quentin shook his head. "No. We came close though. We know how busy you've been so Harper figured she would give you a hand and just take care of it."

Harper tossed him a wink of her eye and smiled brightly.

Troy blew a deep sigh as he sank into the oversize chair. "Thank you. I really appreciate the help."

"You need to focus on your campaign, not the bakery," Harper said. "Quentin and I can cover things here while you handle your business."

"I know," Troy said with a heavy nod, "but the bakery keeps me sane. Sometimes when things get hard, coming home just feels right."

Quentin tossed his wife a look. He shifted forward in his seat. "So, what's bothering you?"

Troy shrugged again, suddenly feeling like the weight of the world was on his shoulders. He didn't speak, unable to find the words to explain all he was feeling. He lifted his gaze to see his brother and sister-in-law staring at him. His mouth lifted in an easy smile.

Quentin leaned and gave his wife a quick kiss on the cheek. Harper tossed her legs off the sofa and stood up. "I need to call my grandmother to check up on her. I'll give you two some space." She kissed her husband one more time and pressed a quick kiss to Troy's cheek as she passed by him.

Troy grabbed her hand. "Thanks again, Harper, and tell Mama Pearl I said hello."

As Harper disappeared toward the back bedroom the two brothers met each other's stare. Quentin asked his brother again. "What's wrong?"

Troy dropped his head into his hands, his elbows resting on his thighs. "I love Amina," he finally answered as he looked back at the man.

Quentin laughed. "Please! I thought you had a real problem. Harper and I know you love Amina."

For a split second Troy was surprised. Then just like that, he wasn't. "So what do I do now?"

Quentin smiled. "I'll tell you like you told me, Big Brother. I have my own issues to deal with. And I really don't have the time or the energy to be worried about yours."

Troy chuckled softly. "I did say that to you once, didn't I?"

"Yes, you did. But just like you, I am worried about you anyway. I don't want to see you get hurt, Troy, and I definitely don't want to see Amina hurt. That wouldn't be cool."

Troy sighed. "I would never hurt Amina."

"I know that. And I know you two have some things you need to get past. But I know that you'll get past them easier with Amina by your side, than without her. You love her and that, Big Brother, is a very good thing. We can all see that Amina makes you feel alive and that you're doing the same thing for her. All your life, Troy, you've taken the right path. Done everything on the up and up. Didn't make waves. Now, if you want to make some noise, make some noise. If you want to make that jump, then jump. Life's too damn short for you to be playing it safe now."

Troy laughed, his brother's advice spinning in his head. "It's good to know that you've been paying attention all these years."

"I learned from the best."

11

Amina had agreed to meet Troy at his Oak Ridge home for lunch. On the drive there she'd questioned the decision more than once but the last time they'd snuck off to share a cup of coffee, holding hands beneath the table, a constituent had rushed him at the counter. The elderly man had been anxious to share his vision for the city with Troy and as he did, she saw their few minutes of alone time dwindle substantially.

It wasn't often that they both had a two-hour window of opportunity, so they were eager to take advantage of it. Troy's home had been the most likely place for them to see each other without having their time compromised. And Troy had insisted, making it clear that he wasn't interested in their hiding.

The spacious home was located in a secluded neighborhood. Situated on a four-acre tract of land it was serene and private with amazing natural living spaces. An open floor plan with lots of natural light through large palladium windows complemented hardwood floors, a stacked stone fireplace, and vaulted ceilings. The décor was sparse with little to no feminine touches. Amina was instantly in lust with the gourmet kitchen that boasted cherry cabinets, quartz countertops, stainless steel appliances, and a double oven.

The house tour had barely been completed when Troy spun her into his arms, cupped her head in his hands, and planted his lips atop hers. He caught her off guard but as soon as his tongue pushed past her lips and began to wrestle inside her mouth, his hands ruffling through her curls, she knew that coming to Troy had been the right decision.

As Troy eased her down atop his king-size bed she could only think about the feel of him against her, his touch consuming. He suddenly rolled onto his back, rolling her with him. His hands gripped the sides of her face as he kissed her intently, his lips like silk against her lips. Amina wrapped her arms around his neck, her hands roving across his neck and head as he licked the curve of her profile, his tongue tasting her skin. She hovered above him, slowly grinding her pelvis against the muscle hardening between his thick legs. His body heat was consuming, pushing her temperature to combustible levels and Amina marveled at the intensity of the sensations.

Troy was nestled deep in the valley between her legs as she pressed her body down against his. He was rock hard, his erection a solid rod of steel grinding beneath her. Amina found herself pushing back against him, meeting his urgent thrusts with her own. Heat raged from the center of her feminine core. The intensity was like nothing she'd ever known. Amina strained against him as she continued to hump his body against hers. He felt fuller and harder and all she wanted was more.

Troy suddenly grabbed the cheeks of her behind and rolled her back over. He reclaimed her mouth and kissed her over and over again. Amina pulled her arms over her head as she gave in to the sensations. Troy's hands danced over her breasts, across her abdomen and back, his pelvis continuing to grind with a vengeance against hers.

He tasted sweet and his mouth was perfection against her mouth. She slid her hands beneath his T-shirt, her fingers burning a heated trail across his skin. She was suddenly pushing her hips upward, her buttocks lifting off the bed as he continued to stroke her through her clothes, his body sending her to the edge of ecstasy.

Her orgasm was explosive, the intensity of it moving her to scream out Troy's name. It rolled off her tongue over and over again as his grinding against her brought her to climax. Troy suddenly cried out with her, his own explosion shooting beneath the fabric of his khaki slacks. Moisture seeped slowly down his leg, dampening the fabric.

He slowly pulled himself from her, his breathing heavy as he gasped for air. He pressed another kiss to her lips before rolling onto his side. "Are you okay?" he asked, concern seeping from his eyes.

Amina nodded, tears of sheer joy clouding her gaze. She smiled, pressing a palm to his chest. "I'm perfect," she said.

"Yes, you are!" Troy pressed another quick kiss to her lips. "I didn't expect us to do that."

"I know," Amina said, understanding the emotion they were sharing.

"It just felt so good to be close to you like that, Amina."

"I know."

"Do you regret it?"

She shook her head. "No. Not at all."

Troy smiled and kissed her again, his lips lingering sweetly. "I think I need to change my pants," he said as he moved toward the master bathroom.

Amina was still trying to catch her breath as she heard him turn on the water in the other room. She slowly lifted her body upward, completely overwhelmed by what had just happened between them. With everything she'd been taught she should have been upset and embarrassed but she wasn't. Not at all. The only thing that could have made the moment more perfect was if she'd allowed herself to completely let go. If she had given herself to him completely. She could only begin to imagine what might have been if they had been naked, Troy's body lost deep inside of hers. Another spasm rippled through her body at the thought.

Troy moved back into the room. He reached for her, pulling her back into his arms as he kissed her again. In that very moment Amina knew that no other man could ever make her feel the way Troy did.

"I'm going to make us some lunch," Troy said when he finally released the grip he had on her, allowing them both to come up for air. "And we need to talk."

Amina sucked in oxygen, fighting to catch her breath. "You kiss me like that, then change the subject to food?"

"If I don't change the subject, we're going to do something we shouldn't be doing. And after what we've already done, you have my head twisted. So I need food," he said as he gave her the most endearing smile.

"I just need to use your bathroom first," Amina said.

Minutes later he was clutching her hand as he guided her back to the kitchen. Pulling out a wicker chair he made her comfortable at the counter.

"I want to talk to you about something," Troy said as he pulled ingredients out of the refrigerator.

"There's something I need to talk to you about, too," Amina responded.

"You first," he said as he reached for a large glass bowl out of the cabinet.

Amina paused as she watched him toss pulled crabmeat, chunks of avocado, sprouts, baby lettuce, and dried cranberries with lime, chopped garlic, onion, cilantro, olive oil, and salt.

"That looks great!" she said.

"I'm an excellent cook," Troy said. He winked his eye at her.

She went back to watching him as he whisked the dressing, ensuring the flavors were just so.

He lifted his eyes and gestured for her to speak as he plated their salads. "So what do you want to talk about?"

She bit down against her bottom lip. "I have a second date tonight with Kareem Fayed."

Troy's hand stalled midair as he was scooping salad out of the bowl. "A second date? I don't recall hearing anything about a first date."

"Date is probably the wrong word because it's not really a date. We're just having dinner. And my brother will be there too."

"And you kept this first threesome encounter a secret from me because . . . ?"

"Because I didn't want you to be upset. You had that fundraising event and you needed to be focused on the election. Not on me. Especially since it was nothing."

"So now you're going on your second dinner date and you figured I wouldn't be upset this time?"

"I figured that it was better for you to know than it would be for you to *not* know. We don't keep secrets from each other, right? And like I said, it didn't mean anything before and it doesn't mean anything now. I wouldn't be going at all if my father wasn't insisting on it."

"So this is something you really don't want to do?"

"Not at all," she said with a shake of her head. "But . . ."

"Then don't go."

Amina met the harsh stare he was giving her. "Are you jealous?" The first hint of a smile pulled at her mouth.

"This has nothing to do with me being jealous."

"Yes, it does." Her smile widened.

He dropped the spoon into the bowl. "Then yes, I'm jealous and I don't want you going on dates with other men."

"Even if I have a chaperone?" Her grin was canyon wide.

Troy shook his index finger at her. "Don't joke, Amina. You know what I mean."

She blew a deep sigh. "I know but I don't have a choice here. My father and brother both are insisting and until this election is over and we can go public with our relationship I think I need to oblige them."

Troy passed her a plate of food and a fork. He moved to the seat beside her. He tossed her a look but said nothing. Taking her hand Troy passed a quick blessing over the food then proceeded to eat. The tension between them was suddenly palpable.

"So you're mad at me now?"

Troy blew a deep sigh. He sat back against his seat, resting his fork on his plate. "No. I'm frustrated. I understand that with you running your father's campaign and me running against him that we have a conflict of interest. Then we have the issue of your father's religious beliefs going against us. We're sneaking around like we're in high school and now I'm supposed to accept you dating men your father would prefer over me. It's just too much, Amina."

Amina didn't know what to say so she didn't bother to respond. She dropped her gaze onto her plate, savoring the delicious meal he'd prepared for them. The quiet was slightly unnerving and tears pressed hot against her eyelids as she struggled not to cry. As they both emptied their plates, Troy moved back to the other side of the counter. He pulled dessert out of the freezer.

"That looks really good," she said as he cut two slices of the frozen dessert for them to taste.

"Quentin made it. It's some kind of frozen berry cheesecake thing. I thought you'd like it." He tossed her a slight smile, the wealth of it easing some of the tension between them.

"So what was it you wanted to talk to me about?" she said. "Before I ruined our good mood."

Troy smiled. "Yeah, I actually wish I'd gone first now."

"Just make a girl feel worse, why don't you!" She rolled her eyes, feigning attitude.

Troy grabbed both plates and moved back to her side. He took a spoon and fed her the first bite of her dessert. She clasped her hand atop his as he guided the cutlery to her mouth. The heat from her touch warmed his spirit. He leaned and kissed her, his mouth dancing lightly against hers.

"I'm sorry," he whispered. "It's just . . ." He sighed, knowing he didn't need to say anything more.

Amina kissed him a second time, her tongue tapping lightly against his closed lips. She pressed her cheek to his, a low gasp blowing past her lips.

"Marry me," Troy said, the words hot against her ear. "I love you, Amina, and I want you to be my wife. Marry me."

Amina drew back in surprise, astonishment shining in her eyes.

Troy nodded, his tone emphatic, the words even more imposing. "I love you. Marry me."

"Troy, you can't be serious."

"I am very serious. I've been thinking long and hard about it, Amina, and we can't go on like this. I can't imagine my life without you. I want the whole world to know how much I love you. Marry me. Today."

"What about my father? The election?"

"I will give up the election if I have to. And I will go to your father and plead my case right now. I will do whatever it takes to be with you, Amina. You just have to want it as much as I do."

Tears were rolling down Amina's cheeks. Troy grabbed her hand, entwining his fingers between her fingers. He pulled her from the seat, leading her into the living room. He sat her on the sofa, lifting an index finger for her to give him a quick minute. He disappeared down the length of hallway toward the master bedroom and when he was out of sight Amina took a deep breath and then a second. She couldn't believe this was happening to her, her mind racing.

Troy suddenly reappeared. He moved back to her side and dropped down onto one knee in front of her. He had a small velvet box in his hand, and held it out toward her. Lifting the lid he exposed a stunning three-carat, princess-cut, diamond engagement ring. He met the look she was giving him, their gazes locking tightly.

"I love you, Amina Salman. Will you marry me?"

"Yes," Amina said, her voice a loud whisper.

"Say it again!"

"Yes!" Amina shouted louder. "I will marry you!"

"Today," Troy insisted.

Amina's eyes widened. "We can't get married today, Troy. I made a commitment to my father and I can't just walk away from that without talking to him. And we have to think about how this is going to impact your campaign. There's just too much we have to consider."

"Okay then, we'll do it tomorrow."

"Troy!"

"Think about it, Amina. This is our future we're talking about. And as you can see by the investment in my hand I didn't just come up with the idea yesterday. I don't plan to change my mind so doing it now makes just as much sense as doing it later. If you marry me now then I don't continue to run the risk of ruining your reputation every time I think about you. Marry me and I will do everything in my power to win your father's respect. I'll even consider converting to Islam."

Her eyes widened. "You would do that?"

"I would earnestly consider it. I've already begun to do some studying and research to learn more so that I have some understanding about the religion and what your family believes. I would only ask that you do the same. Your mother raised you outside your father's religion for a reason."

Amina nodded as she pondered his words. "What about the election?"

"I'll withdraw. I won't let it be a conflict for us."

"Absolutely not! I refuse to let you do that. I know how much you want to win, Troy. I also know that you're well on the way to doing just that despite my best efforts to help my father best you. I will not be responsible for your giving that up. Besides, I kind of like the idea of being the mayor's wife."

"Then marry me now and if it's what you want we'll keep it our secret until after the election. Once the election is over, we'll make the announcement and move you in here."

"But we will still be sneaking around, Troy."

He nodded. "I would much rather we tell everyone the minute it happens but if you're not ready, then I'm willing to give you the time you need. But I would rather sneak around to spend time with my wife, than sneak around to spend time with some other guy's preschool fiancée. And if we get caught, what can anyone say? We'll be legally married."

Amina blew a deep sigh. She didn't know what to think. On the one hand it made all the sense in the world. On the other it was the craziest thing she'd ever considered.

* * *

Amina felt like the third wheel as Kareem Fayed and her brother chatted easily. Once again they seemed to discount her presence at the table. The restaurant was comfortable but there was nothing about the company of either man that had her feeling at ease. She couldn't help but wish she were still with Troy back at his home. She took a deep breath as she looked from one to the other. Kareem tossed her a smile.

"So, Amina, are you enjoying your stay here in Memphis?" Kareem asked.

She nodded. "Memphis is beginning to feel like home."

"I was telling Basil that I'd enjoy taking you around to help you with the adjustment. It will give us an opportunity to get to know each other better. Basil was in agreement."

"You might want to consider asking me if that's something I'd be interested in, not Basil," Amina said.

Kareem smiled. "Forgive me. I forget that you are a woman with a very strong will."

Basil shot her a hateful look. "Brother, I apologize for my sister's rudeness. Amina is still learning our ways and expectations."

Amina bristled. "I am quite capable of speaking for myself, Basil," she said.

Kareem held up a hand toward her brother. "I admire your spirit, Amina. And I know your brother only has your best interest at heart."

There was a moment of awkward silence that dropped down over the table. Amina focused her attention on the serving of pasta before her, wishing she could be anyplace other than where she was. She looked up to find Kareem staring at her, the look in his eyes disturbing. Her heartbeat raced slightly and she suddenly felt like prey that was being hunted. She took a deep breath to ease the sensation.

"So, Basil tells me that you two have done business together?"

Kareem nodded. "I helped your brother acquire some property he was interested in."

"I was telling Amina that the other day. That I want that piece on the corner of Beale Street. With her legal connections she'll be very useful to us."

"I'm still not understanding," Amina said. "You said you already hold the title to some of that property. How'd you manage that? That area is prime real estate. I imagine that would have taken a significant cash investment."

Basil sneered, tossing Kareem a look. "Not necessarily."

Kareem smiled. "Basil utilized the adverse possession laws to his benefit. Most of the property he acquired was vacant or foreclosed and with no true claims of ownership he filed the appropriate paperwork with the register of deeds office."

Amina looked from one to the other, her eyes blinking anxiously. "You're kidding me, right?"

Basil tossed her a look. "Why would we be kidding?"

"Because that's illegal, Basil. You can't just go claim other people's property."

The two men tossed each other a look.

Amina shook her head from side to side. "Don't you know you can go to jail for that?"

"For what?" Basil snapped. "For being creative? For

being ingenious? For getting the job done in a way that you can't fathom?"

"For obtaining property by false pretenses! What you've done undermines the entire real estate process. Why do we need mortgages and contracts when you can just go take someone's property?"

"Stay out of my business, Amina. You need to just do what you're told. Now, I need some paperwork filed downtown for that corner piece on Beale Street. You need to get that done. Kareem will give you the details. It's not your place to ask questions."

Amina leaned forward in her seat. She snatched the veil from her face, wanting to ensure her brother made no mistakes about what she was feeling. Her face was ice. She hissed under her breath. "Not in this lifetime or the next will I risk my legal license for you, Basil. There's a family that owns that property. It's theirs *legally*. You being deceptive, pretending you know what you're doing, won't change that fact."

Basil slammed his cloth napkin against the table. Kareem sat upright, looking from one sibling to the other.

"Basil, I'm sure you and I can address all of Amina's concerns and assure her that we've done nothing wrong."

Amina tossed Kareem a look as he continued. "Amina, all Basil has done is found a lawful way to work the system. People are millionaires all day long for doing that very thing. Essentially, Basil formed a private trust, made himself the trustee, filled out a deed, and had it recorded at the register of deeds office. It was all perfectly legal."

Amina tossed up her hands. "Just because you file

a new deed and put your name on it doesn't make you the exclusive owner! Does Father know about this scam of yours?" she asked, still staring at her brother.

Basil suddenly lunged across the table. He grabbed her by the neck, his hand like a vice cutting off her oxygen. Amina's eyes widened in horror.

"If you breathe one word of this to Father, I will hurt you, Amina. Don't cross me, little girl! I promise you, if you do, you will know hurt like you have never known hurt before!" he repeated before pushing her harshly back against her seat.

Amina gasped for air, clutching both of her hands to her neck as she came to her feet. Tears misted her eyes. Basil stood upright, adjusting his suit jacket around his torso. He tossed a harsh glare around the dining room, eyeing the few patrons who were watching them. His stare was challenging. Kareem stood up as well just as the restaurant manager rushed to the table. Amina recognized the man from the mosque.

"Is there a problem here?" he questioned.

Kareem shook his head. "We apologize, brother. Our sister here was just having a moment."

"It won't happen again," Basil added.

The man looked from the two men to Amina and back. He nodded, and said nothing, as he moved back toward the kitchen.

Basil tossed Amina one last glare as he sat back down, his arms crossed over his chest. Kareem heaved a deep sigh, taking his own seat. He reached into the breast pocket of his suit jacket and pulled out his billfold. He dropped four twenty-dollar bills onto the table, then focused his gaze on Amina.

"Sit down, Amina," he said, his tone commanding. "And fix your veil."

He reached for her arm and she snatched the appendage from his grasp. She hurled her veil to the floor. "Go to hell," she spat. "Both of you go straight to hell!" Then turning, Amina rushed from the restaurant to her car.

12

When Troy had opened his front door Amina had
thrown herself into his arms. Tears had been streaming down her face, her body shaking with rage. She'd
been holding onto him for ten minutes and he still
had no clue what had upset her. He tightened his
arms around her torso and pulled her closer, wanting
to ease whatever was paining her. He felt her body
finally relax against his and he gently kissed her forehead.

He gently cupped his hand beneath her chin and
lifted her eyes to his. "What happened, baby?"

She shook her head, her eyes misting again. She
swiped at her face with the back of both hands. There
was a sadness in the dark orbs that Troy found disconcerting but she seemed unwilling to let him inside.

"I'm sorry," Amina said, still rubbing at her eyes. "I
just . . ."

Troy led her into his family room and eased her
onto a seat. He pulled the ottoman in front of her and
sat down. Leaning toward her he clasped both of her
hands in his. "Talk to me, Amina," he commanded.

She took a deep breath, her gaze locking with his. "Basil," she said, her head shaking.

"I don't understand. Did something happen to your brother?"

Amina slowly undid the pins that held her hijab in place. With methodical precision she unwrapped one side and then the other until she'd released her curls, her hair falling free against her shoulders. She laid the scarf on the table beside her chair. She took another breath then slowly lifted her chin, brushing her fingers across her skin.

Amina's neck was bruised, her pale complexion mottled black and blue. Troy bristled, the concern on his face shifting to something like rage. He stood up so abruptly that it scared her and she gasped loudly, her eyes widening.

"Troy!"

"Your brother did that to you?"

Amina nodded, her tears dropping against her cheeks. She gestured for him to sit back down and told him what had happened. She told him all of it. How Basil was stealing property that did not belong to him. How he wanted her help in doing so. How he'd choked her until she felt like she might pass out from the infraction. She told him and when she was done Troy was angrier than he ever remembered being.

He stood back up and moved into the other room, returning with his cell phone.

"What are you doing?"

"I'm calling the police and you're going to file a complaint against your brother."

"I can't, Troy. Please don't do that!" She reached for the phone in his hand and powered it down.

His expression was incredulous. "What do you mean you can't? You have to, Amina!"

"I can't. It would affect my father. I can't be responsible for the headlines reading that candidate Nasser Salman's son was charged with assault. It would destroy any chance he has in this campaign. And I can't have the record show that the victim is involved with his opponent. Your name can't be tied to this either."

Troy heaved a deep sigh. "And what does your father say about this?"

"I haven't spoken to him. After it happened I came right here."

"And this guy Fayed didn't do anything to help you?"

She shook her head no.

Troy paced the floor, his hands clutching his hips. "Well, I don't care about my campaign. You have to call the police."

She shook her head. "I care, Troy. I care and I need you to support my decision. Please!"

He met her stare, her eyes pleading. His head waved from side to side, something in his gut uneasy with what she was asking of him. Troy wanted nothing more than to wrap his own hands around Basil Salman's neck. Amina's pressing charges against him would be the least of Basil's worries. Doing nothing felt all kinds of wrong.

He sat back down. "So what do you want to do?"

An uneasy silence shifted between them. Since she'd pulled out of the restaurant's parking garage that was all she had thought of. What she should do. What she wanted to do. The questions had played over and over again in her mind until they'd blurred into a raging migraine that had her head feeling like it was about to explode off her shoulders. But even in the midst of all the pain there was only one thing she was certain of.

"Amina?"

She lifted her eyes back to Troy's, easing into the embrace of his loving gaze. She shifted forward in her seat. "The only thing I want to do right now is marry you. I just want to be your wife."

"Enough," Nasser snapped as he slammed his hand against the top of his mahogany desk.

"But Father . . ."

"I said enough, Basil!"

Basil had been pleading his case to his father for over an hour, the patriarch eyeing him with disdain. Nasser had nothing to say as his son blamed his own bad behavior on something Amina had done. Without knowing any details about their confrontation he knew Basil would have lied by omission or he would have just lied outright, embellishing the story in his own favor. If Nasser knew nothing else he knew his son's many flaws and faults. He reached his last level of tolerance when his efforts to contact his eldest daughter failed, Amina not answering his calls. She'd not been seen or heard from and he was past the point of being worried.

Nasser turned his attention to his youngest child. "Rasheeda, have you spoken to your sister?"

Rasheeda shook her head. "No, sir."

"Do you know where she might have gone?"

"No, sir."

Nasser stared at the girl, her eyes focused on the floor beneath her feet. He moved to her side and leaned to kiss her forehead. "Do not worry yourself, Rasheeda. I'm sure that your sister is fine. She is very street savvy. Now, if Amina calls you, you tell her I want her to come home. Tell her everything is going to be fine. Is that understood?"

Rasheeda lifted her eyes to stare at her father. She tossed Basil a look, her brother eyeing her with a narrowed gaze. Shifting her focus back to Nasser she nodded. "Yes, Father."

As Nasser walked out of the room he gestured for Basil to follow him. Before doing so Basil moved to Rasheeda's side. "If she calls you, you tell me where she is first. Do you understand me?" he hissed, his hot breath blowing against her face.

Rasheeda looked him in the eye but said nothing. Basil clenched his fists, his jawline tight. He repeated himself. "Do you understand me, Rasheeda?"

Before she could respond their father called from the other room. "Basil! Now!"

Basil tossed her one last look as he made his way out of the room. Rasheeda blew the breath she'd been holding past her lips. She took an inhalation of air, filling her lungs before releasing it slowly. Moving out of the living space, she headed to her bedroom and closed the door. Changing out of her clothes, she slid beneath the covers and engaged her reader. She had only read two chapters when she heard her father's bedroom door close. She was finished with the fifth chapter when she heard Basil exit the home, his pretty sports car pulling out of the driveway. It wasn't until she finished the ninth chapter, when she was certain her father was asleep and Basil was long gone, that she dialed Amina's cell phone number and waited for her sister to answer.

* * *

Amina was sound asleep in Troy's bed. He looked in on her for the umpteenth time, needing to assure himself that she was safe and well. They had talked for a good while and despite his finally agreeing to handle things her way he found himself second-guessing his decision.

Early in his legal career he'd done some pro bono work for a women's shelter located in downtown Memphis. Too many of their clients had been women who'd been abused by a man they had trusted to protect them. Husbands, fathers, even a son or two had been guilty of some sort of physical assault and in too many cases the women had refused to prosecute.

Troy had grown weary of the excuses, many of them founded in fear. His last case had been the hardest. The young woman had barely been twenty-four, pregnant with her third child. Her boyfriend had only slapped her the first time. Dragged her by the hair the second. Troy first met her after she'd been burned with a hot iron, the scar a reminder every time she looked in the mirror.

The young woman had blamed herself, believing that things would have been different had she not been the woman she was. Thinking that her love had not been enough to calm the beast that claimed her man's soul. Excuses for every bruise and broken bone had rained from her mouth like water from a faucet. The last time her boyfriend had hit her, also flinging her eight-year-old son down a flight of stairs, had been her moment of reckoning. Troy was pleased to say the boyfriend was doing a twenty-plus-year sentence for his many crimes and the young woman and her children were thriving.

As he looked down on Amina, her body curled into the fetal position around one of his pillows, he found himself second-guessing himself and her. He blew a deep sigh as he pulled a cashmere blanket up and over her shoulders and leaned to press a light kiss to her cheek.

Moving out of the room Troy eased himself into the kitchen for a cup of coffee. He didn't imagine that he would be able to get any sleep so he saw no reason to try. As he waited for the Keurig coffeemaker to brew him a hot cup of brew, Amina's cell phone vibrated against the countertop where she had left it. Earlier, it had rung nonstop and she had refused to answer it. Then there'd been silence. Despite his insistence, Amina had adamantly refused to call home. As it rang again Troy fathomed someone might be worried about her. So he answered the call, pulling the device to his ear.

"Hello?"

Silence greeted him on the other end.

"Hello?"

There was a long pause, a loud moment of quiet trolling across the phone line. Behind the quiet came the sound of someone breathing, a hint of curiosity in each breath.

"Hello? Is anyone there?" Troy asked for the third time.

Rasheeda cleared her throat, her voice a low whisper into the receiver. "Yes, hello. I'm trying to reach Amina Salman. Have I dialed the right number?"

"You did. Is this her sister?"

"Yes, I'm Rasheeda Salman. Is this Troy?"

He smiled ever so slightly, mildly surprised that Amina's sister knew his name. "Yes, it is!"

"Is my sister okay? Basil didn't hurt her badly, did he? I was worried about her."

"She's fine. She's a little shaken up but she's going to be okay. She's sound asleep right now. Do you want me to wake her?"

Rasheeda blew a sigh of relief. "No, let her rest. I just wanted to make sure she was okay. I know she's safe with you."

Troy nodded, then remembered she couldn't see him through the phone. "You don't have to worry. I promise you I'll make sure Amina is okay."

"Thank you."

"How about you?" Troy asked. "Are you okay? We don't need to be concerned about your safety, do we?"

There was a moment's hesitation before Rasheeda responded. "I'll be fine. Don't let her worry about me."

Reflecting on her tone, Troy wasn't altogether sure that he believed her. "Okay, but if you need anything from either one of us, you just call. Take my cell number," he said as the seven digits rolled off his tongue. "Anything, Rasheeda, and I mean it. Or, if for any reason you can't call, just find your way back to the bakery. You'll be safe there."

"Okay," Rasheeda answered.

"Promise me," Troy intoned.

"I promise."

There was another moment of hesitation between them. Troy broke the silence. "I'll tell Amina to call you as soon as she wakes up."

"Thank you. And Troy?"

"Yes?"

"Please, tell my sister I love her."

13

Amina finally made her way to her father's office. For two days straight she'd hidden out at Troy's home, pondering her next move. And despite his best efforts Troy had been unable to help her with the decisions she needed to make. Amina had kept him at arm's length knowing that it would not have served either of them well had she not been able to resolve her problems by her lonesome.

That first day had been the hardest as she'd assessed the pros and cons of their situation. The second day had been easier as she'd paused, thinking she might second-guess her decisions. When she hadn't, knowing wholeheartedly that she was doing the right thing, she'd put on her favorite Anne Klein suit and headed to campaign headquarters. As she walked into her father's office, her convictions firm, Amina knew nothing and no one was going to change her mind about what she wanted.

"Amina!"

She moved to her father's side and kissed his cheek. "Good morning, Father."

"Where have you been? I have been worried about you."

"I needed time to think. I've been staying with a friend. I apologize for not letting you know where I was."

Nasser nodded. "I understand that there was a situation between you and your brother?"

"Basil attacked me and if he were not my brother I would be pressing charges against him."

Nasser tensed his jaw tight as he clenched his back teeth together.

Amina continued. "But he is my brother and because the negative publicity would not serve your campaign well I can't do that to you."

Nasser took a deep breath. "I don't know the details of what happened, Amina, but I don't think it was Basil's intent to do you harm."

"Father, you don't know Basil and you don't know half the things he's done. Basil will hurt anyone who is in his way. If you hope to win this election and have a successful term as mayor, I would strongly advise you to distance yourself as far from Basil as you can."

Nasser came to his feet, moving around his desk to stand in front of her. "Basil is my son, Amina."

"And I am your daughter. As well as your campaign manager. And as a licensed attorney and officer of the court I would not steer you wrong."

"Daughter, I wish you had a better understanding of how things should be with family; between a father and his children, men and women. Your mother did not serve you well to turn you away from Islam. I forgive your behavior, Amina, because I know you have not been taught better."

Amina shook her head. Her tone was terse. "This is

not about my mother or how I was raised. There is nothing my mother could have done differently or that the Nation of Islam can do now to change any of that. This is all about Basil, his illegal activities and his destructive behavior. It has nothing to do with your religion or my beliefs. You don't know half of what you son has been up to and you need to."

Nasser moved back to his leather chair and sat down. "I don't want to discuss this further, Amina. I expect your obedience. I will deal with your brother and his behavior. Now we have work to do," he said. He looked back down to the papers on his desk and Amina knew she had been dismissed.

She stood quietly for a few minutes, then rounded the desk to her father's side. There were tears in her eyes as she leaned to kiss his cheek, wrapping her arms around his neck. She allowed her lips to linger against his skin as she wished a quick prayer skyward. As she stood straight she met his gaze and smiled, a sweet bend to her lips. She loved her father with everything in her. In that moment she knew that he would never know how much.

"I'm sorry, Father," she said. "I can't continue on as your campaign manager. I wish you much success and pray that Basil will be able to serve you well. But I'm handing in my resignation."

Nasser stared at her for a brief moment, then nodded. "That is probably for the best, Daughter. This will allow you more time to focus on your commitment to Kareem; to prepare yourself to be a good wife and mother."

Amina shook her head. "No, sir. Kareem is not the man I want to spend the rest of my life with. He's self-centered, egotistical, and a coward. He will never have my heart. I know that I would never be safe with Kareem and I don't trust that he would protect me if the need arose. I refuse to marry him."

"That is totally unacceptable!" Nasser exclaimed. His eyes were wide and his nostrils flared in anger.

"I'm sorry that upsets you, Father, but I want better for myself. I would hope that you would want better for me as well."

"How can you think that I do not have your best interests at heart, Amina?"

Amina's tears finally rained down her cheeks. "If you want what's best for me, then accept that Kareem is not it. Support my decision."

It was on the tip of her tongue to tell her father about her relationship with Troy but as he stood staring at her, Amina knew that her father would never be accepting of her choices. She felt a sliver of her heart crack in two. She took a deep breath and held it.

"We can discuss this further at home," Nasser said, his tone dismissive.

"I won't be coming home," Amina said, blowing warm air past her lips. "I leave for Atlanta tonight and I'll be gone for the weekend. If you want to talk more on Monday I would love to meet with you but I won't be moving back into your home when I return."

Nasser shook his head. "You disappoint me, Amina."

She forced another smile to her face. "I'm sorry you feel that way, Father," she said. As she moved out the door, she tossed him one last look. "I'm disappointed in you, too."

Rasheeda had never flown in an airplane before. The flight from Memphis to Atlanta was one new experience after another. For most of the one-and-a-half-hour flight she felt like a deer caught in the headlights. If it were not for Amina in the first-class seat beside her she imagined she'd have been completely lost.

Amina seemed to read her mind as she smiled in her sister's direction. The woman's excitement was infectious and Rasheeda smiled with her, feeling slightly vulnerable without her veil.

"Mother is going to be so surprised," Amina chimed. "I can't wait to see her face. I can't wait for her to see you," she said as she pressed a hand to her sister's cheek.

"It's been so long," Rasheeda gushed. "Do you think she'll like me?"

Amina laughed. "Mother loves you. And yes, I think she's going to *like* everything about you."

"I'm really happy that you asked me to be your maid of honor, Amina."

"I'm really happy that you agreed to come and stand up with me."

"I like Troy. I think he's perfect for you. And I wouldn't miss your wedding for anything in the world."

Amina grinned. "Troy is perfect!"

She paused for a brief moment, excited by the prospect of becoming Troy's wife. Saying yes to Troy had been the easiest decision she had to make. And although she had hoped to be of help to her father in his campaign she knew she had to step aside. She knew that eliminating that conflict of interest was necessary for her and Troy to move forward.

And they were moving forward. Troy had one last political commitment that afternoon before he and his family would be on their own plane to Atlanta. A quick phone call to her mother had gotten the wheels rolling, a wedding ceremony planned for the following day. They'd only have a day and a half to honeymoon before they would have to fly home and have Troy back on the campaign trail Monday morning.

Amina had done much soul-searching to get to this point. She had never been foolhardy, rushing into anything without some serious thought first. When Troy had first asked her to marry him, she hadn't wanted to give it any consideration. It was too soon. There were too many challenges. It couldn't possibly work. Questions and doubts had been like fodder, the wealth of it fueling every fear she ever had. But with all her reservations and concerns what kept leaping to the forefront of her mind was how much she loved Troy.

She loved him with every ounce of breath in her. She loved him more than she had ever thought possible. Loving Troy had made her final decision easy. And loving Troy would have taken her down the aisle days earlier if such a thing had been possible.

Despite the rush of it, Amina had only one regret. Not having her father or even her brother to share in her joy broke her heart. Her sister didn't miss the look of sadness that crossed her face.

"Father will come around," Rasheeda said softly as she pressed a warm palm against the back of Amina's hand. "It will be hard in the beginning but he does love us."

Amina nodded. She really hoped that was true.

Laughter could be heard outside the front door. The crowd inside was consumed with laughter when

Troy and his family found their way to the home of Rebecca Brewer. The wealth of it was contagious as Harper broke out into giggles and Troy and Quentin both found themselves smiling.

When Amina swung the door open, her own excitement spilled out the entrance as she threw herself into Troy's arms, kissing him eagerly.

"Hi!" she finally exclaimed as she looked from Quentin to Harper and back to Troy.

Greetings rang in perfect sync as they traded hugs and kisses. From somewhere in the back of the ranch-style house, Amina's mother called out to her, using her family nickname.

"Mimi! Let that young man come up for air so we can meet him, please!"

Troy laughed. "Mimi?"

"Only my mother calls me that. If you call me Mimi, I will hurt you!" she said as she laughed with him. She took his hand and pulled him inside, gesturing for her new family to follow.

Amina led them down the hall into the open family space. The laughter subsided abruptly as everyone turned to stare. Troy suddenly felt shy with all eyes on him. He tossed Quentin and Harper a dazed look and Harper giggled warmly.

"Hello!" Troy chimed, his hand waving slightly.

Amina's mother jumped from her seat and rushed to his side. Standing on tiptoe she wrapped her arms around his torso and hugged him warmly. Pulling back, her hands gripping his shoulders, she studied him intently. Troy's eyes widened, words stuck somewhere deep in his throat.

"You are as handsome as my girls said you were!" Rebecca exclaimed.

Troy blushed profusely. "Thank you!"

Amina shook her head. "Troy Elliott, this is my mother, Rebecca Brewer. Mom, this is Troy. And this is his brother, Quentin, and Quentin's wife, Harper."

"Welcome to my home!" she said. "I'm so excited to have you all here. Come sit! Make yourselves comfortable!"

As the family pointed them to empty seats, Amina continued the introductions. "These are my uncles, Manuel Brewer and Nico Brewer and my aunt, Rochelle Hines. The three gossips in the corner there with Rasheeda are my cousins Alisa, Alaina, and Abigail. And somewhere in the other room watching the game are more cousins; David, Prentiss, Alonzo, and Brighton."

"And Mamie!" Uncle Nico added. "My wife loves a good ball game."

The young woman named Abigail called out loudly, "Please, please, please tell me that you two have more brothers. At least one. Please!"

The women all laughed.

"Sorry," Troy said. "It's just us two."

"Damn!" Alisa exclaimed as she snapped her fingers.

"And you're really happily married?" Abigail asked, her gaze falling on Quentin as she licked her lips.

Harper laughed as she eased her arm through her husband's. "He's very happily married!" she said. "And take your eyes off my man!"

The room burst out laughing again.

Amina shook her head. "Please excuse my cousins. They're all desperate!"

"I would not define us as desperate, thank you very much!" Alaina said.

"We're desperate," Abigail interjected.

"Speak for yourself," Alisa chimed.

"We're all so excited to meet you and your family, Troy. Every time my Mimi says your name her eyes light up. I have never seen her so happy."

Troy smiled. "I feel the same way. Your daughter has made me the happiest man in the world."

Quentin nodded. "Would anyone mind if I made myself happy watching that game in there?"

"Really, Quentin?" Harper chimed.

Quentin leaned to kiss her lips. "Really!"

Rebecca gestured him on. "Just make yourself at home. If you want to watch the game, baby, you go watch the game," she said.

An elderly woman poked her head into the room and looked around. "I heard voices," she said as her gaze rested on Troy.

"Oh, Grandmother!" Amina exclaimed. "I forgot you were in the kitchen.

"Me and Bettina was finishing up the fried chicken," the matriarch said as she moved into the room, coming to stand in front of Troy. She eyed him intently. "So, dis be him?"

Amina nodded. "Yes, ma'am. Troy, this is my grandmother, Ann Brewer. Grandmother, this is my fiancé, Troy Elliott."

Troy rose from his seat, leaning to wrap the older woman in a warm hug. "It's very nice to meet you, Mrs. Brewer."

She patted him warmly against the back as she hugged him in return. "Everyone calls me Grandmother." She leaned back to stare up at him. "Ain't you just the prettiest thing! Amina, he is just the prettiest thing!"

The room laughed again. The banter continued from room to room as the two families all got to know one another. The mood was easy and comfortable and the Elliott family was made to feel completely at home. After an hour or so Amina's uncles came to their feet and gestured for Troy to follow.

"Let's give the women some space," Uncle Nico said. "Give us men some time to get to know each other better," he said.

Troy tossed Amina a wink of his eye and leaned to plant a light kiss against her lips. She smiled brightly as he disappeared with her uncles through the sliding glass doors to the backyard. When all the men were out of earshot, the women converged. Talking over each other they tossed questions at Amina faster than she could answer them. Both Rasheeda and Harper sat back like two flies on the wall, Harper amused and Rasheeda completely overwhelmed.

Rebecca eased over to their side and gave them both a warm smile. She wrapped her arms around her younger daughter's shoulders. "You're not used to all this feminine energy, are you, baby?"

Rasheeda shook her head. "No, ma'am."

"Baby doll, don't ma'am me! Ma'am makes me feel so old!"

"Yes, ma'am."

Harper and Rebecca both laughed. Rebecca shook her head as she kissed her daughter's cheek. "You don't know how happy I am to have you here."

Rasheeda smiled, a hint of red coloring her cheeks. Rebecca winked as she headed toward the kitchen. "Let me check on that food. I know everyone has to be hungry."

Harper shifted her gaze to Amina's sister. "You look a little overwhelmed. Are you doing okay?"

Rasheeda nodded. "I really am. This is just so different from my life in Memphis. I've never seen people laugh so much!"

Harper giggled. "You and Amina are very lucky. You have a wonderful family!"

"I wish I'd had this growing up," Rasheeda said with a deep sigh.

Harper nodded. "You have it now. That's all that matters."

The two women talked for a few minutes more before they were interrupted by Rebecca's calling the family to dinner. Amina gestured for them to head to the kitchen and dining room as she moved outside to reclaim her man.

Troy and Quentin both were standing in deep conversation with her uncles and her cousin Brighton, the group debating politics. Her uncle Manuel, a staunch Republican, was making a point about taxation that the others weren't receiving well. It was a passionate exchange and Amina hesitated for a brief moment as Troy made his point, her uncle giving him his due.

"You right, you right, you right!" the elder man was saying, his head bobbing excitedly.

Amina chuckled warmly. "Grandmother says you all need to come eat."

"Don't have to tell me twice," Uncle Nico said. He extended his hand toward Troy. "Congratulations, young man. She's a good girl, my niece. I trust that she'll be in good hands."

"Thank you, sir," Troy responded.

"Amina, this one's a keeper," he extolled as he wrapped her in a deep bear hug. "Don't mess it up!"

Amina laughed. "I won't, Uncle Nico."

As the men headed back inside, Troy and Amina took a quick minute to themselves. Troy wrapped his arms around her torso and pulled her close. He kissed her easily, his lips dancing like silk across hers. Amina purred ever so softly, savoring the taste of him.

"So, do you women have all of our wedding plans under control?"

Amina nodded. "We do. My mother has been calling in favors and pulling strings since I got here. You'd think she was the one getting married."

"As long as you're happy with everything."

"I really am and thank you for faxing your documents over to the courthouse. I picked up our license and you'll just have to sign it in front of Judge Colter tomorrow before the ceremony."

"I'm excited to meet Judge Colter. I've heard good things about him."

"He was my mentor in law school. And in some respects, a substitute father figure. He taught me everything I know."

"Then I'm even more excited about meeting him," Troy said.

Amina's grin was a mile wide. "My family thinks you're great! Everyone loves you. In fact, if she were a few years younger I think my grandmother might try to give me a run for my money."

Troy laughed. "I wasn't going to say anything but I think your granny tried to goose my bottom."

She laughed with him. "I'm *sure* my grandmother tried to goose your bottom!"

* * *

There was just a sliver of a moon in the late-night sky when Troy stepped outside to take in the view. Inside, the Brewer family was still going strong, a game of bid whist being played at the kitchen table and an old Tyler Perry movie playing on the DVD player in the family room. He had just sent a prayer of thanksgiving skyward when Amina's mother joined him out on the patio.

"What a beautiful night!" Rebecca exclaimed.

Troy smiled warmly. "It is. You couldn't ask for better weather."

"It'll be perfect for the wedding tomorrow!"

"I really want to thank you for everything you've done. Amina couldn't be happier."

"My daughter is happy because of you, Troy. I'm sure that if you were to take her down to town hall for the ceremony and then to lunch at McDonald's she would be just as excited."

"I love Amina very much. I hope you know that there isn't anything I wouldn't do for her. I want the very best for her and I promise you I will make every effort to be the best husband that I can be."

Rebecca crossed her arms over her torso, hugging herself tightly. Her eyes misted with tears. Her head bobbed up and down against her shoulders. She shifted her gaze, staring up at that sliver of moon as she paused in reflection. "I didn't want Amina to go to Memphis. But if she hadn't she wouldn't have met you."

Curiosity crossed his face. "Why didn't you want her to go?"

"I was afraid that being there with her father

wouldn't be a good thing for her. Nasser loves his faith more than he has ever loved his family."

Troy turned to stare at the woman as she continued to speak. The dim light cast a shadow across her face but Troy could still see the concern that blanketed her expression.

"Please don't think I'm bashing my ex-husband because I try not to. And I do know how much he loves our children. I just think he loves Islam more."

"Is that why you left?" Troy asked.

Rebecca hesitated, seeming to choose her words carefully. "I left because I couldn't be myself with Nasser. He had an image of how a good wife and mother should be and how a woman was supposed to conduct herself. I wasn't comfortable in that mold."

"But you left Rasheeda and Basil with him?"

"Yes, I did. Nasser was in a position to be the better parent. He was stable. I was not. I did what I thought was in my children's best interest. I left Amina too but she is very much her mother's daughter. She refused to settle herself into that mold. For Nasser it was easier to send her to me and let the chips fall where they did than to deal with how spirited she was."

"Amina wants her father's approval. It's very important to her."

Rebecca blew a sad sigh. "Pleasing Nasser is almost impossible and the only way to get his approval is to do what he wants and not what you want."

"Well, I hope that he wants Amina happy and that he'll eventually accept the two of us being together."

"Amina tells me that you were willing to consider converting?"

"I was but I don't think it's for me. Amina understands that I have to follow my heart and do what I think is best. But I'm willing to support her choice and what she wants for herself. Ours would not be the first interfaith relationship."

Rebecca nodded her head. "I'm happy that you love Amina as much as you do because she's going to need to trust that when her father turns on her. And trust me when I tell you, Nasser will turn his back on her for marrying a man he didn't approve first. It'll be more about his need for control than anything else."

Troy had only a quick minute to ponder the woman's words when she suddenly tossed up her hands.

"Look how late it is!" she exclaimed excitedly. "It's almost midnight! Go kiss my daughter good night, then get out. It's your wedding day and you're not supposed to see the bride before the ceremony!"

14

That next day, at one o'clock in the afternoon, Amina Salman and Troy Elliott vowed to honor and cherish each other as husband and wife. As their two families looked on in support, the couple professed their love, promising each other fidelity and respect for as long as they lived.

Amina's mother had secured space at Frogtown Cellars winery. The event facility was located an hour from Atlanta, at the foot of the north Georgia mountains. The main building was a timber-frame structure with cathedral ceilings, hand-carved Tennessee flagstone walls, and Brazilian cherry floors. Its natural setting, quiet ambience, and breathtaking views of the mountains and vineyards had been perfect for their impromptu ceremony.

Troy had been awestruck when Amina stepped outside onto the large deck. Her gown was a sleeveless design with a deep V-neck made in vintage lace. The simple A-line silhouette was stunning on her petite frame. She was beautiful and she glowed. Joy misted her gaze and Troy's only regret was that he had not followed his intuition and married her even sooner.

They were a beautiful wedding party; he and Quentin in black suits, white dress shirts, and matching black-and-yellow print neckties. Rasheeda had stood by her sister's side in a simple yellow dress and headscarf. Family friend and district court judge Patrick Colter officiated. Everything about the ceremony and the afternoon meal at the reception had been ideal. The two families celebrated into the early evening and when it was all done Amina and Troy both knew that they wouldn't have changed one thing.

Troy had made reservations at the Four Seasons Hotel in Atlanta's midtown district. As he checked them into the Presidential Suite Amina could feel the butterflies in her stomach begin to quiver. She pressed a hand to her stomach, hoping to stall the tremors that suddenly had her trembling unabashedly. As the desk clerk ran Troy's credit card and processed their key cards to the room, Troy pulled her to him, wrapping his arms around her torso. He kissed her forehead, his lips lingering as his warm breath brushed her skin. She pressed a palm to his chest as her body eased into his side.

"Would you send a bottle of champagne to the room, please?"

"Do you have a preference, Mr. Elliott?" the clerk asked.

"A bottle of Moët, please, and if you could please have the spa send up a foot tub for me as well, I'd appreciate it."

"Yes, sir." She gestured for the concierge first, passing on the order as Amina eyed Troy curiously.

Amina's knees were weak as Troy guided her to the elevator and up to the nineteenth floor. When they were settled inside their suite he nuzzled his face into her neck, inhaling the scent of her. The light fragrance she wore was perfect for her, delicate and intoxicating and it made his desire for her increase tenfold. He took an abrupt step back, clenching his hands together tightly against his sides.

"What's wrong?" Amina asked, a stunned look on her face. "Did I do something?"

"I suddenly want to rip that dress off of you, that's what's wrong."

Amina threw her head back and let out a peal of laughter. "I could just take it off," she said, her tone coy and teasing.

Troy felt every muscle in his body harden, his erection lengthening hungrily. Before he could respond there was a knock on the door, room service delivering his champagne and foot tub.

He met her curious stare. "You're wondering what all this is, aren't you?"

She nodded. "So are you going to share?"

Troy guided her to a cushioned seat. He pulled the ottoman over beside her and sat down. "I had a dream about you last night," he said as he lifted her feet into his lap. Her legs were bare, her toes perfectly manicured and polished a brilliant shade of pink.

Amina gasped as his hands gently caressed her calves, snaking beneath the hem of her gown. His touch was electric as he eased one high heel and then the other off her feet. She took a swift inhalation as she remembered to breathe. She blew it out slowly before she spoke. "Really? What did you dream?" she purred softly.

He lifted his gaze to hers for a quick minute as he continued to massage her soles. "We were old and our grandchildren were playing in the yard."

"Grandchildren?"

"Two little girls and they were the spitting image of you."

Amina smiled then gasped as Troy struck a nerve, his hands caressing the back of each calf, tickling the creases behind her knees. "What . . . what else?" she said as her breathing became shallow.

"It was all perfect. I was gray and had a potbelly and you were still as beautiful as you are now. There was just so much love between us and we had the happiest home. And our grandchildren were laughing in our front yard."

Troy's hand suddenly teased her inner thigh and Amina jumped at his touch. The smile on his face was seductive. Amina leaned forward, clasping his face between her palms. She pressed her mouth to his and felt her body grow warm and languid as she kissed him intently. When she finally pulled back, breaking the connection, Troy blew a soft sigh.

He opened his eyes to stare at her. His passion was reflected in her gaze. "I love you so much!"

"I love you more!"

Troy reached for the foot tub and a towel he'd taken out of the hotel's bathroom. She watched as he popped the cork on the bottle of champagne and emptied it into the foot tub. He pushed her gown up around her thighs and pressed a kiss to her knees as he gently eased her feet beneath the moisture. Amina's eyes widened.

"Mrs. Elliott . . ." Troy paused as they both let the sound of her new name settle comfortably against their ears. "Mrs. Elliott, I love you. And today, I promised to love and honor and cherish you for the rest of our lives. But I want to promise you something more."

He gently rubbed her feet in the cool liquid, the effervescent moisture tickling her toes. "I promise you that our life together will be an unending adventure. Like this champagne bath, we will have moments that will be outrageous and moments that will be decadent. As I live and breathe you will want for nothing. I want you to trust that I will support every one of your dreams and wishes. And you can trust that when it's necessary I will wash every one of your fears and hurts away."

Tears misted Amina's eyes as she pressed her palm to his cheek, her fingers dancing along his profile. Troy lifted her feet back onto his lap, drying them with the towel. He leaned to kiss her toes, leaving a trail of damp kisses across the top of her foot. Before she realized what was happening Troy swept her up into his arms and carried her from the living space into the bedroom. The king-size bed featured luxury linens and a mountain of pillows. He placed her onto her feet as he dropped his mouth to hers. His kiss was urgent and searching as her body melted against his.

When they finally broke the connection the tears that had pressed against her lashes had fallen onto her cheeks. "I'm scared," she whispered softly.

He shook his head. "I won't hurt you. And I won't do anything you're not comfortable with."

She pressed herself closer against him. "No, I'm not afraid that you'll hurt me. I'm scared of disappointing you. I want to please you."

He kissed her again, his touch light and easy.

"Just relax. We're going to please each other," he whispered back.

Amina took a deep breath and then a second as Troy turned her around in his arms until he was standing directly behind her. He kissed the nape of her neck, trailing kisses along the curve of her profile as she tossed her head back against his shoulder. One by one he undid the pearl buttons along the back of her dress. When they were all undone Amina spun out of his arms and stepped away from him. He watched as she pushed one arm and then the other out of the gown, the garment falling to the floor beneath her feet. Troy was riveted as he watched inch after inch of lush flesh being revealed. Her breasts were bare and she stood in nothing but a pair of white-laced, boy-cut shorts. Troy suddenly had a vision of himself buried in her sweetness, the taste of exquisite ecstasy against his tongue. He was panting heavily as he pulled her back into his arms. With one hand he snatched the bedspread and tossed it to the floor, then lowered them both to the sheet-covered mattress.

Amina shivered as he kissed her fingertips one by one, his mouth skating across her palms. He grabbed her by the wrists, pulling her arms up and over her head as his kisses moved back to her mouth. He lifted himself up to stare down at her, reaching to brush a few stray strands of hair out of her face. He kissed her again, his mouth open, and she slid her tongue inside. Troy shuddered as he tasted her, the two locked in a wet and fiery embrace, every fiber of their being surging with electricity.

Troy suddenly moved himself from her. He tore at his shirt and tie, pulling his clothes from his body. As he undid the zipper to his pants Amina's eyes widened.

When he pushed them past his knees, her pulse surged with a vengeance. The protrusion between his legs pressed against his boxers, straining for release. Crawling back onto the bed Troy wrapped one arm around her waist as he moved above her, his lips latching back onto hers.

They kissed for an eternity, tongues licking, tasting, and dueling in his mouth and then hers. His hands danced over her body, his fingers searching every crease and crevice. Amina could barely stand it as desire surged from the pit of her stomach deep into the core of her feminine spirit. Her nails dragged across his broad back as she clutched him hungrily. Her mouth latched onto his shoulder and she bit him gently. He jumped, pain and pleasure coursing through his body. Her tongue danced from his shoulder to his neck, settling in that spot beneath his chin as she nibbled his flesh. Troy savored the sensations. Her breath was light, her touches easy; the featherlike caresses teasing his senses.

He suddenly dropped his head to her chest. Her breasts were just a handful, orange-size treats topped with dark, Hershey's Kiss nipples. His mouth watered as he leaned to lick the succulent treat. Her fingers danced against his head as he sucked one past his lips. He could feel her heave and writhe beneath him as he grabbed the other with his hand, kneading the nipple between his fingers. His mouth danced from one to the other, and Amina moaned. His touch was the sweetest torture.

In one swift motion Troy snatched her panties, ripping them from her body. She gasped loudly as her eyes locked with his. His touch was suddenly possessive, his hands claiming every last part of her. He slid a finger down her belly, past the tuft of pubic hair that curled neatly between her legs. He eased his fingers across the door of her most private place and air caught tight in her chest, Amina unable to breathe. Moisture seeped past her opening and his fingers danced through the slickness. Troy suddenly slid one finger across her folds and then a second. He teased her, gently caressing her sweet spot. He felt her begin to push against his hand, wanting more of him.

Amina had only imagined what it might be like to have a man touch her so intimately and what she imagined hadn't come close to the wealth of sensations that Troy was eliciting from her. She had also imagined what it might be like to touch a man. To reciprocate the ministrations. She eased her hand across the curve of his back, around his waist and into his boxers. Troy shifted his body to allow her unfettered access.

The slightest sheen of sweat dampened his skin. His entire body was a wall of hardened muscle. His stomach was flat and hard and he flinched as her fingers grazed his flesh. She was transfixed by his nipples as they hardened beneath her fingers. Troy paused as he let her explore his body at her own pace. His member was rock hard and the engorged muscle twitched in anticipation.

Her fingers slid slowly down, the dark brown protrusion peeking past the waistband of his shorts. As she watched, Troy pushed his underwear off his hips and down his legs, kicking them from his feet. The hardened length bulged past a nest of tight curls. He was uncircumcised, the shiny head of his cock pushing past its hiding place as his foreskin began to stretch back. His swollen member seemed to grow fuller and fuller in the palm of her hand.

Troy's gaze met hers, a smile pulling at his mouth. She giggled ever so slightly, enthralled by the transformation, as she likened herself to a snake charmer luring a snake out of its hiding spot. Troy moved his hands down to grab his shaft and he commenced to pumping his organ up and down. The motion was slow and easy. Amina placed her palm over his hand, following the rhythm. He moved his hand away, allowing her free rein and as she stroked him his tongue pressed against his lower lip. She suddenly drew her fingertips across his testicles. They were dangling like two succulent sweet lemons. Troy bit down hard against his bottom lip, her touch throwing another log onto the fire burning in his groin. His breathing was heavy and raspy as he tried to fight the rising sensations.

Troy kissed her again, then slid his mouth to her ear. He drew his tongue along the outer edge, then plunged it deep inside. Her whole body shuttered in response to the sensation. Amina gasped loudly as her arms tightened around him.

"I *need* to make love to you," he whispered as he rolled above her.

Amina nodded, her own arousal at a feverish pitch. Troy moved with an effortless grace between her opened legs, a provocative vivacity creeping across his face. He eased himself toward the center of her core, one hand clutching the cheek of her buttock as the other braced his weight above her. Amina held her breath as she felt him pushing against her entrance. There was a moment's hesitation as he entered her. He felt her tense beneath him and he paused for a split second before pushing himself past the barrier of her virginity. There was a brief moment of hurt and her fingers dug into the flesh across his shoulders until it passed and he was settled tightly against her. She inhaled swiftly as Troy's mouth recaptured hers, his tongue twirling around her tongue.

She was tight and her muscles constricted even more around his member. He began to pump himself slowly in and out, gently over and over again. Completely enthralled by the murmur of her low moans, her rock candy nipples, and the sheen of perspiration that dampened her skin, he felt his own orgasm building, the taut muscles pulsing as he pushed and pulled against her body. Amina bit down against his shoulder again as she pushed her hips to meet his strokes. Heat surged through her midsection, her inner lining throbbing in perfect sync with each thrust.

Troy felt his blood begin to boil and surge, his whole body quivering as he fell off the edge of ecstasy. His movements were erratic, controlled by pure lust as he poured himself into her. He was suddenly overwhelmed by the intensity of his orgasm, the rush of it like nothing he'd ever known.

Amina's body suddenly heaved and she cried out, her own body exploding with his. The tremors were consuming, every ounce of control lost as she gave in to her quivering nerve endings. She started to laugh and cry at the same time. Troy dropped down against her, his arms wrapping her in a warm, loving embrace. It was joy and bliss, the beauty of it like the sweetest balm.

Amina eased her body off the bed, trying not to wake Troy from the deep slumber that was holding him hostage. Her first steps were cautious, the tenderness between her legs giving her reason to pause.

After their third time making love she'd lost count of how many times Troy had been inside of her. He'd vigorously marked his territory, claiming her heart and body and Amina had never felt more loved.

In the bathroom she turned on the shower, adjusting the spray until the water temperature was hot. Stepping into it she relished the sensation as the warm water rained down across her shoulders and back and dripped over her breasts and abdomen. It was refreshing and she felt instantly invigorated. She blew a loud sigh as she tilted her head into the spray, the water pulsing against her face. She rinsed her mouth, taking two large mouthfuls of water to wash away the morning film across her teeth.

The bathroom door opened slowly as Troy peeked inside. "Good morning, Mrs. Elliott!" he called, his voice raised over the sound of the shower.

"Good morning, Mr. Elliott!" Amina chimed back as she peered through the glass doors. She greeted him with a wide smile.

"May I join you?"

"You better!"

As he moved into the tiled space, she heard her new husband relieving himself in the commode. She was suddenly aware of all the intimate and personal things they might share now that they were married. The thought made her smile as Troy flushed, moving to the sink to rinse his hands.

A wave of cool air blew into the shower as he opened the door and stepped inside. He eased himself against her backside and looped his arms around her torso as he kissed her cheek.

"How'd you sleep?"

"Like a baby. Did you know you snore?"

Troy laughed. "That was you!"

Amina laughed. "I do not snore!"

"Oh, yes, you do," he teased.

"Well, we both slept well then."

"I know I did. And I loved falling asleep with you in my arms."

Amina turned, easing her body around his so that he could enjoy the full force of the shower spray. She rested her small hands against his hips as he leaned into the downpour, the water washing over his face and chest.

"I see you like your water hot!" Troy exclaimed.

Amina laughed. "I don't like it cold!" She grabbed the bar of lavender-scented soap and drew it across his body, lathering him until his skin was coated white with suds. When she was done, Troy returned the favor.

Troy nodded. "So what's on our agenda today? What would you like to do?"

"Do we have to do anything? I was thinking we could order all of our food in and just lounge in bed all day long."

"We can definitely do that!"

"Good," she said with a soft chuckle. "'Cause there are some things I need you to teach me."

Troy turned and looked at her curiously. "What things?"

She gave him the most seductive smile as she reached between his legs and grabbed his manhood. "Things!"

Heat flickered between his thighs as he found himself craving the sweetest temptations. He nodded. "I think I can handle that."

They laughed as she stepped into his arms, her body nestling nicely to his. He pressed his cheek to hers, gently rubbing the hint of morning stubble against her skin. Then he kissed her eyelids, her cheeks, her nose, finally coming to a stop as his lips glided against hers. Amina could feel her sexual energy rising all over again. She felt insatiable, wondering if she were ever going to get enough of Troy.

Troy was thinking the same thing as his muscles tightened, his manhood surging beneath her palm. His kiss was enthusiastic and teasing. Troy leaned back against the tiled wall, pulling her against him. His hands traced the line of her body from her hips, across her buttocks, up the length of her back. One hand nestled into her hair, his fingers teasing the nape of her neck.

Troy finally broke the connection. "So what things would you like to learn first?" he asked.

Amina's eyes widened. "I figured I'd let you choose the curriculum. I'm just going to be the good student."

Troy chuckled. "You might have homework and a pop quiz, or two."

"I do good homework," she said as she continued to slowly stroke him.

Troy leaned to kiss her again. "Yes, you do," he said, his voice a deep guttural timbre.

He reached his own hand down between their two bodies, easing his fingers against her. He slid a finger into her and her back arched easily. Her body tightened, the muscles clenching around his finger. He slid a second, then a third finger in, as he slowly pumped his hand into her. Amina moaned, then flinched, a hint of pain crossing her face. Troy pulled his hand away.

"Did I hurt you?"

She shook her head. "I'm just a little tender."

"Baby, you should have said something."

"I know it'll go away."

He hugged her to him. "My poor baby! I don't know what I was thinking. I'm so sorry!"

She pressed her head against his chest. "There's nothing for you to apologize for!"

"Well, lesson number one, your comfort comes before all else. Don't you ever forget that."

"But being with you feels so darn good."

Troy smiled slyly. "I can still make you feel good without you hurting."

Amina smiled with him, her gaze curious. "Is that going to be lesson number two?"

"Lessons number two, three, and four!"

Troy kissed her again. It was slow and heated, his tongue darting between her lips and past the line of her teeth. He eased his way down her body, his tongue trailing over her skin. He kissed the round of each breast, a nipple, the dip in her belly button, then dropped to his knees in front of her, his tongue trailing a slow, decadent path. He planted a gentle kiss on the edge of her mound, the patch of auburn hair soaked with the scent of lavender and her rising need. His fingers trailed gently through the curls.

Amina took a deep breath and held it. Her eyes were wide with anticipation. Troy kissed her again and she moaned. She closed her eyes as he pushed her legs open, easing one up and over his shoulder as she balanced herself on the other. Her hands pressed against the tile walls.

Amina's body suddenly quivered as Troy's hands slid farther down, wrapping around her body as he clutched her buttocks and pulled her to his mouth. She gasped loudly as he eased his face closer and licked her for the first time. The intimate kiss sent a shock wave coursing through her body. Her sweet spot was engorged and it glistened with her secretions, her fluids hot with wanting. Troy dove into her sex, licking her gently, his fingers kneading the cheeks of her behind.

A low rumble rushed past Amina's lips as she purred, her voice echoing through the room. "Mmmm," she moaned softly as his lips darted over her folds, teasing as he tasted her. She dropped her hands to his head, the swollen nub of her clit throbbing for his touch as he licked the flesh around that tender spot, purposely avoiding that button of love. She surprised herself as she tried to guide his mouth to her clit, her need intense and urgent.

Without warning, Troy's tongue eased past her slit and penetrated the throbbing cavity. The pleasure was volcanic and Amina almost fainted from the intensity. As she fought to catch her breath he began to suck her secretions, his tongue finally flicking back and forth over her clit. She was grinding herself against his face, his lips nudging and sucking until her orgasm ripped through her, her sex throbbing with vengeance, the pleasure invading every part of her body. She cried out, calling his name over and over again, as if she were in prayer, and when her spasms finally ceased, Troy was still bathing her with his tongue. His ministrations continued until she'd climaxed three more times and her legs were nothing but rubber.

* * *

"Have I told you how beautiful you are?" Troy asked as he lay with his head in Amina's lap, the two relaxing after a full meal.

She laughed. "You did. Did I tell you how incredible you are?"

Troy hesitated, his eyes shifting from side to side. "I'm not sure I heard that from you," he said, his tone teasing.

She giggled a second time. "Well, you are the most incredible man, Mr. Elliott!"

He laughed with her. "I'm also stuffed. I shouldn't have eaten that last slice of cheesecake."

"But it was good cheesecake."

"It was very good cheesecake!"

Amina shifted her legs beneath the covers. Troy lifted his head ever so slightly before resting himself back into her lap.

"Did you call your brother?" Amina asked.

"Nope!"

"You should check in."

"I'm honeymooning. He knows what I'm doing. I don't need to check in."

"Well, I called my sister. I wanted to make sure she was okay and things were going well with Mother."

"And?"

"And she's having a good time. They've really hit it off."

"That's a good thing."

"It is." Amina paused for a brief second. "I also called my father," she said, her voice dropping an octave.

Troy opened his eyes to look at her. "Did you tell him?"

Amina shook her head no. "He didn't answer."

Troy blew a deep sigh. He twisted his body upright, shifting to sit beside her. He wrapped his arm around her shoulders and pulled her against his body, her head dropping onto his chest. He didn't need her to say anything to know that Amina's heart was broken when it came to her father. They'd talked for hours about her frustrations, how she'd moved to Memphis hoping to establish a bond with the man. How much she regretted the distance between them. Her heart was broken and the weight of that wore heavy on his own spirit.

"Why don't we plan on going to see him together when we get back? I owe him a conversation and just because we're not going public with our relationship just yet doesn't mean we can't share the news with your father, especially since you've quit his campaign."

"We can do that?"

Troy nodded. "I need to apologize to him."

"For what?"

"For stealing his beautiful daughter without asking his permission first."

Amina smiled. "You didn't steal me."

"I imagine that if some man we don't know suddenly marries our daughter before we've had a chance to determine whether or not he's worthy, we're going to feel like he stole her. I owe your father that apology."

Amina nestled her body closer to his. She knew beyond any doubt that she'd hit the jackpot to have a man like Troy love her the way she knew he did. She suddenly couldn't imagine her father not feeling the same way.

15

"So, where is she?" Kareem questioned. His arms were crossed over his chest, his tone voicing his displeasure.

Basil shook his head. "Apparently she went to Atlanta to visit our mother. Rasheeda went with her."

Kareem was not amused. "I thought you had her under control?"

"You saw for yourself how obstinate Amina can be. She has always been a problem. Rasheeda would make a better wife."

"Rasheeda doesn't have a law degree and isn't licensed to practice law in this state," Kareem hissed. "Rasheeda is of no use to me!"

"No, she isn't. So you need to let me handle Amina, my way!" Basil hissed back.

Kareem cut an eye at the man. "We can't afford to have any problems, Basil. Amina knows too much. And we need her to file the paperwork on that last piece of property where that bakery, Just Desserts, sits. We needed that done yesterday."

Basil blew a heavy sigh. "Don't you think I know that?"

"Then act like it!" Kareem snapped. "Let me explain this to you again, Basil. This deal is worth *millions*. That entire area will soon be rezoned and once the city puts their official stamp of approval on that change, we can flip those titles to our buyer before anyone knows what happened. The new owner's name will be on those deeds and by the time anyone figures out what we've done, we'll be long gone and extremely rich."

The two men stood toe to toe.

"I said I will handle my sister," Basil said, spittle flying out of his mouth as he snarled.

"Then do it! And your sister and I need to be married before the end of the month."

"Why so soon?"

"Because if anything goes wrong a wife can't be forced to testify against her husband. And as long as she can't testify against me, and obeys what I tell her, then she won't be testifying against you, either."

Rasheeda was taking longer than normal to check her bags. Amina became concerned when they called for the early morning flight to begin boarding. She and Troy had arrived at the airport before dawn, their short honeymoon ending to get him back onto the campaign trail before he was missed. His brother and Harper had flown home the morning before, Quentin needing to get back to the bakery to get a jump on the week's baking. While she and Troy had lounged in the lap of luxury at the hotel, Rasheeda had spent the weekend with their mother, the two women getting to know each other. And now she was late.

Just as Amina was thinking she might have to search her sister out, Rasheeda rounded the corner, waving in their direction.

"There she is," Troy said, pointing toward the young woman. He dropped an arm around Amina's shoulder.

"You made it!" Amina exclaimed as Rasheeda moved to her side.

"I'm sorry. I should have called or at least sent you a text."

"That's okay. You're here. We need to get in line. They started boarding already."

Rasheeda shook her head. "No. I mean I should have let you know sooner that I won't be flying back to Memphis with you."

A look of surprise crossed Amina's face. "Why not? What's wrong?"

Rasheeda shook her head, smiling brightly. "Nothing. I've just decided to fly to Baltimore to visit Todd. Then I'm coming back here to spend more time with Mother."

Amina nodded, her own smile showing her approval. "Good for you!"

Rasheeda nodded. "My flight leaves from Gate Fourteen in an hour. But I wanted to see you and give you a hug before you left."

"Awww! I love you!" Amina said as she reached her arms out to her sister.

Rasheeda hugged her tightly, planting a kiss against her sister's cheek. "You were a beautiful bride, Amina. And you look so happy now!"

"I am happy," Amina replied, her eyes shifting to stare at Troy.

Rasheeda moved to give her new brother-in-law a hug also. "You two have a safe flight and please keep taking good care of my big sister. I like having her around to look up to."

Troy nodded. "Definitely."

The last call for boarding Flight 1462 echoed over the intercom. The two sisters hugged one last time.

"When do you think you'll come back to Memphis?" Amina asked.

Rasheeda shrugged. "I'll be honest. I really don't know if I want to come back."

Amina shook her head. "If you do you can always stay with us." She tossed her husband a quick look. "Right, Troy? She can stay with us?"

"Of course! That will never be a problem," he said.

Rasheeda nodded. "Thank you. Now go before you miss your flight."

Amina reached out for her sister's hand and squeezed it gently. "I'll call you tonight to make sure everything's okay. And you tell this Todd guy that we've got our eye on him so he better do right by you!"

Rasheeda laughed as they moved through the gate, Troy passing the flight personnel their tickets. She was still waving, a bright smile on her face, as they disappeared from sight.

The morning crowd at Just Desserts was more animated than usual, everyone in a particularly good mood for a Monday morning. Had Troy not known better he would have sworn that their secret was out, everyone celebrating his and Amina's good news.

Miss Alice was the first to rush them as they came through the bakery door. Round, plump and gregarious, her extroverted spirit and youthful exuberance made her seem like a three-year-old on a sugar overload. She enveloped Amina in a deep bear hug, her gaze narrowed over Amina's shoulder as she glared in Troy's direction.

"You could have told me!" she said loudly.

Troy tossed a quick look around the room, hoping that no one was paying them an ounce of attention. "Sorry, Miss Alice," he said, his voice dropping to a whisper.

She held up her index finger. "I'll get to you in a minute," she said.

Troy rolled his eyes. Behind the counter Quentin was laughing heartily, clearly amused that the older woman had his brother hemmed up.

Miss Alice drew back to stare Amina down. "You're forgiven, baby girl. You didn't know any better. This one though"—she tossed Troy another look—"he knows better."

Quentin looked like he'd gotten caught with his hands in the cookie jar. He shook his head as he introduced the two. "Amina, this is Alice Moore. Miss Alice helped raise me and Quentin. She's like our surrogate mother. She's also mean and bossy. And she really has a hard time keeping a secret!"

Miss Alice's eyes narrowed even more as she eyed him, her mouth pursed to give him one good lashing.

Troy continued. "But we love her very much because even when we mess up she continues to love us back." He gave Miss Alice a wide, toothy smile.

"That's better," she murmured. "'Cause I know you wasn't talking bad about me!"

"Miss Alice, this is Amina Salman-Elliott. My . . ." He tossed another look over his shoulder before turning back to the old woman and mouthing the word "Wife!"

Miss Alice chuckled warmly. She hugged Amina one more time. "Come sit," she said. "Let me get to know you, baby!"

She led the way to the corner table, pulling Amina along behind her. Troy watched as the two women sat huddled together in conversation. Amina's eyes were wide and bright and laughter bubbled from her midsection. He moved to the counter where Quentin and Harper stood watching.

"Sorry," Quentin said as he tossed up his hands in surrender. "You know I can't lie to Miss Alice."

Troy shook his head. "Like you've never lied to Miss Alice before."

Harper laughed. "Well, I know you've never lied to Miss Alice," she said.

Troy nodded as he leaned in, his voice dropping one more time. "I'm scared of Miss Alice. She would hurt me if I ever lied to her," he said.

The trio burst out laughing again. Across the way, sensing that she was being talked about, Miss Alice gestured for his attention. As he approached the table the matriarch whispered something in Amina's ear and the two women laughed cheerfully.

Troy tossed up his hands. "Really?"

Amina laughed.

Miss Alice gestured for him to take the seat beside her. "I like this one," she said as he sat down. She tossed Amina a quick nod. "I like her a lot."

Troy reached for Amina's hand and squeezed it. "She's a very special woman, Miss Alice."

Miss Alice smiled. "I just know you two are going to have a very nice life together. But I have to say one thing." She met Troy's stare, her own expression turning serious. "Secrets ain't never good for nobody. If you love this woman she ain't supposed to be no secret. Get yourself together and do right," she said as she stood up. "'Cause I can't be voting for a man who ain't doin' right."

Troy took a deep breath. "Yes, ma'am."

He and Amina locked gazes as the matriarch bid them good-bye. When Miss Alice was across the room giving Quentin and Harper their own hard time, Amina gave him a soothing smile.

"So what now?" she asked.

Troy smiled back. "We go tell your father as soon as we can and have ourselves an announcement party by the end of the week."

Rachel was surprised to find Amina Salman waiting in the conference room of Elliott and Harris, Esq. when she returned to her office from court. Surprised because she'd had no contact with the woman since their first meeting and because Amina didn't have any appointment that she was aware of.

Rachel passed her briefcase to her assistant with instructions to hold her calls and to get her a chef salad with bleu cheese dressing and a Diet Coke for her lunch.

"Amina, how are you," she said, greeting her warmly as she made her way into the conference room.

Amina came to her feet, extending her hand. "Rachel, it's good to see you again."

"Did we have an appointment?"

Amina shook her head. "No, we didn't. I'm actually meeting Troy here. He said he needed to stop by to pick up some paperwork and I was on this side of town."

"Oh! I apologize. My secretary made it sound like you were here to see me specifically."

"I had asked if you were around. I was hoping to ask you a question. I know you're busy so if this isn't a good time I can definitely schedule an appointment."

Rachel gestured for her to retake her seat, dropping into the chair across from her. "Now is as good as ever. If you schedule an appointment I'll have to charge you. I'm on lunch right now so you get a freebie."

Amina laughed. "Troy said you were all business."

"I'm sure he didn't put it that nicely."

"No, he didn't."

Rachel smiled. "It looks like you two have gotten quite close."

Amina met Rachel's curious stare, her own smile ever so slight. "Troy isn't the reason I asked to see you," she said.

Rachel's eyes narrowed, her eyebrows lifting curiously.

"I've recently resigned from my position as campaign manager for Nasser Salman's campaign. With Troy likely to win this election I thought you might be in need of another attorney to help fill that void when he's gone."

"So you need a job?"

"I *want* a job. I'm a really good attorney but then

you already know that. And with my high-profile background I would be an asset to your organization."

"So let me understand this. You think Troy is going to win so you're pulling out of your father's campaign to keep from being associated with a losing team. And now I should hire you?"

"I've left my father's campaign because we don't agree on his political agenda and I can't help him win if he refuses to follow my advice. And he has adamantly refused to do just that. Troy is going to win because he has a stellar team that he respects and whose advice he follows. And you should hire me because I'm darn good at what I do."

"We really weren't thinking about taking on a new partner."

"I'm not interested in a partnership. Not right now. But I am interested in a legal position that will afford me the opportunity to do what I do best, as well as enable me to familiarize myself with the Memphis judicial system."

Rachel nodded, pondering the opportunity. "I could use another pair of hands around here and you are good."

"I'm better than good. I'm one of the best."

"Have you discussed this with Troy?"

"No. I came to you first."

"Because you and Troy dating might be a problem. I mean, what happens if you two break up?"

Amina's smile widened. "I don't anticipate that happening anytime soon."

"You sound pretty confident about that."

"Confident about what?" Troy questioned, making a sudden appearance in the conference room's doorway. "What does Amina sound confident about?"

Rachel smirked as she crossed her arms over her full bustline. "About you not breaking up with her anytime soon."

Troy nodded. "She's right. I won't be."

Rachel looked from one to the other. "I don't want to be a Debbie Downer but you two should know better. This isn't high school. I mean things might feel great right now but once that honeymoon period is over and life gets real, things could go downhill."

Amina nodded. "They could, but they won't. I am committed to Troy for the rest of our lives."

"And I'm committed to Amina," Troy said as he moved behind her, both hands dropping against the curve of her shoulders. "But why are you two having this conversation?" he questioned.

"Amina wants a job."

Amina tilted her head back to stare up at him as Rachel continued talking.

"She thinks you're going to win this election and that she should come work for us and take over your cases."

Troy met Amina's gaze. "I hadn't thought about that but it's a great idea."

Amina smiled. "I'm full of great ideas."

"Well, I'm not so sure," Rachel interjected.

"Why not?" Troy questioned. "We've talked about hiring another attorney. Amina comes highly recommended. I can personally attest to her many skills. It's a win-win for all of us."

"Until Amina finds out your winning personality isn't all it's cracked up to be and I have to deal with your relationship-gone-bad attitudes. You know workplace romances never end well!"

"What about workplace marriages?" Troy asked.

"Excuse me?"

"Workplace marriages. You sit on the board of your husband's business. You two have done some major work together and neither of you is having a problem. Are you?"

"But Dwayne and I are married," Rachel said.

Amina held up her left hand and waved the diamond ring on her finger in the air. "So are we," she said, her face beaming.

Rachel's eyes widened. Her gaze skated from one to the other. "Married? You two got married?"

Troy nodded. "Amina made an honest man out of me this past Saturday," he said.

Rachel jumped from her seat, moving quickly around the table. When she reached Troy's side she gave him a hard punch to his shoulder. "You got married and didn't tell me!"

"Ouch!" Troy took a step back.

Amina laughed. "I'm sorry but that was my fault. It was a quick decision."

Rachel shook her head. "You and I are starting off on the wrong foot," she said as she leaned to give Amina a hug. She tossed Troy another harsh look. "I can't believe you did that to me. Me! We're family! I'm like your sister. I should kick you in your knees!"

Troy laughed. "Why me? Kick her!"

Rachel rolled her eyes. She reached out and punched Troy a second time.

"I'll make it up to you," Troy said, a wide grin across his face as he rubbed the hurt from his shoulder.

"Unless I'm the first to know ten minutes after you conceive your first child, you can't make this up. You have really hurt my feelings."

"I'm sorry," Troy said as he wrapped her in a warm

hug. "But if it's any consolation we didn't tell Miss Alice either. She found out this morning."

Rachel laughed. "I hope she gave you hell!"

"She did and you know better than anyone that she's just getting started."

"Serves you right."

"Really though," Troy said. "I know how we can make things right."

"How?"

"We need someone to host an announcement party for us. And you'd be the perfect person."

Rachel grinned. "Can I hire a band?"

Amina smiled. "You can do whatever you want."

Rachel reached to give Amina another hug. "Amina, I'm liking you more and more," she said as she maneuvered toward the door.

Amina laughed. "Enough to hire me?"

Rachel's head bobbed eagerly. "Girl, I had you on the payroll when you said hello!"

16

Amina had been tossing and turning for over an hour. Troy and Mike had been downstairs strategizing for most of the evening and Troy had not come to bed yet. She found it amusing that she had grown comfortable with sleeping in a king-size bed with him right next to her. The twin bed at her father's was nothing but a faint memory and she couldn't imagine herself sleeping alone in a bed ever again. She blew a deep sigh suddenly missing Troy's being there with her.

It had been a good day, she thought. Troy had made all of his political commitments on time. His friends and family had continued to celebrate their good fortune and she was once again employed. The only thing they still had not done was talk with her father.

Nasser had not answered or returned any of her calls and when she'd stopped by the house no one had been home. She'd briefly considered showing up at a political dinner he was scheduled to attend but had changed her mind, refusing to put her father or Troy in any awkward situations. They had tomorrow and she hoped to catch him right after his morning prayers, before his public day started.

Amina sat upright in the bed as she heard the front door close. Minutes later Mike's car pulled out of the driveway, his tires screeching down the road. The house grew hauntingly quiet save for the soft beat of the stereo playing in the other room. The music was jazz, a rhythmic infusion of things she was just beginning to discover.

Tossing back the covers Amina moved to the bathroom to check her reflection in the mirror. She rinsed her mouth with cool mint mouthwash and passed a damp washcloth over her face. With one last glance she pulled her fingers through the length of her hair. Moving out of the room, she wore nothing but an oversize T-shirt and bikini-cut panties. She eased herself toward the family room where Troy was still pouring over some paperwork.

She paused in the doorway for a brief moment, watching him as he sat engrossed over a series of charts and financial statements. Deciding not to disturb him from his work, she turned an about-face.

Troy spied her out of the corner of his eye and looked up from what he was doing. "Hey, you."

Amina turned back toward him. "Hey."

"Did Mike and I wake you?"

She shook her head. "No, I couldn't sleep. But I didn't mean to disturb you. You look busy."

"You aren't disturbing me."

He gestured for her to come to him, crooking a finger in her direction. Amina smiled sweetly as she sauntered to his side.

"What are you working on?"

Troy shrugged. "I forget. You've got me distracted with your sexy self."

She tossed her head back as she laughed. The lilt of it made him laugh with her. Troy pulled her onto his lap and she straddled her legs around his body. He pulled her close, her pelvis kissing the nature that had risen in his pants as he nuzzled his face against her neck. He licked her skin and it was sweet with a hint of salty against his tongue. He slid both hands beneath her T-shirt, his fingertips tracing the curve of her backside. He slowly kneaded her buttocks, the softness of her skin like silk against his palms.

Amina wrapped her arms around his neck, locking her hands behind the back of his head. She captured his mouth with her own, her touch gentle at first, like the lightest brush of a feather. As Troy kissed her back she opened her mouth to him, the kiss becoming more passionate. She put her hands against his face and gently caressed his flesh with her thumbs as their kiss deepened ever more.

Troy's hands were still dancing beneath her shirt, his fingers grazing the sides of her waist, her back, her tummy. He pushed it up and as he eased it past her breasts and around her neck, she lifted her arms and pulled it over her head. Tossing it to the floor behind them Troy moved his hands back to her body, both palms pressing against her breasts. Her nipples hardened against his fingertips. Amina's lips continued to dance against Troy's lips, their tongues doing a sensuous tango in his mouth. His hands trailed down her sides and back to her hips as he pulled her against himself, lifting his body ever so slightly as he pushed himself against her.

Amina suddenly needed to feel his skin against

hers. She trailed her fingers across the white dress shirt he wore, undoing the trail of buttons down the front. Her fingertips were heated and warmth surged through his torso with each stroke of her hand. She pressed her body to his, her nipples brushing against him. Troy wrapped his arms around her, his hold tight.

He kissed her neck and she closed her eyes, a low moan rushing past her lips. She was even more beautiful, he thought as she fell into a state of sensual bliss, her cheeks heated with desire. His mouth moved back to hers, his kisses more intense, his wanting surging through every nerve ending in his body. He felt himself break out into a sweat, perspiration beading against his skin.

Amina's eyes were closed and she was breathing harder. Troy trailed his lips across her chin, down her neck, leaning until he took one of her nipples into his mouth. He sucked on it gently, his tongue swirling around the hardened bud while his hand massaged and teased the other breast. Amina moaned again, the sensual sound further inciting his desires.

He snaked a hand down to the waistband of her panties and Amina opened her eyes, her gaze locking with his. Her breath was hot, coming in heavy gasps, and she bit down against her bottom lip. His fingers tapped against her waist, resting there as he teased her, his gaze still locked with hers. He continued his journey down to the elastic band and eased his fingers inside. Amina gasped as he touched her, his fingers teasing and taunting her sex.

Amina reached between them and pulled at his pants. A slow, easy smile pulled at her lips, her intent registered in the light that shimmered in her eyes.

He shifted forward enough for her to pull at his zipper to release him. With Amina propped in his lap he inched up enough to pull his pants from around his hips and with her help pushed them past his knees, the fabric tangling around his ankles. The protrusion of flesh between his legs was rock hard, twitching for attention. Amina wrapped her hand around him, savoring the sensation of his manhood throbbing against her palm.

Troy gestured with his eyes, his gaze guiding her movements. Amina lifted her body until she was hovered above him. With one hand she pulled the satin fabric of her panties to the side, then lowered herself slowly down against him. As her inner walls welcomed him in she gasped, a swift inhalation of air that filled her lungs. She held her breath as the moist cavity clasped and tugged at him, drawing him deeper and deeper into her. She blew the air past her lips as he filled her, the wealth of him tucked tightly against the inner satin of her feminine spirit.

He recaptured her mouth, his tongue pushing past the line of her teeth. His touch was passionate, the sweetest moment of nirvana. He began to push and pull himself from her, the skin-to-skin contact encouraging his thrusts. Amina was grinding her hips against his, a rhythmic give and take that took his breath away. He gasped for air, her name teasing the tip of his tongue. Every muscle pulsed and tensed and clenched until they were both aching with pleasure.

Time stood still as they both fell into an indulgent trance. Troy knew that she wouldn't last much longer and he pulled her closer. Her gyrations became harder and swifter as she slammed her body against his. He met her stroke for stroke, his own desires surging with a force that would not be contained.

Amina suddenly screamed, her body arching as she convulsed around him. His own body surged as they both dove into a state of frenzied ecstasy. Clinging to each other the two felt like they were soaring sky high, the moment overwhelming.

Minutes later Troy continued to caress her, his own body still lost deep inside of hers. His nerve endings were still firing waves of aftershocks and she was still twitching, her body pulsing slow and easy. Her face was full of passion and pleasure, moisture glistening against her skin. He leaned forward and kissed her again.

He suddenly lifted them both from the sofa, still holding her tightly against himself. He carried her into the bedroom and fell down onto the bed, his body covering hers. With renewed vigor he pumped himself into her, the last lines of his erection stretching eagerly. He wanted more and he took it as Amina gave it to him willingly. He stroked her over and over again until they both came a second time, Amina's screams like balm to his spirit.

They lay side by side both breathing heavily. Air felt like a precious commodity that only the two shared. It was sweet and nourishing as he inhaled when she exhaled, both panting in sync with each other. Time suddenly resumed, the hands on the clock beginning to spin again.

"That was wonderful," Amina said, her words a faint whisper. She pressed her mouth to his again and thrust her tongue inside. The kiss was quick and easy.

Pulling back she leaned into him as his arms tightened around her. Troy smiled as she lay against him, her head on his shoulder. His hands lightly rubbed her back and in no time at all, both were fast asleep.

Kareem Sayed slammed the local newspaper down onto the mahogany table. The front page of the society section was folded up; a quarter page, color image of mayoral candidate Troy Elliott and his new bride smiling up at them. The newlyweds had made the announcement at a party hosted by their family friend and Mr. Elliott's legal partner.

Everything on the tabletop shook from the infraction; a plate flying, water spilling, papers falling. Kareem's face was beet red, ire like bad makeup across his cheeks and forehead. Basil jumped, his friend's rage startling. The two men stood staring at each other until Basil turned his attention back to the legal documents he'd been reviewing. He said nothing until Kareem kicked a large hole in the drywall of his home.

"Man, you really need to get a grip."

"You assured me that you had this under control."

"I do."

"I'm sorry. Did you miss the announcement that your sister married someone else?"

"It's not like you actually liked her. I don't see it as a loss. This is fixable."

Kareem glared. Moving swiftly in Basil's direction he knocked him from the stool he was sitting on.

"What the hell! What's your problem?" Basil shouted, jumping to his feet. He stood defensively, his hands raised.

Kareem swiped a hand over his face, his fingers pulling at his nose. He inhaled swiftly as he focused his narrowed gaze on Basil's face. "Screw this deal up for me and you're a dead man. We stand to make a lot of money if we pull this off so you better get it right."

Basil slowly nodded. "I told you. I'll take care of it."

Still glaring, Kareem stormed out of the room. Basil kept his eyes on the man until he was out of sight, Kareem heading down to the basement. The tension in his shoulders finally relaxed when he heard his heavy footsteps fade off into the distance.

Basil blew a heavy sigh, pulled the news article into his hands, and read it for the second time. He had never trusted his sister to do what was expected of her. Amina had always had a mind of her own, even as a child, refusing to play nice in the sandbox when he told her to. Her spirit was enviable and there were times he wished he was more like her. Being jealous of Amina was why he did half the things he did. Rasheeda would have been a better choice to marry Kareem if he'd been looking for an obedient wife.

He tossed the paper off to the side. Kareem was high-strung and unpredictable. He also had issues with anger. Basil had once thought his friend needed medication but he'd been reluctant to say so. Despite those flaws though, Kareem was a brilliant con man. He took the art of theft to new heights and Basil was hoping to learn as much as he could from him.

His father would be disappointed if he ever found out, but Basil was going to make sure Nasser never got wind of the things he'd had to do. His father would be proud of him when all was said and done and Basil wouldn't have to hear about his sister Amina's accomplishments. Nasser would never be able to rub her success in his face ever again.

* * *

For the first time Nasser looked old to Amina. As she stood watching him she was surprised by how aged her father suddenly seemed, his youthful posture a semblance of what she remembered it to be. It unnerved her and she felt herself begin to tremble. Sensing her anxiety, Troy grabbed her hand and gave her fingers a fast squeeze. Nasser cast a quick glance in their direction. He didn't seem surprised to see them both standing there.

"Good morning, Father."

"Mr. Salman, it's a pleasure to finally meet you in person, sir," Troy said. He extended his hand in greeting.

Nasser pushed his chair back from his large desk, rising to shake Troy's hand. "Mr. Elliott, welcome to my home."

"Thank you."

Nasser sat back down, clasping his hands in front of himself. He turned his attention back to his daughter. His tone was abrupt, his demeanor almost hostile. "Where is your sister?"

Amina was slightly stunned. "Excuse me?"

"Where is Rasheeda?"

Her gaze skated back and forth. "I honestly don't know. I left her in Atlanta. I know she had plans to visit her friend Todd in Baltimore, then she was going to head back to Atlanta to spend time with Mother. But I haven't spoken with her."

Nasser bristled ever so slightly. "And you didn't try to stop her?"

"Why would I? She's an adult and that's what she wanted to do."

Nasser took a deep breath and exhaled loudly. "It is inappropriate for her to be traveling alone to spend time with any man unchaperoned."

"But she's spending time with the man you selected for her to marry. A man she seems to care about."

"And Todd Bashir will not marry her if she does not adhere to tradition. What decent family will want her if she does not practice the decorum she's been taught?"

Amina shook her head. "I don't think Rasheeda would do anything to disrespect herself, or you, Father. I'm sure that she is properly veiled and appropriately clothed. Rasheeda would never disappoint you."

Her father shook his head. "I do not appreciate your tone, Amina."

Troy interjected, slightly disturbed by the attitude Nasser was showing toward her. "I don't think Amina meant you any disrespect, Mr. Salman. I think she wanted to assure you that Rasheeda is more than able to take care of herself and that you can trust she will do everything to ensure her safety and her modesty."

Nasser narrowed his gaze on Troy, clearly not amused. He said nothing, turning his attention back to his daughter.

Amina took a deep breath, taking a step closer to where he sat. "I apologize, Father. I didn't come to fight with you. Troy and I have something important that we wanted to share with you."

Nasser moved onto his feet. He reached for the newspaper that rested on his desk, the announcement in the society page folded open. He waved it in the air. "And I spoke to your mother. She was very excited to tell me that you had married without me knowing."

Amina took another breath, her stomach twisting

into a tight knot. "Troy and I had hoped to tell you ourselves." She tossed Troy a quick look.

Troy's head waved ever so slightly from side to side. "Amina, will you give me a moment alone with your father?" He leaned and kissed her forehead.

When her father said nothing, she nodded. Both men watched her as she exited the room, closing the door behind herself. Troy began to speak as Nasser sat back down, staring at him intently.

"I want to apologize, Mr. Salman. I should have come to see you sooner and I was wrong for not doing so."

"You and Amina have not known each other long. Is that correct?"

Troy nodded. "Yes, sir, that's correct. But we've known each other long enough to know that we've made the right decision. I love Amina with everything in me. I want to spend the rest of my life taking care of her, ensuring her happiness. She means the world to me. I understand that you don't know me but I hope that you'll give me an opportunity to prove myself to you. To show you just how much love and respect I have for your daughter."

"Are you Muslim, Mr. Elliott?"

"No, sir. I'm not."

"Do you plan to convert?"

"No, sir. I gave it some consideration but Amina and I both agreed that it was not for me."

Nasser nodded. "I was very happy when my older daughter finally came home to me. I was not happy with how her mother raised her and felt that this was an opportunity for things to be right in her life. She was making an effort to learn our ways and follow our teachings and then suddenly she stopped. I imagine that was when she became acquainted with you. If I'd had any idea I would have interceded. I would have ordered Amina not to see you and she would have obeyed. Now Amina had done the unthinkable, the ultimate taboo for a good Muslim girl from a good Muslim family."

"I can't say that I agree with you, Mr. Salman. Amina followed her heart. She loves me and she trusts I will be good to her."

"As her father I know what's best for my children when they do not know what's good for themselves. I believe in a patriarchal society and there are traditional roles charged to men and women that need to be followed for our own preservation. The family lineage passes through the father. The father establishes religion for his children. As head of the household the husband provides leadership for the family. A Muslim woman does not follow the leadership of someone who does not share her faith and values. When a Muslim woman marries outside our faith it impedes the growth of our community.

"I know nothing about you, or your family's history. I don't know that we share the same values and I should have been able to ensure that the man who married my Amina was an honorable man. All I know of you, Mr. Elliott, is that you have challenged my political agenda and questioned my ethics. Then you sneak in and steal my daughter from me and you expect that I should toss up my hands and be happy about that. Well, I'm not happy. Not happy at all. My trust has been betrayed."

"I understand your concerns, Mr. Salman, but I have to respectfully agree to disagree. I love Amina. I want her to be happy and I am going to do everything I can to ensure that. If it's her desire to continue

200   *Deborah Fletcher Mello*

to follow her Muslim ways then I will support that. I have no expectation that she should give up her religion if she does not want to. Nor do I expect that she will follow mine if it does not serve her well."

Nasser stared at him with reservation, saying nothing. He finally nodded. "What's done is done. I would naturally have preferred Amina to marry someone who shared my principles. But ultimately it is her choice. As a father I have done all I can do. I have worked to ensure she knew and understood my values. Amina should have trusted that. Her choices, however, indicate I did not serve her well."

"I'm sorry you feel that way, sir."

Nasser swiped a large hand over his face. "Mr. Elliott, I pray that Allah blesses you both in your choices."

Nasser called out Amina's name. When she came back into the room she looked from one to the other, nothing about either's expression giving her reason to relax.

"Yes, Father?"

"I have concerns about the influence you seem to have had on your sister, Amina. I fear that you and your mother both have not been good for her. When I talk to Rasheeda I will insist that she return home immediately and when she does she will be forbidden to have any contact with you. Rasheeda has always been obedient and I anticipate that she will continue to honor my commands. I hope that you will respect my decision and not make this difficult for her. You are to stay away from your sister."

Tears rose to Amina's eyes. "But Father . . ."

Nasser held up his hand, stalling her words. "I love you, Amina, but I have to do what I think is best."

He moved from his seat to her side, cupping her

face in the palms of his hands. He kissed her on one cheek and then the other. *"Assalamu alaikum,"* he said, wishing her peace and blessings.

"Wa'alaikum assalaam," she responded, bidding him the same as well.

And just like that, Nasser dismissed them both, moving from the room as he asked them to leave his home.

Amina wept. The last time she'd cried that hard was when her mother had left them, her feeling as if her whole world had exploded beneath her. Nothing Troy could say or do was of any consolation. Her heart was broken. Her father's rejection yet another explosion that she found difficult to bear.

As he sat alone in the kitchen Troy could hear her sobbing in the bedroom. It broke his own heart to hear her so completely devastated. He took a deep breath and then a second as he reached for his coffee mug. His cell phone suddenly vibrated in his pocket. Pulling it into his hand, he saw that it was Amina's mother, calling again to check on her. They'd spoken three times since he and Amina had left her father's home. This time he ignored her call, having nothing new to tell her. He pushed the appliance back into his pocket, turning off the ringer.

Mike had been calling him as well, annoyed that Troy had cancelled all of his appearances for the day. Feigning an illness, Troy had begged the afternoon off, imploring his friend to extend his apologies to the Memphis Rose Society, the Women's Foundation for Greater Memphis, and the Tennessee Historical Society. Until things were well with Amina, Troy was willing to put his obligations on hold, his wife being his one and only priority.

Her sobs had gone quiet. Troy sat with his coffee for a moment longer, then made his way into the bedroom to join her. Amina was sitting in the center of the bed, shaking the cell phone in her hand.

"What's wrong?" he asked. "What's wrong with your phone?"

"This stupid thing just froze on me," she said. She swiped her hands over her eyes.

"Here, you can use mine," he said as he reached back into his pocket.

She shook her head. "I just reset it. It should be okay in a minute."

He met her gaze as she lifted her eyes ever so slightly. "Are you feeling any better?" he asked.

She shrugged her narrow shoulders. "I'm angry. Angry at my father. Mad with myself. I shouldn't let him get to me. My mother warned me. But it still hurts my feelings."

"You only wanted your father's approval. Most people know what that's like. I know I understand it."

"I did. I love my father. I also know that he's a little unrealistic about some things. I tried but he never once gave me credit for my efforts and now he says I'm a bad influence on Rasheeda. That makes me really mad!"

Troy smiled. "Have you spoken with her?"

"I was trying to call her when my cell phone froze up."

"I'm sure you two will be able to work things out but I don't want you to be upset if Rasheeda decides to follow your father's orders."

"Do you think she will?"

"I don't think Rasheeda would defy him if he told her to stay away from you."

Amina fell back against the mattress. She felt like crying again but didn't have a tear left to cry with. Troy crawled against her, wrapping his arms around her torso. He hugged her close, planting a damp kiss against her cheek. She blew a soft sigh, sinking into the warmth of his body.

"Did I ever tell you that Rasheeda wants to go back to school?"

"Back?"

Amina nodded. "She has a bachelor's degree in social work from the University of Memphis. She wants to get her master's."

"She should."

"Father won't let her go back. One of the reasons she likes this Todd person is because he supports her dreams."

"Then why don't they go ahead and get married?"

Amina blew a deep sigh. "She's not ready. She wants to work and live on her own before she commits to any man and I have great respect for that."

"And she wants to work in her field?"

"She does. She really is an advocate for at-risk populations. She gave a presentation to the women at the cultural center where she spoke about domestic violence against women. She explained how it's really a global problem and that all men needed to rise up and protect their women and children. She made everyone understand that violence against women is not the monopoly of any single group. That domestic violence affects all segments of society irrespective of race, religion, or socioeconomic status. She spoke so eloquently and with such genuine concern. I was so proud of her!"

"I'm sure she knows that and I have no doubts that you two will be able to continue to support each other."

Amina blew a deep sigh. "I really wish I could have been the woman my father wanted me to be."

"Your mother raised you to be your own woman. Even your mother found it difficult to be the woman your father wanted."

"I know that but I wanted things to be different. I wanted what Rasheeda had."

"And what's that?"

"When I saw how Rasheeda and the other women at the mosque embraced Islam, I imagined myself being able to do the same thing. Many of us have a very deep misunderstanding of the religion. Even I did, at first. But then I imagined myself being this Muslim-American attorney who'd help rectify that misunderstanding. My father convinced me that I could help people to see me not as an exception to Islam; that I wasn't a decent person despite my religion, but that all the good things I am are because of Islam. I wanted to educate people and I didn't want to let constant prejudice deter me or anyone else from doing whatever we wanted to do. And I wanted my father to be proud of me for doing so."

"I guess what you need to ask yourself, Amina, is if that was what you really wanted for yourself, or if it was your father's dream and you bought into it to make him happy. Because if that's what you want, you can still do that. No one is stopping you. But I get the impression that you were somewhat willing to embrace the principles of the religion but you didn't necessarily embrace the sentiment behind it. You might need to ask yourself why."

Amina blew another sigh. "It's too much. I suddenly feel broken."

Troy kissed her forehead. "You are not broken. You are overwhelmed trying to be all things to all people. Take a step back and pray on it. Think it through, then pray on it again. You're an intelligent woman. You'll figure it out."

She pondered his comments as he held her. Minutes passed without either of them saying anything at all. Amina suddenly sat up, turning to stare down at Troy. The man was beautiful and she couldn't imagine loving him more.

"I need chocolate!" she exclaimed.

Troy smiled. "I might have an M&M in the cabinet."

She shook her head. "I need *good* chocolate! I need your brother's chocolate cookies."

"That's going to require a trip to the bakery."

Amina jumped from the bed. "Shotgun!"

17

Tears misted Rasheeda's eyes, her brother's screams pounding through her head. His verbal attack was mean-spirited and unnecessary but she knew he was only being this way because of Kareem. She clenched her hands into tight fists as he snatched her by the arm and threw her into the backseat of Kareem's car, the other man eyeing her with disdain.

She folded her body into the corner, pulling her knees to her chest as she wrapped her clothes tight around her body. Her tears dripped past her lashes, saturating the edge of her veil.

"You should be ashamed of yourself," Basil hissed as he eased into the passenger seat, securing his seat belt around his torso. "Father is so disappointed. What did you think you were doing?"

Rasheeda didn't bother to respond, instead curling her body into a tighter ball.

Basil shook his head, continuing to rant. For ten minutes all Rasheeda heard was what she'd done wrong. She'd been mortified when Basil had found her and her friend Todd in the hospital cafeteria enjoying a quick cup of coffee before Todd had to return to his shift in the emergency room. Todd would never have known anything was wrong with the performance Basil had put on, her brother pretending to be concerned about her well-being. Todd had kissed the back of her hand before sending her off with him. Rasheeda had wanted to protest but would never have caused a scene. Even when Basil escorted her back to her hotel for her belongings she didn't say anything, not wanting to draw attention to either of them. The door to her room had barely been closed when her brother had threatened to hit her, throwing a punch against the wall instead. It had scared her to death. She'd barely caught her breath before his fist smashed into a lamp on the table, sending it straight to the floor. Her head was still spinning from his yelling at her. She felt battered, her entire spirit bruised.

Like every time before, Basil had blamed her for what he'd done. It was her fault that he was mad, thinking it was okay to threaten to cause her harm. It was her fault that he'd been made to reprimand her. It was her fault that he'd caused her pain, hurting her feelings. And like every time before, Basil had wiped her tears away, berating her to be good and dutiful so that he would not have to be mean to her ever again. But things were different this time and Basil didn't even begin to know. Rasheeda blew a deep sigh as she laid her head down on the seat.

"So what now?" Kareem snapped.

"I need to get her back home and then we need to deal with Amina."

"She's married!" he spat, the ire of his having lost

painting his expression with pure rage. "How do we deal with Amina?"

Basil cut his eye toward his friend. "She can still be of use to us. She married an Elliott. His name alone will allow us to still do this deal."

"How do you figure that?"

"We'll transfer the property into her new name. No one will think twice about the property moving from one family member to the other. She can say her husband transferred it to her as a wedding present."

"And how do you think you'll be able to make her do that?"

Basil smiled. He waved Rasheeda's cell phone in the air. Since he'd arrived there'd been no fewer than thirty calls from Amina trying to reach her sister. He gestured into the backseat. "She'll do anything to keep our baby sister safe and happy. Nasser says Rasheeda can have no contact with Amina. I will make sure she wants to. And I'll make sure the only way she will ever know whether or not Rasheeda is well is if she does what I say, when I say."

"Neither one of us can afford for this to go wrong, Basil. I have some serious reservations."

"So do you have a better idea?"

"Yes. I think we need a little more insurance. So Rasheeda will marry me. And she'll be an obedient wife. Because if she's not, she'll pay the price. That should give your sister a little more incentive."

Basil nodded, a slight grin rising to his face. "Father would approve of Rasheeda marrying you, especially after the embarrassment that Amina has caused us all. Rasheeda can say that she realized she felt more for you after our sister betrayed you."

"We don't need an elaborate ceremony. We'll tell

everyone that Rasheeda thought long and hard about committing to her boyfriend in Maryland and realized that she and I were a better fit for each other. There was no reason for us to wait. And you need to make sure everyone at the mosque knows how treacherous Amina was; how she dishonored both of our families with her marriage to that man."

Basil tossed his sister a quick look. "This is for the best, Rasheeda. Your submission will serve you well. You will marry into a wonderful family!"

Rasheeda had been listening intently. She met the stern stare her brother was giving her, her own eyes devoid of any emotion. Knowing that there was nothing she could do from the backseat of Kareem's car, Rasheeda closed her eyes. It would be a long ride back to Memphis. She had at least fourteen hours to figure out what she needed to do to make all of this right.

Amina, Harper, and Rachel were seated at a booth at Bonefish Grill after an entire day of shopping at Carriage Crossing. They'd dropped their credit cards at Abercrombie & Fitch, Caché, Ann Taylor, Chico's, Talbots, Soma, and at least six other stores; the trunk of Rachel's SUV looked like its own clothing warehouse.

The waitress had just delivered two chocolate martinis and an iced tea to the table when Amina lifted her cell phone to try Rasheeda's number one more time. Her frustration showed on her face when she got no answer.

"It's been three days now and she hasn't answered any of my calls!"

"Who?" Rachel asked as she took a sip of her drink.

"My sister."

Harper shook her head. "You don't think anything's wrong, do you?"

Amina blew a heavy sigh. "Everything's wrong. I would never have thought she would allow my father to do this to us."

"What about your mother?" Harper asked. "Has she talked to Rasheeda?"

"She hasn't heard anything from her either."

"That's not cool!" Harper chimed.

There was a pause in their conversation as the waitress came to take their orders. Rachel was excited to try the Chilean sea bass and Harper and Amina both ordered the pecan Parmesan-crusted rainbow trout, sautéed and topped with artichoke hearts, fresh basil, and lemon butter.

They made small talk while they snacked on the restaurant's signature Bang Bang shrimp. When their entrees were on the table, everyone enjoying the meal, Rachel resumed their conversation about Rasheeda.

"Why don't you just go to your father's house and talk to your sister? I find that if you corner someone unexpectedly you leave them no other choice but to talk to you," she said.

Harper laughed. "Or knife you. You can't box everyone in a corner and expect it to turn out all right."

"I would but I've been banned from the property. My father doesn't want me talking to Rasheeda so I'm not allowed to see her."

"Can you go to the mosque?"

"I thought about that but I ran into one of the church mothers and my name is mud in the community. Apparently I disgraced the family name when I married Troy."

Rachel and Harper both shook their heads from side to side. "That doesn't make any sense," Rachel said.

"I'm an only child," Harper started, "so I don't exactly know what it's like to have a sister although I claim my best friend Jasmine. But Jasmine does have a younger sister. There's a four-year age difference between the two of them and I don't think they've ever had a close relationship. They grew up in the same house together and you and Rasheeda are closer than those two ever were."

"I wish Rasheeda and I had grown up together. Our relationship started out a little rocky but once we got comfortable with each other, it was really good between us. She's my baby sister and I love her to death and I'm definitely protective of her."

"I wish I could say that about Jasmine. She and her sister Taya don't talk. I have seen them together at family events where they don't speak to one another. And Jasmine has even refused to go places she knows her sister will be at."

"What could be so bad that they don't even speak?" Rachel asked.

"Taya's a little different. Opinionated, condescending, judgmental, competitive, and a tad evil."

Rachel laughed. Amina shook her head for emphasis.

"I actually think there's some emotional disorder going on with her that makes it hard to get close to her," Harper added.

"That's not good," Amina said, "but I still don't understand what could be so bad."

"It's not good." Harper took a bite of her fish, chewed, and swallowed before talking again. "About six years ago they got into a heated argument on Mother's Day. Heated! Taya was having a bad day and

she snapped at Jasmine the wrong way. They got into
it. Things were said that couldn't be taken back and
Taya called her sister everything but a child of God.
Their parents were mad and Jasmine walked away
saying that she'd had enough. For a minute there
everyone thought they might make up, then Father's
Day rolled around. Taya wanted to celebrate at her
house and apparently Jasmine didn't respond fast
enough. Then Taya pitched a fit because Jasmine
took her parents to dinner the week after and didn't
give her enough notice. It was all childish and stupid
and you would think the two of them would be over it
but Jasmine says she can't do it anymore. She feels
like she has always had to coddle her sister's feelings
and not once has her sister given her feelings any
consideration. She cut Taya from her life and hasn't
looked back."

"That is so sad," Amina said, unable to fathom not
having Rasheeda in her life. She suddenly felt tears
burning behind her eyelids.

"What's really sad is that their parents indulge the
behavior. My grandmother says that Mrs. Holt should
have put a stop to that mess when they'd been little.
Instead it's almost like she enjoys parenting them sep-
arately."

"Everyone has some kind of family drama," Rachel
said. "It's just a shame."

"Well, I don't want to think about me and Rasheeda
never talking again. I need to figure out how to fix
this."

"I'm just glad that with everyone else's drama me

and my man are getting along just fine," Harper said as she sipped the last of her martini.

"Me, too!" Rachel said with a snap of her fingers.

"Me, three!" Amina chimed.

The three women burst out laughing. They talked for another hour, sharing secrets and advice. When the last refill was delivered to the table Rachel lifted her glass.

"Let's toast, ladies!"

Amina lifted her iced tea and Harper lifted her martini in salute.

"I don't have a sister but I consider you both to be my family. To good times with good friends, good sex with good men, and whatever else good we can think of!"

"Hear, hear!" Harper chanted.

Amina laughed. "You two have had a little too much to drink. I'm driving us all home!"

Troy laughed as Amina replayed the afternoon for him. She'd been giggling since she'd walked in the door. He was glad that she'd allowed herself an opportunity to relax and he appreciated Harper and Rachel's taking her mind off the things that were bothering her.

They'd been lying in bed, trading easy caresses as they shared their respective days. Troy was concerned about his numbers, the polls showing the slightest dip in his popularity based on his very liberal views on the definition of family and marriage. It was the one issue where Amina's father had a loyal following, his values popular with an ultraconservative, Southern mind-set that agreed with him in principle.

"So what does Mike recommend?" Amina questioned.

"He doesn't think it's a problem. His answer is to ignore it and focus on those issues where we've captured public opinion."

"I don't agree."

"What do you think? How would you advise me to handle it?"

Troy massaged her foot as she pondered his question. She closed her eyes for a brief moment as he applied just the right amount of pressure against the ball of her foot, his fingers pressing around the heel and moving her toes to curl. When she opened her eyes he was staring at her, his fingers gently teasing her calf.

"You can't ignore it. It's a hotbed issue right now for all politicians and you can trust that someone is going to bring it up wherever you go. I'd advise you not to hide from it. You believe what you believe and you can agree to disagree. You don't need to argue your opinion. You state it and move on. But you always end that conversation by saying everyone needs to do what makes them comfortable. That way you're not pushing your opinion on anyone and you validate what someone else might be feeling or believe."

Troy was nodding his head slowly as he moved on to her other foot. "So do you want to come work for my campaign, Mrs. Elliott?"

Amina laughed. "No, Mr. Elliott. I start my new job tomorrow and I'm very excited."

"Don't let Rachel bully you because she can be a bully."

"Rachel and I will be fine together."

"I'm just warning you," he said.

"Duly noted," Amina replied as she leaned forward to kiss his mouth.

"Did you eat?" Troy asked. "Are you hungry?"

"I'm antsy," Amina said as she shook her body from side to side.

"Do you want to go to the gym and work out?"

Amina thought about it for a quick moment. "I think I really just want to walk."

"Then let's walk," he said as he slid his body off the bed, pulling her along behind him.

After slipping on their running shoes the duo headed outside. There was a full moon floating in the late night sky. It shimmered bright like an oversize pearl in a sea of black silk. Side by side they walked the cul-de-sac, occasionally peering into their neighbors' homes when curtains were open and lights were on.

"Does Mrs. Turner ever speak to you?" Amina asked as they passed the one-story home at the end of the roadway.

Troy glanced toward the Turner home, Mrs. Turner fussing about something as she stood in the center of her dining room. "All the time. She's always been very sweet to me."

"I don't think she likes me. She gave me the dirtiest look the other day."

Troy laughed. "You know, I hadn't thought about it but she probably thinks we're shacking up. She's old-school so I'm sure not knowing we're married has her thinking all kinds of things about the two of us."

"Well, we need to get that straight then."

He laughed again. "Don't pay her an ounce of attention. If she wants to think we're having wild, wicked sex, let her."

"But we are having wild, wicked sex," Amina said as she tapped him against his backside.

"Keep that up and I'm going to show you wild and wicked!"

Amina's giggles vibrated through the cool air. Even with the concerns she had on her mind she felt more at ease than she'd felt all week. Being with Troy felt like home no matter where they found themselves. She gave him a sidelong glance and she sensed he was deep in thought. As her gaze washed over his profile she couldn't imagine herself ever loving any man more. She gently bumped against his shoulder and when he turned his head she gave him the sweetest smile.

Troy grabbed her hand, entwining his fingers between each of hers. The walk back was an easy stroll as their arms swung between them. The air had just a hint of a chill to it, a cool breeze blowing over them. He lifted her hand and kissed the back of her fingers. Wrapping his arm around her shoulders, he pulled her into his side and held her close. He pressed a kiss against the top of her head, nuzzling his face into her curls. The sweet scent of vanilla and coconut teased his nostrils as he inhaled deeply.

As they made it to the end of their driveway Troy spun her body against his and dropped his mouth to her mouth, kissing her earnestly. She tasted like mint ice cream and he savored the sweetness. Before either realized it Amina was sprawled across the hood of

Troy's 7-Series BMW, his body nestled nicely against hers. They kissed and kissed, so lost in the moment that neither noticed Mrs. Turner standing in the roadway, leash in hand as her cocker spaniel sat with its little head cocked to the side, staring at them.

18

Amina waved as Troy pulled out of the driveway, pointing his car in the direction of the bakery. His day was starting an hour earlier than hers; he needed to finish some paperwork for the business. As he tooted the horn and waved back, she grinned, her face lit with joy. Troy's black sedan would forever be a favorite memory for her, their scandalous behavior just hours earlier teasing her sensibilities. She could only imagine what might have happened if their nosy neighbor hadn't made her presence known. Imagining made her grin all over again.

She tightened the belt that closed her bathrobe as she walked to the end of the driveway to collect the morning newspaper. The morning air was chilly and she felt a shiver spiral across her spine. She took a deep breath and then a second, the cold air invigorating her lungs.

Pausing to scan the morning headlines, Amina had just turned to head back inside when her brother, Basil, suddenly moved to her side, gripping her harshly by the elbow. Startled, his sudden presence made her jump, her breath catching in her throat.

"Basil!"

Tossing a quick glance around the neighborhood Basil dragged her toward her front door and inside the home, slamming the door shut behind them.

"What are you doing here?" Amina snapped as she snatched her arm from his grip.

"Is that how you greet your brother, Amina?" he asked as he turned to look at her.

"What do you want, Basil?"

"I want you to remember your family responsibilities. That's what I want."

Amina crossed her arms over her chest, hugging herself tightly. "How dare you come into my husband's home and . . ."

"Your husband!" Basil snapped back as he took two hasty steps toward her.

Amina stepped back quickly, grabbing for the house phone that rested on the table in the foyer. "I will call the police," she warned, her finger prepared to push the emergency speed dial number.

Basil stopped short, his gaze narrowed. He inhaled deeply, his lips pushed forward, annoyance painting his expression. He took a second breath then stepped back, both hands rising as if he were surrendering. "I apologize," he said. "May I please sit down?"

Amina eyed him with reservation, intuition warning her not to let her guard down. Without waiting for an answer Basil moved into the family room and took a seat on the sofa. He crossed one leg over the other as he waited for her to join him. Amina followed behind him, the phone still in her hand. She paused in the doorway. "What are you doing here?"

"We need to talk about Rasheeda."

Her eyes widened with trepidation. "Is she okay?"

"She will be as long as you do what I need you to do."

"I don't understand."

"I told you, Amina, I need that Beale Street property."

"I don't care what you told me, Basil. I'm not having any part of that sham."

Something in Basil's stare made her take a step back, prepared to flee if he came at her. She took a deep breath.

Basil nodded, his gaze flitting back and forth as he leaned back against the cushions. She could see him relax, the tension in his body fading ever so slightly. He took another breath, then lifted his eyes back to hers. "Father was hurt by what you did, Amina. You disappointed him and you disgraced our family name. This marriage to Troy Elliott is a travesty and you need to repair the harm you've done before it's too late. Unfortunately, Rasheeda is having to pay the price for your disrespect."

"What have you done to Rasheeda, Basil?"

"Nothing. Yet. And as long as you do what I tell you to do Rasheeda will continue to enjoy a very blessed life. She will be a dutiful wife and mother and have much given to her."

"I want to talk to her."

"Soon."

"I want to speak with her now, Basil, or I'm not going to entertain this conversation for one minute more."

Basil shifted forward in his seat. Still holding tight to the house phone Amina cut her eyes toward the kitchen counter and crossed to where her cell phone was resting. She dialed her sister's number from the mobile device. Seconds later the cell phone in Basil's pocket vibrated loudly, Rasheeda's ringtone echoing through the room. Basil shook his head, a sardonic grin across his face.

As she depressed the phone's off button Amina blew a deep sigh, frustration tensing her muscles as her brother's mocking expression taunted her. He pulled the phone from his pocket and dialed a number. A minute later someone answered on the other end.

"Put her on," Basil commanded. He set the phone on the coffee table and pushed it toward Amina. He sat back in his seat and gestured for her to pick it up.

Still holding on to the house phone Amina eased in his direction. When she reached the edge of the table she snatched the other device from where it rested and took ten steps back before pulling it to her ear. Her eyes were still locked on her brother.

"Hello?"

"Amina?" Rasheeda's voice rang on the other end.

Amina could hear the tears in her sister's voice. "Rasheeda, where are you? Are you okay?"

"Please, Amina," Rasheeda started before the phone was snatched from her hands and the call disconnected.

Amina frantically depressed the redial button but no one answered when it rang. She flung the phone in Basil's direction, the man's malevolent laugh moving her heart to race.

"What are you doing, Basil?" she shouted. "She's our sister!"

He stood up abruptly. "I'm doing what I have to,"

he snarled. "And all of this can be done and finished if you do what I tell you to do," he said, enunciating each word slowly. "I'm going to leave some papers with you, Amina. And you are going to go down to the courthouse and file them with the clerk's office. That's all you have to do. Once that's done I'll make sure you and Rasheeda have a wonderful reunion. I'll even make sure Father changes his mind about the two of you spending time together. That is, of course, if her new husband permits it."

"What new husband?"

Basil cackled a second time. "See how much you're missing out on, Amina. Your baby sister is marrying a man of great faith, a man our father approves of. He's a good and honorable brother and you aren't there to support her. Such a shame!"

Basil moved toward her and Amina felt herself tense. Like one of two boxers squaring off she widened her stance and shifted her weight, preparing herself to fend off whatever he might throw at her. As he reached her side he paused, pulling a legal-size envelope from the inside pocket of his suit jacket. He held it out to her and waited for her to take the mailer from his hand. "File the papers, Amina. I wouldn't want to see Rasheeda hurt any more than she has been. And you don't want to be responsible for anything else that might happen to her."

Amina stiffened as Basil leaned and kissed her cheek. He pressed his mouth close to her ear, his breath repulsive against her skin. "Don't you dare breathe a word of this to Father, Amina. You will regret it if you do," he said, his voice low and composed.

She took a breath and held it. Basil smiled. From

his nonchalant expression you would have thought he was sharing news of some award-winning event with her. He made the little hairs on the back of her neck rise.

"You might want to keep your new husband in the dark about this as well. It would be bad for his health for him to know, Amina. This is family business. Salman . . . family . . . business. Besides, something like this might not be good for his political career. I'd hate to see it ruin his chances for election."

He took two steps toward the door and stopped. "And congratulations. It looks like you've done very well for yourself," he said, taking one last glance around her home.

Then without saying another word he moved back into the foyer and out the front door. Racing behind him Amina engaged the lock and the alarm, ensuring the door was tightly secured. Sinking to the marble floor she gasped for air, suddenly feeling like she couldn't breathe. She fought back tears, wanting to cry. Instead, she dialed the phone in her hand and waited for her father to answer the line.

Amina tilted her face into the spray of hot water, allowing the shower to rain down over her head. Moisture saturated her thick curls until the fullness lay flat against her scalp, the length reaching toward her waist. Her tears finally mixed with the water flow as the shower wet her skin.

Her father had refused to entertain the idea of Basil harming Rasheeda. To hear him tell it, Basil could do nothing wrong, having always been a model son. He had assured her that all was well with

Rasheeda, his baby girl happy and healthy. According to Nasser he personally had his eye on the young woman and there was nothing out of sync in his home. Nothing Amina said had convinced her father that things were not as they seemed; the man rejecting everything she claimed.

When she had asked to speak with her sister, Nasser had told her no. Amina was still persona non grata in his home. He earnestly believed that she was a greater threat to Rasheeda than anyone else ever could be. The absurdity of the situation ignited the tears that burned behind her eyelids. Amina knew her brother was dangerous and she couldn't begin to figure out how to protect them all.

She had thought to call Troy right after Basil had left the house, managing to partially dial his number three or four times. And each time she'd dialed she'd changed her mind, disconnecting the call. She didn't want Troy to worry and she didn't want Troy to do something they would both regret. She knew her husband was still unhinged about Basil putting his hands on her before. This would send him over the edge and she couldn't let that happen.

Amina reached for the bottle of Coconut CoWash, squeezing a palmful into her hand. The cleansing conditioner was her go-to formula to detangle and nourish her hair. Massaging the rich formula through her locks was therapeutic and as she gently worked the cream against her scalp and along the thick strands she was able to relax and see things with more clarity.

It took no time at all for Amina to dress. Her designer suit was stylish and fit her perfectly. The heels weren't too high and her only jewelry was a simple pair of diamond studs gifted to her by her mother.

Just a hint of foundation and a quick shake of her head completed the look. Right on time, Amina was out the door, heading to her first day of work.

The law offices of Elliott and Harris, Esq., employed a team of six attorneys, an office manager, and a support staff of nine other employees who helped with the day-to-day functioning of the office. Amina was pleasantly surprised to find that Rachel and Troy had decorated office space especially for her. She couldn't help but smile when her new secretary escorted her to a door with her name engraved on a platinum doorplate. Inside, the décor reflected her favorite colors and Troy had placed one of their wedding photos and a large bouquet of yellow roses on the desktop.

"There's a staff meeting in thirty minutes," Gail, her new assistant, advised. "Ms. Harris left your first cases on your desk to review and two of our paralegals have been dedicated to help you with the transition. Would you like coffee?"

Amina moved to the executive's chair and took a seat. "I would really love a cup of tea with lemon and no sugar."

"Not a problem. They usually have a table of pastries at the morning meetings but if you want something else, I'll gladly get it for you."

"I appreciate that, Gail, but the tea is more than enough."

"Yes, ma'am." The young woman made her exit, blowing a low sigh of relief as she closed the door.

Amina had to smile. She understood the girl's anxiety, her own nerves skipping like crazy. She was confident though that they'd be comfortable with each other in no time at all. Seconds later Gail knocked on the door, returning with a large mug of hot tea.

"How long have you been with the firm?" Amina asked as she gestured for Gail to take a seat.

"Mr. Elliott hired me two years ago. I've assisted two of the junior attorneys previously. Now you," she said with a bright smile.

"Well, I look forward to our working together. I'm sure we'll make a great team."

The young woman smiled. "I'm very excited."

"That's a beautiful scarf you're wearing," Amina said, admiring the deep burgundy wrap draped around her neck and shoulders.

Gail smiled ever so slightly. She suddenly looked embarrassed. "It's my hijab. I pull it down while I'm in the office."

"You're Muslim?"

She nodded. "You probably don't remember me, but I know your family from the mosque."

"My goodness!" Amina gushed. "I apologize but I've met so many people since I moved here."

"My parents are Julian and Amsa Bashir."

Amina paused in reflection, trying to recall the familiar names. "Todd's your brother?"

Gail nodded again. "He is so crazy about your sister."

Amina tensed, fighting to keep a smile on her face. She prayed that nothing showed in her eyes. "What a small world!" she exclaimed softly. "I know Rasheeda is head-over-heels about him, too."

"He was so excited when she flew to see him the other week. Apparently they made a lot of plans for their future, which is why he's so surprised about her not answering his calls. He's been worried that something might be wrong."

Amina's brow furrowed with concern. "She hasn't been answering his calls?"

Gail shook her head. "I'm sure it's nothing but I thought if you talked to her you could slip in a good word for him? I can vouch for his character. I know I might be a little biased but he really is a good man. And he loves her to death!"

Amina forced another smile. "I will definitely see what I can do the next time she and I talk."

For a brief moment Amina didn't know what to think. Basil had taunted her about not knowing that Rasheeda had plans to marry. If she wasn't answering Todd's calls then how could they be making plans? And if she wasn't preparing to marry Todd, then who? Her anxiety level was rising again and she struggled to regain some control over her emotions. She had to stay calm if she was going to be of any help to Rasheeda. She took a deep breath.

Gail glanced to the clock on the wall. "You should head to the conference room. We don't want you to be late on your first day."

Amina nodded, the two women both moving back onto their feet. As Gail reached the office door, Amina called after her.

"Yes, ma'am?"

"Why don't you wear your hijab in the office?"

Gail smiled. "I was reporting to attorney Spaulding and it made him uncomfortable."

"Did he say that?"

"No, but I could tell and I didn't want it to be a problem. I really need this job."

Amina nodded. "Well, from this point forward if you don't wear your hijab let it be because it's something you just don't want to do. Do what's right for you. If anyone here has a problem with it, point them in my direction. And I'll deal with attorney Spaulding personally."

Gail's grin widened. "Thank you!"

"Don't thank me. I'm just doing what's right. If you were a Jewish man and wanted to wear your yarmulke, I would stand up for that right as well."

"I look forward to learning from you, Ms. Salman."

Amina smiled and with a quick nod she headed toward her meeting. She was surprised to find Troy in the conference room, seated in conversation with Rachel. The two greeted her warmly.

"Everything okay?" Rachel asked. "Are you getting all settled in?"

Amina nodded. "I am and thank you for the flowers," she said, turning her gaze toward Troy. She would have given anything to rush into his arms to be held.

He winked an eye at her and it made her blush.

Rachel rolled her eyes skyward. "Don't you two get me started," she said.

Amina and Troy both laughed.

"How long are you going to be here?" Amina asked. "There's something important I need to speak to the two of you about."

"I have a meeting at ten. I wasn't planning on being here for the whole meeting, just long enough to introduce you to everyone."

"Well, I can fill you in later tonight."

"Are you sure?" Concern seeped from Troy's eyes.

Amina nodded. "I'm positive."

Before anything else could be said, the staff began

to fill the space, everyone welcoming Amina warmly. The meet and greet was short and sweet with Troy making the formal introduction, then giving everyone a brief synopsis of her résumé, focusing solely on the skill set she was bringing to the table. When he was done he extended his apology for having to rush off, moved to where she was sitting, boldly kissed her lips, then extended his good-byes. Amina blushed profusely, acutely aware of the raised eyebrows that suddenly sat around the conference-room table.

Rachel chuckled softly as she took command of the meeting. "Allow me to put everyone's wagging tongues to rest before you all start spreading false rumors. Our esteemed partner Mr. Elliott and our new associate Ms. Salman were married recently. Amina here is the boss's wife but that's not why we hired her. We hired her because she's an extraordinary attorney and I like her. Y'all know I don't like too many people so that says a lot. But I have every confidence that attorney Salman will quickly prove herself to be a valuable asset to our organization.

"Now, Mr. and Mrs. Elliott will officially announce their marriage at a party I'm hosting this coming Saturday at Just Desserts Bakery down on Beale Street. Everyone's invited and in lieu of gifts please feel free to make donations to one of the nonprofit foundations that the happy couple supports. Or not."

There was a round of applause until Amina held up her hands to stall the ovations. "Thank you," she said. "I appreciate everyone's kindness and I look forward to getting to know you all."

"Now on to business," Rachel said.

For almost an hour there was a roundtable discussion as each attorney updated the status of the cases on their plates. When Rachel was satisfied she dismissed them, sending everyone off to do whatever it was they needed to do. When the door was closed behind the last person, she moved to the seat beside Amina and blew a deep breath.

"So what's up?"

Amina pushed a manila folder in her direction. "My brother, Basil, has illegally acquired the titles to some significant properties in the downtown area. He and his business partner, Kareem Fayed, are now trying to manipulate me to turn Just Desserts over to them."

"How?"

"Basil is threatening to harm my sister, Rasheeda, if I don't claim the deed and file the title in my name. I think something has happened to her and I'm not sure what to do. I spoke to my father twice and he assures me that Rasheeda is fine but something doesn't feel right and I'm worried."

Rachel flipped through the documents Amina had passed to her, sitting upright on the edge of the seat. "And you say he's pulled this stunt with other properties?"

"Yes. I haven't had an opportunity yet to find out just how many but I'm thinking it's significant."

Rachel nodded. "What do you want me to do?"

"I need to discover how extensive this is, then I need you to go to the district attorney with whatever I find."

"What about your sister?"

"I'm going to try to get to her at the town hall meeting tomorrow. One of the topics up for discussion is family values and I know my father will have her and Basil both there for show. If she's not there then we take everything to the police as well and I'll file a missing persons complaint."

"This could get very messy for your brother and anyone else who might be involved. Are you going to be able to handle the fallout?"

"There's nothing weak about me, Rachel. My brother is about to find out just how tough I am."

"Why are you bringing this here?"

"Because there are going to be some pissed off property owners who are going to need legal representation when this comes out. I have no doubt that most of them will want to be represented by the law firm that uncovered the travesty."

Rachel smiled. "Earning your keep already! That's what I'm talking about!"

19

Amina knew that this would be their very first fight. Despite his best efforts to contain his anger, Troy was finding it difficult not to rage. He paced from room to room, moving between the family room and the kitchen. Amina sat where her brother had sat hours earlier. Her hands were clasped together and folded in her lap. It had taken her less than ten minutes to tell Troy what had happened and fill him in on the details. It felt like it was taking him forever to get past it.

As he moved back into the room, finally dropping onto the seat beside her, she blew a deep sigh.

"Why didn't you call me when it happened, Amina?"

She cut an eye at him. "Because I didn't want you to overreact."

"Overreact? Did you really just say that to me?"

"I was afraid that you would be angry just like you are now and that you'd go looking for Basil and do something that we wouldn't be able to fix."

"That's right. I would have gone looking for your brother and given him a taste of his own medicine. I should have done it the first time he put his hands on you."

"No one is going to vote for a mayor who has anger management issues."

Troy's jaw tightened. "When are you going to understand that you mean more to me than this election? Your safety and happiness are paramount and nothing and no one comes before you."

Amina dropped her hand against his thigh, caressing the flesh with a heavy palm. "Troy, I know how much you love me and I appreciate that you want to take care of me but there are going to be times that I'll have to make decisions that protect you, too. Taking care of you is just as important to me. I'm not going to let you throw your dream away when I know we can handle this another way."

She felt the tension in his body begin to slowly subside but she knew he was still unhappy about the situation.

He blew a heavy sigh. "So what next?" he finally asked.

"I'm filing a legal complaint against my brother for the property fraud. And as soon as I find my sister and I know she's okay, we'll figure out the rest."

"And you think it's going to be that easy?"

"I think that it's a start and if it keeps you from punching Basil out and destroying your mayoral chances then it's what I'm going to do."

Troy wrapped his arm around her shoulder and pulled her to him. He hugged her close as she melted into his side. He kissed her forehead, his lips warm and tender against her flesh. If anything happened to her, he thought, he didn't know what he would do. What he did know was that it wouldn't take much

more for him to bust Basil Salman in his face when he
next saw him.

Basil struggled to contain his annoyance. He'd
known Amina would call their father. She wasn't half
as smart as she thought she was. And she wasn't smarter
than him. He'd also known that it was only a matter of
time before his father would be asking him questions
he had no interest in answering. He shook his head as
he endured the interrogation.

"Really, Father?" he said as he shook his head. "Why
would I hurt Rasheeda?"

"Amina seemed quite sure of herself," Nasser answered, eyeing his son sternly.

"Amina has been nothing but a problem since she
came to Memphis. She's overly dramatic, emotional,
and she has not been good for any of us, Father."

Nasser nodded. "That may be true but I do not
need your sister making such irrational claims so close
to the election. Where is your sister? I want to speak
with her."

"She is with Kareem's mother. Mrs. Fayed thought
that with Amina turning her back on the family that
Rasheeda would benefit from a little motherly inter-
vention. She's been wonderful with her and very supportive."

Nasser leaned back in his seat, clasping his hands
together. "That is good. Rasheeda needs positive
female influences. But I want to speak with her. I tried
to call but she's not answering her phone."

"Rasheeda had so much going on that she left without taking her cell phone with her. I found it on the
counter in the kitchen. But we can call the Fayeds.

Here, I'll dial the number for you," Basil said as he reached for his own phone.

Nasser nodded. He stole a quick glance down to his wristwatch. "It's actually late. We shouldn't disturb Mr. and Mrs. Fayed. But I expect to see Rasheeda at the town hall meeting tomorrow. I expect you both to be there. I will speak with her then."

Basil smiled. "Of course, Father. We wouldn't miss it."

Rasheeda pounded her fists against the locked door. The room she was confined had no windows and the one light bulb in the center of the ceiling was flickering on its last filament. When no one responded, she moved back to the twin-size cot against the wall and lay back down. She was angry and desperate to see anyone who wasn't Basil or Kareem. The two had been holding her hostage since returning from Baltimore and she was starting to get scared.

Hearing Amina's voice earlier had been the first hint of hope that she'd had for days. But then Kareem had snatched the phone from her and that thin line of hope was dashed. Kareem was not a nice man and her brother was foolishly following behind him like a lost puppy. Basil wanted to rule the world without working for the right to do so. He wasn't willing to pay his dues believing his wanting it was enough for him to have it.

But Rasheeda had wants, too, and she wanted desperately to go home. She couldn't imagine that no one was looking for her, concerned about her disappearance, but she also knew the lengths Basil would go to get something he coveted. Her brother was a master manipulator and a crafty liar. She could just imagine the tall tales he'd already told about where she was. But Rasheeda trusted Amina would be able to see through him. Her big sister would help get her back home.

Hours later she was dreaming about Todd. He looked dashing in a black tuxedo, standing in wait as she walked down an aisle toward him. He had the sweetest smile and made her laugh. He had never seen her face and she was hopeful he would find her as beautiful as she felt. Because in that moment she felt like the most beautiful girl in the world. Her sweet dream suddenly turned into a nightmare when Todd disappeared and Kareem stood leering at her. Rasheeda didn't care about being beautiful anymore as she turned, desperate to run as far and as fast from the man as she could.

Rasheeda was still running when Basil and Kareem stepped into the room. She had drifted off into a deep sleep when she woke with a start to find them both staring down at her. She jumped, drawing her body upright, her back pressed against the wall. She adjusted her veil across her face as Basil smiled.

"I thought you'd be hungry," he said softly. "Kareem and I bought you some food." He pointed to a tray on the end table. There was a yeast roll, some type of meat and gravy, steamed broccoli and creamed potatoes on the plate. A wrapped brownie sat on the side and there was a tall glass of iced tea.

She reached for the roll, snatching the bread into her hand as she nibbled the end of it. Basil smiled.

"You know I love you, Rasheeda, don't you?"

She stared up at him, knowing he wasn't interested in her answer.

"And that I only want the very best for you, right?"

She dropped her eyes into her lap, fear beginning to tighten a large knot in her stomach.

"Well, here's the thing. Amina needs to learn a lesson, so I need you to go along with this."

Tears fell from Rasheeda's eyes, the roll in her hand nothing but mushed dough as she crushed it beneath her palm. She waved her head from side to side. "Please, Basil, don't do this," she whispered, her low sobs just beginning. "Why would you do this to us? We're your family."

Basil pulled her up on her feet. He wrapped his arms around her and hugged her. "Hush, now," he said as her tears dampened the front of his shirt. He gently pulled her veil from her face and kissed her cheek. "You really need to trust me. You know I won't let anything bad happen to you."

Kareem sneered. "You should listen to your brother," he snapped.

Rasheeda shook her head. "I want to go home, Basil. Let me out, now!"

"Just a little longer," Kareem said, his face twisted in annoyance. Then we'll marry and everything will be perfect."

Kareem suddenly grabbed her hand, kissing the back of it. His lips were like sandpaper against her skin. Rasheeda cringed, bile swelling full and thick in her mouth as she struggled not to vomit. She tried to snatch the appendage back but Kareem held on tightly.

"Leave her alone," Basil snapped. "You haven't exchanged vows yet. He narrowed his gaze on the other man.

Kareem laughed as he released his hold on the young woman. Rasheeda backed herself into the corner, settling her back against the wall. She cut her eyes from one to the other.

Behind them Basil was dialing his phone. When the party on the other end answered, he held it out, engaging the speaker function. Amina's voice rang through the room.

"Why are you calling me, Basil?"

"I told you not to talk to Father, Amina, and you didn't listen. I bet you even told your husband, didn't you?"

"I'm calling the police, Basil."

"No, Amina, you're not."

Kareem suddenly grabbed Rasheeda's arm, twisting it harshly. Pain shot through her and she screamed. "Get your hands off me!"

Amina gasped. "Rasheeda! Is that you? Rasheeda!" she shouted into the phone.

Rasheeda cried out, calling for help. "Amina!"

Both men walked out of the room, Kareem closing the door. Basil turned off the speaker function. Rasheeda's screams were still ringing in the background as she banged on the door, calling for her sister. He pulled the phone to his ear. "I told you, Amina. If you won't listen to what I tell you, Rasheeda will suffer for it."

"Leave her alone, Basil, please!" Amina begged, her own tears flowing. "Please!"

"File the papers, Amina!"

"I'll file the papers, just don't hurt her!"

"And keep your damn mouth shut. Do you understand me?"

"Yes."

"Let me hear you, Amina!"

"Yes, I understand!" she said loudly.

"Good. I'm glad you've finally gotten it!" he snapped.

"You're a monster, Basil!"

Not bothering to respond, he disconnected the call.

The two men locked gazes.

"You're soft," Kareem said.

Basil shook his head. "I don't have to really hurt Rasheeda. I just need Amina to think I am. It's nothing but smoke and mirrors, my friend. Smoke and mirrors."

"Until she figures it out and then what?"

When Troy stepped out of the shower Amina was still holding her cell phone in her hand. Tears were streaming down her face. He jumped across the bed, moving quickly to her side.

"What's wrong?"

She shook her head from side to side.

"Tell me, Amina. What is wrong?"

Amina met his intense stare, wrapping her arms around his neck. She couldn't begin to tell him about Basil's call or everything that was bothering her and she couldn't lie. She didn't say anything at all until Troy pressed her again for an answer.

"I'm just scared for Rasheeda," she finally said, beginning to sob.

Troy embraced her, pulling her tightly to him. He held her as she cried against his shoulder. When she was all cried out he kissed the side of her face. "Everything is going to be okay," he said, rocking her gently.

"We'll see her tomorrow and you'll be able to see for yourself that she's okay."

Clinging to Troy, Amina desperately wanted to believe that was true. With everything that was happening, she suddenly wasn't so sure anymore.

"I hate you, Basil," Rasheeda muttered, her face pressed into the thin blanket wrapped around her shoulders.

Basil brushed a hand across her face. "I'm sorry, Rasheeda. I really am. But it was necessary. Amina needed to learn that I mean what I say."

Kareem stared at her from the corner, his arms crossed over his chest. His dick had hardened as he'd stood watching her. If Basil were not there, he would have taken great joy in wiping away her hurt; in turning her pain to pleasure. He was suddenly looking forward to the prospect of Rasheeda being his wife. Her obedience and staid demeanor would serve him well.

Her slim body had a coltish innocence to it, everything about her petite and small. Her face, streaked with tears, had a youthful appeal undefiled by makeup. Her long, reddish-brown hair had natural full body, waves that had the appearance of carefree grooming. Her breasts were small, like two ripe lemons beneath her clothes and the slight curve of her hips and bottom were perfection. But tears streaked her café au lait complexion, her dark eyes bloodshot from crying. She was too pretty a girl to bear the hurt of being bullied. He would make that up to her once they were married, he thought, and he said so out loud.

Rasheeda's eyes narrowed as she returned the look he was giving her. Hostility and anger gleamed from her eyes. Hell would freeze before she would ever agree to marry him. Kareem Fayed could promise her the world and she would settle for a life of deprivation before she accepted. She bit back the urge to tell him so, the words curdling on the tip of her tongue.

Basil wiped her face, the cool rag comforting against her skin. Kneeling in front of her he looked her in the eye. "This didn't have to happen like this, Rasheeda. We both know that. Now, tomorrow is going to be a test for us all. If you do everything just like I tell you, then you'll be able to go home. You've always been a good girl so I know you wouldn't disappoint Father. I know how much you love him. And just think, when this is all over you'll be able to start planning your wedding and I promise you'll be happier than you ever imagined. The money we get from this business deal is going to make us all very, very rich. Don't you want that for us?"

Rasheeda shifted her gaze to stare back at her brother. She lifted her mouth into a polite smile and nodded. "Whatever you say, Basil!"

20

Troy maneuvered his car toward his law office. He took a quick glance at the digital clock on the dashboard. He needed to be headed to the high school for the town hall meeting but Rachel had insisted on seeing him first. He hadn't been able to reach Amina and he'd been trying to call her for over an hour, his calls going directly to voice mail. He imagined she was already at the municipal building waiting for her family to arrive.

She hadn't slept well and her restlessness had made it difficult for him to sleep. He sensed that there was more wrong than she'd been willing to tell and that bothered him. They had each sworn to never keep any secrets from the other but there was something Amina was afraid to tell him. There was little that scared his beautiful wife so he could only begin to imagine what was tearing at her spirit. As he pulled into his designated parking space he blew a heavy sigh.

Rachel was pacing the conference-room floor when he arrived, her high heels clicking harshly against the wood floors. Her expression was strained and he knew her well enough to know that her mind was racing.

"Hey, what's up?" he said as he moved into the room, his gaze meeting hers.

"Your wife has uncorked one hell of a firestorm. That's what's up," Rachel said.

Troy sighed again, his warm breath blowing past his full lips. "Fill me in."

"Have you heard of the Broadman Gaming and Entertaining Group?"

Troy pondered her question for a quick minute. "David Broadman. He owns a consortium of hotels and casinos around the world. He and his group filed an application a few years back to build a casino here in Memphis."

"He did and it was initially denied."

"Okay."

"It was denied because the property he wanted to build on had zoning restrictions and the powers in place at that time refused to revise the city ordinances."

"So what does that have to do with Amina and what her brother is doing?"

"The city council will soon be voting again on that ordinance and with the right mayoral support it will likely pass. Based on a new application recently submitted by Mr. Broadman he should be able to get it passed. It's projected to be a two-hundred-and-ten-million-dollar project that will create over nine hundred jobs and inject more than sixty million in wages here in Memphis. Jobs and wages that are greatly needed.

"Last year David Broadman approached Dwayne about purchasing that old warehouse he owns around the corner from the bakery. Dwayne turned him down because he was hoping to acquire your property and expand Just Desserts into the national food market. It would have been ideal since the bakery would have been its anchor point. But when Harper decided not to sell neither one of us gave it a second thought.

"Well, it seems that a few months ago the title to my husband's property was transferred to Basil Salman. As well as most of the property that David Broadman was interested in acquiring to build his casino. Almost two whole blocks of property with deeds registered to Basil Salman."

"Well, I'll be damned."

"It gets better. Dwayne talked to David Broadman and someone named Kareem Fayed is negotiating the sale of all that property to him; a sale that will net Basil Salman close to one hundred million dollars."

"Wouldn't the title searches have exposed him?"

"It probably wouldn't have been caught until after the fact, especially if the rightful owners didn't know what was going on."

"So what now?"

"The district attorney has everything. I filed a lawsuit this afternoon on Dwayne's behalf and we're contacting all the rightful owners to let them know what's going on."

Troy nodded. "Unbelievable. How did he think he could get away with this?"

"He might have if Amina hadn't gotten involved. They would have bilked the Broadman Group out of a lot of money and been long gone. But that's not why I called you."

"What?"

"Doesn't Amina have some connection to this Kareem guy?"

"Yeah, she was supposed to marry him."

"Well, I did a little digging and Mr. Fayed was investigated for his involvement in a similar scheme in Vegas ten years ago. They weren't able to tie him to it so charges weren't ever filed. But during the investigation Mr. Fayed's second wife died of suspicious causes, although her death was ruled an accident. Apparently she'd taken a nasty fall down a flight of stairs but the autopsy showed that she had previously suffered multiple contusions and broken bones that were never explained."

Troy stared at her. "His second wife?"

Rachel nodded. "No one can find anything on his first wife. Not even their divorce papers."

"Okay, so why is that important?"

Rachel reached for the morning newspaper resting against the conference-room table. She flipped it open to the society section. The announcement was in the bottom corner of the front page: news that mayoral candidate Nasser Salman was announcing the engagement of his daughter Rasheeda Salman to Kareem Fayed.

"There's something else," Rachel said as she met the stare Troy was giving her. "Amina transferred the deed for the bakery into her name this morning."

Amina looked around the crowded room. There was no sign of Troy or any of the other candidates and she reasoned that they were all in one or more of the classrooms waiting for the event to begin. She looked around for her brother but there was no sign of him or Rasheeda either. She bit down against her bottom lip, her nerves completely on edge. She spun back toward the entrance, looking to the parking lot for any car she might recognize. Mike suddenly rushed her, his own anxiety apparent.

"Where's your husband?" he whispered. "Doesn't he know he's supposed to be here?"

"I'm sure he's on his way," Amina said as she gave the man a quick hug. "He's probably stuck in traffic."

"This is not the time for him to be stuck anywhere. This event could win or lose him this election. I need him here focused."

She nodded her understanding. "He'll be here. And he'll be fine. You know he's prepped and ready." She took another glance around, searching the new faces that had come for the Q&A session. "Are the other candidates here?" she said, asking about the remaining contenders.

Mike nodded. "I saw Mr. Salman and his family, our esteemed public defender and his partner, and the bookstore guy who's running as an independent. The only person I haven't seen is Troy!"

"Well, here comes Quentin and Harper," she said as the family pushed through the doors, greeting them warmly.

"Hey, we're not late, are we?" Quentin questioned.

"The only person who's late is Troy," Mike said as he paced from side to side.

Amina shook her head. "Mike is having anxiety. I'm sure Troy will be here any minute now."

Mike shook his head. "Since you three are the only ones here, let me review things with you. There are reserved seats for each candidate's family members. Troy will introduce you and all you have to do is smile nice, give the audience a little wave, and applaud loudly every time he makes a brilliant point. Any questions?"

Quentin and Harper tossed each other a look, wide grins crossing their faces. "Mike, you seem a little tense," Harper teased.

Mike cut his eyes at her. "I'm going to kill him if he doesn't get here. You will all see me commit premeditated murder. I'm telling you now."

Amina laughed with the other two. "He'll be here. But I need to go find my family. Where are the candidates waiting?" she asked.

Mike gestured down the length of hallway. "The classrooms back that way."

Amina nodded, tossing her new family a quick glance.

"We'll wait here with Mike," Quentin said.

Harper nodded. "We'll keep him calm until Troy gets here."

Amina smiled as she turned and moved toward the holding area. Her eyes shifted back and forth as she looked for her father and Rasheeda. She saw Basil first. And then Kareem. The two men were standing in a huddle outside a science room, pretending to be standing guard. Both eyed her warily as she rushed to their sides.

"Where's Rasheeda?" she asked Basil as he stepped in front of her.

"Do you have something for me?" Basil questioned.

The two eyed each other, Amina's expression ice cold. She reached into her oversize handbag and passed him a manila folder. As he flipped through the documents inside a wide grin slowly filled his face. He cut an eye at Kareem, nodding his head slowly.

"Very good, Amina. I knew I could trust you."

"Where's Rasheeda?"

Basil stepped aside and gestured for her to enter the room. Rushing inside Amina found her sister sitting piously in a chair by her father's side. She barely lifted her eyes to look in Amina's direction. Nasser moved to his feet as she eased her way over to where the duo had been talking.

"Father!"

Nasser nodded, dropping his hands against her shoulders as he kissed his daughter's cheek. "Amina. I see you came to support your new husband."

"I came to support you both, Father," Amina responded. She turned her attention to her sister. "Rasheeda, are you okay?"

"Of course she's okay," Kareem interjected, moving to Rasheeda's side. He dropped a heavy palm against the young woman's shoulder and squeezed it.

Amina saw her sister wince ever so slightly. The two women locked gazes briefly before Rasheeda dropped her eyes back to the floor.

"I've been trying to reach you," Amina said. "I was worried."

"I told you she was fine," Basil interjected. "She's been very happy. Perhaps you heard. Rasheeda and Kareem will be marrying this weekend."

Amina's eyes widened in surprise. She looked from one to the other. Kareem's expression was caustic. Rasheeda's distant, as if she were someplace other than in her own body. Her posture was different, stiff and heavy, something about her giving Amina reason to pause.

"Rasheeda, can we talk alone, please?"

Kareem shook his head. "That's not going to happen," he stated. He looked toward Nasser for assistance.

Her father cupped his hand beneath her elbow and guided her toward the door. "Amina, this is not the place for this conversation. You need to go support your husband. I will not have you trying to influence your sister's decisions. You made your choice. Rasheeda has made hers."

"Did she? Did she choose this? Or is this all Basil and Kareem's doing? They won't even let her speak for herself!"

Rasheeda's voice suddenly broke through the tense atmosphere. Her tone was crystal clear and strong. She stood up, meeting her sister's concerned stare. The hint of a smile pulled at the edges of her eyes. "You should go be with Troy, Amina. Everything is going to be okay. I'm going to do the right thing. I promise."

The two women stood staring at each other, a silent exchange passing between them. Amina nodded her head as she gave her sister a warm smile. "I promise, too," she said.

As Amina moved out the door Basil rushed behind her. When they were out of their father's eyesight he yanked her arm, spinning her around to face him. "You're doing really well so far," he hissed, his mouth pressed against her ear. "Just keep your mouth shut now and you and Rasheeda both will be fine."

Neither of them expected Troy when he suddenly

grabbed her brother. He pushed him back into the classroom, slamming him hard against the green chalkboard. Chalk dust spewed behind Basil's back as Troy slammed his fist into the man's stomach, following it with a left hook to Basil's chin.

"What's going on here?" Nasser said, his voice raised. "Basil?"

"Troy!" Amina cried out, shock splattering her face.

"If you ever put your hands on my wife again, I will hurt you," Troy said, holding Basil by his collar. "You already got one pass. You won't be so lucky if it happens again."

She called his name a second time. "Troy, baby, don't, please!"

Troy threw one last punch before he released the hold he had on Basil, the man's body sinking to the floor. He adjusted his suit jacket around his torso then turned toward Nasser. "Your son has a problem with hurting women. Now, you might not be able to keep him in check but I will if he ever hurts Amina again. Do we understand each other, sir?"

Nasser nodded, his jaw locked tight. He tossed a glance toward Basil and then to his daughter. Tears misted Amina's gaze, frustration creasing her brow.

Mike and another man suddenly appeared in the doorway. Mike's eyes widened, his mouth opened in surprise. The other man stepped inside, assessing the situation.

"Is there a problem here?" the other man asked. He looked down at Basil who was still reeling from Troy's assault.

Nasser shook his head. "No. No problem. My son tripped and fell. Mr. Elliott was showing his concern."

The stranger eyed them all warily. "Well, the meeting is about to start. We need all the candidates to gather by the entrance," he said.

Troy slid one hand into Amina's curls, his fingers resting against the back of her head. His other hand slipped around her waist as he pulled her to him and kissed her forehead. He pressed his cheek to hers and held her tightly for a brief moment. When he pulled away, Amina smiled.

"I love you," she whispered.

Troy nodded. "I love you more!"

Mike grabbed both their arms. "I've got love for you both and I don't want to ever know what happened here."

Troy smiled. "Why not?"

"Plausible deniability," Mike said with his own chuckle. "We need to move it."

Amina tossed her sister one last look. Rasheeda took a step forward and Kareem grabbed her by the back of the neck, his grip tight as he stalled her steps. His grin was malevolent as he pulled her closer to his side. Amina's gaze shifted from one face to the other.

Rasheeda nodded. Something in her eyes made Amina smile, her own head bobbing against her neck. She pulled herself from Kareem's grasp and eased to her father's side. She grabbed the patriarch's hand and leaned to kiss his cheek. As they stepped past Basil, Nasser didn't bother to look in his son's direction.

The atmosphere in the large auditorium was energized. The crowd was eager to talk one-on-one with the candidates and each of the candidates was impressive. Amina was still in awe of Troy's actions and as she glanced to the empty seat beside Rasheeda and Kareem she knew that no one had ever bested her brother like that before.

As the crowd clapped, Amina clapped with them. When Quentin, Harper, and Mike cheered, she joined them but truth be told she hadn't heard one word any of the candidates had spoken. She was unable to focus on the discussion, her attention drawn to Rasheeda who was sitting stoically, her body tense. Kareem had an arm resting against the back of her chair and she was leaning as far from him as she could manage. Some thirty minutes into the meeting, Basil finally made an appearance, the dust brushed from his clothes, the beginnings of a black eye forming on his face. He sat down beside Kareem and the two fell into a whispered conversation.

The two sisters locked gazes and held it. Amina's heart began to race and she leaned forward in her seat. Rasheeda stood up abruptly and suddenly rushed toward the exit. Before either man realized what was happening Amina was on her heels, both heading in the direction of the ladies' room. When they were safely inside, Amina locked the door, just as Kareem slammed his shoulder against the wood.

Amina wrapped her arms around her sister's shoulders and the two women hugged each other tightly. They clung to each other as Rasheeda began to cry, tears streaming down her face.

"I knew you weren't okay," Amina finally whispered. "I knew something was wrong."

"I've been locked in a room in Kareem's basement.," Rasheeda whispered. "Today was the first day they let me out."

Amina gasped. "We're calling the police."

There was a sudden slam against the bathroom door and both women jumped. On the other side Kareem was banging harshly as he called out Rasheeda's name.

Amina fumbled inside her purse for her cell phone. She had just dialed the nine and the one when the door suddenly flew open. Kareem and Basil both rushed into the room behind it, Basil snatching the phone from her hand.

Inside the auditorium Nasser and Troy both had watched as the two women rushed from the room. Neither man had missed Kareem rising to follow, Basil on his heels just minutes later. By the end of the meeting when none of them had returned both men became anxious. The evening's moderator brought the session to a close. Both Nasser and Troy avoided the salutary handshakes and rushed to the front of the building. When he couldn't find either of his daughters Nasser pulled out his cell phone to call his son. Troy called the police.

21

Amina and Rasheeda were still holding tight to each other when Kareem slammed the basement door, leaving them alone in the dimly lit room. When they heard footsteps fading off into the distance Amina moved to the door and tried to pull it open. Frustration washed over her expression as she tried to fathom how they'd managed to be in such a precarious situation.

Rasheeda pulled her knees to her chest, wincing as she slid down on her side, her head resting against the pillow. Amina moved to her side, brushing her fingers across her sister's forehead.

"You're running a fever," she said.

Rasheeda shrugged. "I don't feel good. My insides feel like they're on fire."

"They'll find us," Amina said, trying to sound confident. "Troy won't stop looking until he finds us."

Tears suddenly rained down Rasheeda's face. "Oh, don't cry. Please don't cry," Amina said as she crawled onto the bed and wrapped her body around her sister's. She held her tightly. "It's going to be okay. We are going to get out of here," she said.

Rasheeda shook her head. "Todd doesn't know where I am. They put that marriage announcement in the newspaper and I bet he thinks I turned my back on him."

Amina shook her head. "No, he doesn't. He loves you. And as soon as we get out of here you're going to be able to tell him how much you love him."

Rasheeda wanted desperately to believe Amina. She suddenly felt like that was all she had to hold on to. She winced as a twinge of pain shot like a bolt of lightning through her midsection. She squeezed her sister's hand, tightening her grip on the other woman's fingers.

"Todd has never seen my face," Rasheeda suddenly said. "Isn't that crazy? I could look like the back end of a baboon and he wouldn't know it."

Amina smiled. "Well, you're absolutely beautiful so he won't have anything to complain about."

"That's it though," Rasheeda exclaimed. "I don't think it would matter to him. He loves my personality and my spirit and he likes being my friend. He makes me feel so special and I like that."

"So do you ever plan to let him see your face?"

Rasheeda tried to lift her mouth in a slight smile. She winced again. "On our wedding day. When I was in Baltimore we had set a date and then Basil showed up and forced me to leave. Kareem threatened to break Todd's hand and I was afraid he would hurt him. Todd's studying to be a surgeon and he can't have a broken hand!"

Amina blew a strained sigh. She tried to lighten the moment, making conversation to pass the time.

"Well, I can't wait until you get married then. Do you plan to wear the veil after you marry?"

"No. I only wear it now because of Basil and Father. And I think if I said I didn't want to wear it Father wouldn't have a problem with it. I will continue to wear my hijab though. That was the other reason I went to see Todd."

"I don't understand."

"Todd was having a crisis of faith. He was thinking about leaving and I needed to know how he felt about that."

"And now?"

"He's worked through it and he's happy now."

Amina felt Rasheeda's forehead a second time. She was hot and her skin was clammy.

"Are you and Troy happy?" Rasheeda suddenly asked.

Amina nodded. "He's the best thing that could have happened to me."

"That's good. I like Troy. I think he's good for you."

"I'll tell you a secret but you have to swear to me that you won't tell anyone else."

Rasheeda tried to lift her head. "I . . . prom . . . prom . . . prom . . ." she stammered, suddenly unable to get the words out. It was harder for her to breathe and she was panting lightly.

"Rasheeda! Are you okay?"

Rasheeda sighed, a low grown easing past her lips. "So . . . tired," Rasheeda finally whispered. "So . . . tired . . ."

Basil was pacing the floor, his mind racing. He should never have allowed Rasheeda to attend the town hall meeting. From the moment they'd arrived things had gone from bad to worse. He had trusted Amina would have done one thing she'd been told and she'd managed to screw that up for him. He raged, a loud scream the momentum behind a soft punch. He was breathing heavily as he stared at the dent in Kareem's living-room wall.

Kareem moved into the space with a suitcase in hand. After opening the wall safe behind a painting in the far corner, he removed his passport, a portfolio of legal documents, and stacks of cash, tossing everything into the leather carrier.

"What are you doing?" Basil questioned.

"What do you think I'm doing? I'm getting the hell out of town."

"We can still make this work!" Basil shouted.

Kareem shook his head. "Are you crazy? This is over and I'm not about to hang around to see how it blows up."

"What do we do about my sisters?"

"Your sisters are a liability. I don't leave problems around to burn me later."

"Where are you going?"

"Far away. And I strongly suggest you do the same," Kareem said matter-of-factly.

The two men stood staring at each other for a brief moment before Kareem grabbed his suitcase and headed to the car in the garage. Minutes later he returned with two full containers of gasoline.

Troy was finding it harder and harder to control his emotions. He knew he needed to stay calm but he was finding that more difficult to do. Since the police had arrived he'd had Mike in one ear reminding him about his public image. Then Harper had found Amina's cell phone smashed on the floor in the women's bathroom and all his control had been lost. Troy had suddenly become a husband whose wife was missing and he was willing to do whatever he needed to get her back.

After giving his last statement to a uniformed officer he moved to Nasser Salman's side. The man was no longer his opponent but his father-in-law, his loss cutting even deeper than Troy's. The two men locked gazes, Nasser tossing Troy a nod of his head.

"Do you have any idea where Basil would have taken them?"

Nasser shook his head. "No, I'm sorry but I don't. I don't know why Basil would do something like this."

Troy sighed. "Do you know anything about Basil's business dealings with Mr. Fayed?"

"No. It was my understanding that Kareem was teaching Basil the ropes. Helping him build his own real estate business. I never got specifics."

Troy nodded. "Mr. Nasser, you might want to sit down," he said.

"I don't understand . . ."

"Well, it seems that . . ." Troy started as he laid out the details of real estate fraud Basil had committed with Kareem Fayed's assistance. Troy told the man everything Rachel and Amina had told him, including the suspicion that Kareem might have been involved in the disappearance of his first wife, and the death of his second.

"He's been married twice?"

Troy nodded. "Yes, sir. There are two marriages that we're aware of."

Nasser shook his head, his spirit suddenly broken. "I trusted him. I trusted him with my daughters."

"How about his parents? Would he have taken them there?"

"His parents are living in London. They returned to the UK after they learned about Amina's marriage to you. I gave the officer the one phone number I have for them. I also gave them the only address I had for him as well."

Troy blew breath past his lips, the air rushed. "The officer said they checked his apartment and his office but there's no one there."

"I don't know anywhere else to look," Nasser said, his own frustrations beading sweat across his brow.

The two men stood together in solidarity for another ten minutes, until the police had spoken with everyone who might have seen something. When the officer in charge instructed them both to go home and wait, neither moved. Quentin broke through the quiet they'd fallen into.

"We can all go back to the bakery to wait. The police have your cell phone numbers and they can reach you both there."

Troy nodded. Nasser looked hesitant.

Harper placed a gentle hand against the man's forearm. "Mr. Salman, we're all family and we need to be together to support each other. Amina and Rasheeda both would want you to be with us right now so that we can support you."

Nasser nodded. "I don't have a car. Basil drove . . ." He paused, his voice catching deep in his throat.

"That's okay, sir," Troy said. "You can ride home with me."

Basil's eyes were skating frantically back and forth. "What the hell are you doing!" he snapped.

Kareem cut an eye at him, not bothering to respond. He continued to douse the floors and furniture in gasoline, moving from the bedrooms, down the hall through the living room, and into the dining area.

"What about my sisters?" Basil yelled.

Kareem said nothing as he moved back to the garage and tossed the now-empty red containers into the washroom.

He came into the house one last time, turning on the gas stove and oven.

Kareem came toe to toe with Basil, his narrowed gaze cold and calculating. "Your sisters are on you. But if you're smart you'll let them *vanish* and you'll do the same thing. Disappear, Basil. Forget this life. Forget your family. And you damn sure better forget you ever knew me."

Before Basil could respond Kareem flicked the Zippo lighter in his hand and slung the flaming unit into a puddle of fluid. The gasoline ignited, flames shooting with a vengeance across the floor. Basil's eyes widened as he watched Kareem head for the door, tossing him a glance over his shoulder. "Disappear!" Kareem snapped one last time.

Racing to the front yard, Basil turned to stare back at the house. Flames were beginning to shoot out the side windows, glass shattering from the heat. The neighbor next door suddenly rushed to his side.

"I called the fire department. They're on their way!" she shouted as she held tight to a small poodle tucked under her arm.

"What?" Basil tossed her a look, his eyes swinging back to the house and then down the road where Kareem's car had disappeared.

"The fire department. They're on their way," the woman repeated.

Basil could hear the sirens in the distance, sounding like they were miles away. He tossed the woman another look. His heart was racing, perspiration dripping from his pores.

He suddenly shouted, "They're my family! Tell them my sisters are inside!" And then he tore across the lawn and back inside the house.

Troy was pacing the floor, twisting his hands nervously. Nasser sat in a corner, Miss Alice keeping him company. Harper crossed the room, coffeepot in hand, as she refilled everyone's cup with brew. Quentin rested a tray of sandwiches and baked goods on the table, encouraging everyone to eat.

Staring out the bakery window Troy was reminded of the first time he'd laid eyes on Amina, her energy like a tornado spinning around her. Her bright eyes had reflected her spirit and he'd fallen head over heels in love. The memory pulled an easy smile on his face.

There was a knock on the bakery door and he turned to see Rachel, Dwayne, and the baby standing in the entrance. Quentin moved to let the family in.

"Any news?" Rachel asked.

Troy shook his head. "Nothing. I'm about to go crazy."

Dwayne tapped him on the back. "They'll find her."

Miss Alice gestured toward them. "Bring me that baby! Let me cuddle her," she said as she waved her arms.

Rachel rolled her eyes as she moved to drop her infant daughter into Miss Alice's arms. She extended her hand to Mr. Salman. "It's a pleasure to meet you, Mr. Salman. I'm Rachel and this is my husband, Dwayne."

"It's very nice to meet you both," Nasser responded.

"And this delightful little munchkin is Joanna," Miss Alice cooed.

Nasser smiled. "May I hold her?"

Rachel nodded as Miss Alice placed the baby into his arms. She smiled as Nasser cooed softly, rocking Baby Joanna in his arms. Rachel moved back to where Troy was standing.

"A warrant's been issued for Basil's arrest. Thus far there's nothing to connect Kareem to the real estate fraud."

"I don't even know where to begin to look for them," Troy said, throwing his hands up in frustration. "The police have looked everywhere."

"Not everywhere! She's out there and she'll be home," Dwayne said.

"I hope so. I wouldn't tell everyone this, but I'm scared," Troy said. "I'm really scared."

"I don't know if this will help you or not, but I found something interesting when I was researching those titles," Rachel said as she reached into her bag and passed him a sheet of yellow lined notepaper.

"What?"

"There were two residential properties on the list in Basil's name. Both were foreclosures. One deed was transferred to another couple who were both arrested on trespassing charges last month. They allegedly removed a lockbox from the front door of the building and changed the locks, then forged sale documents and moved into the residence without permission. Apparently they'd been squatting there for some time."

"And the other?"

Rachel shrugged.

"Call that detective and give him the address," Harper chimed.

"Yeah," Quentin added. "The police can get there faster than you can."

Troy pushed the speed dial on his phone, the line connecting to the detective assigned to try to find Amina and her sister. The conversation was brief when Troy suddenly shot a look in Nasser's direction as the color drained from his face. He moved toward the door and gestured for Nasser to follow him.

"What's wrong?" Quentin exclaimed, the room growing quiet as they all turned toward him.

"Did they find her?" Harper asked.

"They don't know. But the detective says there's a fire burning at that address I just gave him."

22

Amina was having the sweetest dream. She'd been dreaming about Troy. Troy had been by her side, telling her how much he loved her, how he would always be there for her, that he would never leave her. She imagined that his kisses were like butterflies flitting against her cheeks and eyelids. His warm touch was gentle and loving. Troy kept calling to her, begging her to open her eyes and come back to him but she was scared.

Amina was afraid that if she opened her eyes Troy would be gone and she would find herself back in that room, the smell of fuel and sulfur in her nostrils, smoke blinding her eyes. If she woke up Amina feared her beloved sister would be gone and she and Basil would be fighting back the flames that had been burning around them. Dreaming of Troy made her feel better and so she drifted back into a state of bliss, refusing to let him go.

Troy dropped his forehead against the back of Amina's hand. For two days he'd been by her side, refusing to leave until she opened her eyes again and smiled. He took a deep breath, unable to comprehend how any of this could have happened to them. He drew his fingers against her arms, over her neck, along her profile, lightly grazing the side of her face with his fingertips. He reached to kiss her nose, her cheeks, her lips, then laid his head back against her.

There was a light knock on the room door and Quentin peeked his head inside. Sitting upright Troy gestured for his brother to come on in.

Moving to his side, Quentin dropped a palm against Troy's back. "Hey, you need to take a break. Why don't you go home and get a shower. Maybe take a nap. I'll stay here with Amina until you get back."

Troy swiped a large hand over his face. "No, I'm good. I'm not leaving until she wakes up. When she opens her eyes I plan to be right here."

Quentin nodded. "Well, I thought you would want to know that Rasheeda just got out of surgery. They finally got that bleeding stopped. The doctor says she should make a full recovery."

"That's good. Too bad the poor girl had to go through three surgeries to get there though. How's Basil?"

"Mr. Salman says he's doing well. The burns are all minor and he responded well to the oxygen therapy for his smoke inhalation. They'll probably release him tomorrow. Then he'll be transferred to the county jail and arraigned."

Troy nodded. "How is Mr. Salman holding up?"

"He actually asked me the same question about you," Quentin said, smiling. "But he seems to be doing okay. Your father-in-law is one tough bird."

Troy smiled. "That's what Amina loves most about her father—his strength."

"Well, you and Mr. Salman are a lot alike. I imagine that's one of the qualities she loves about you, too."

Troy nodded. "I really admire him. He's been roaming from one room to the other, like clockwork. I'm sure having one child in the hospital is stressful. Having all three of them here is unfathomable. I can't begin to imagine what he must be going through," Troy said. He blew a deep sigh. "Worrying about one child is bad enough." He pressed his palm against Amina's abdomen, his head waving from side to side.

Quentin nodded his understanding. "It's going to be okay. You and Amina will be able to celebrate any day now."

Troy met his brother's stare. He could only hope Quentin was right. The news had come as a complete surprise to them all. They had been pacing the linoleum floors in the hospital's waiting room for news on the siblings' condition. The trio had been pulled from the house fire and rushed to the Delta Medical Center hours earlier. They had already been told that Rasheeda had been rushed straight to surgery but there was no news at all on Amina, or Basil. Then the doctor had called for Amina's family.

Troy had stood toe to toe with Dr. Bernard Strand as he explained that Amina was suffering from smoke inhalation and a concussion from a fall. The doctor advised that she was already undergoing therapy to help her lungs and that her head injury, although serious, was not permanent. He predicted that it might take up to two weeks for her to regain consciousness but that she was stable and well on her way to recovery. And then he'd congratulated him on the pregnancy, shock registering on Troy's face.

"I'm sorry, Mr. Elliott. I thought you knew. Your

wife is only a few weeks along. Thus far it doesn't look like the trauma has had any negative effect on the pregnancy. But we're going to keep an eye on her."

Harper and Rachel had jumped with excitement. Miss Alice hadn't been able to contain her squeals.

Mr. Salman had shaken Troy's hand, congratulating him. "I'm going to be a grandfather!" he'd exclaimed.

The moment had been bittersweet. Troy had wanted to jump with joy but he had wanted Amina to jump with him. Since then, he'd not left her side. He nodded, tossing his brother a slight smile.

Quentin squeezed his shoulder one last time before he made his exit. "If you need me, Big Brother, I'll be right here."

As the door closed, Troy resumed his light caresses, gently massaging her limbs. His hand skated across her stomach. He slid a warm hand up the length of her arm. Then, resting his forehead back against her side, he whispered the mantra he'd been whispering religiously since she'd been admitted. "I love you, Amina. I'm right here, baby. I'm not going anywhere. Open your eyes, darling, and come back to me."

Basil hung his head, unable to look his father in his eyes. A glass partition separated the two men. A prison guard stood behind Basil's right shoulder, a crass reminder of where he was and why. Nasser reached for the telephone receiver on the wall beside him and waited for his son to do the same. There was a moment of pause before Basil did, slowly pulling the device to his ear.

"Hello, Father."

"Hello, Son. How are you?"

Basil shrugged, finally lifting his gaze to meet Nasser's. Contrition painted his expression as tears welled in his eyes. "How are the girls?"

"Rasheeda is good. She'll come home tomorrow. Amina is still unconscious but the doctor says she and the baby are doing fine. They're hopeful she'll wake up soon."

"Baby?"

Nasser nodded. "Your sister and her husband are expecting a child."

Basil closed his eyes, his head waving from side to side. The news of Amina's pregnancy suddenly made him feel even worse. He was embarrassed by his own bad behavior and it showed, the weight of it heavy against his shoulders.

He had vivid memories of the last time he'd seen his sisters. He had run back into the house but the flames were already spreading too quickly. He'd barely been able to get past the fire to reach the door and steps that led down to the basement. When he had, the door handle had burned his hands, the heat having sealed it shut tight. Rushing back out he'd raced to the backyard and the metal door that gave him access to the lower level. The smoke had been thick and the space was dark.

He'd struggled to find his way to the room in the back. The key to the padlock had been in his pocket and as he pulled it into his hands, he'd dropped it to the floor. He'd fallen down on his knees, his hands palming the concrete surface until he found it, unlocking the entrance.

When he'd pulled the door open Amina had been on her knees in prayer, tears streaming down her face. Her eyes had lifted with hope when she saw him and she'd flung herself into his arms, hugging him tightly around his neck. "There's something wrong with Rasheeda," she'd cried.

Sweeping his baby sister into his arms he'd admonished Amina to stay close to him, to hold tight to the back of his shirt. Breathing was difficult and he was panting heavily, trying to suck in oxygen. His eyes burned and he couldn't see through the thick gray cloud that fogged the space. It took every ounce of energy he had to make his way back to the basement door and when he finally pushed his way through, Amina was no longer behind him.

Someone, a fireman maybe, took Rasheeda from his arms. Someone else had tried to grab him but Basil had shaken off the arm and had thrown himself back down the basement stairs, screaming out his sister's name. Crawling on his hands and knees he tried to find his way back to her. It was only when he had absolutely nothing left, not an ounce of energy to keep him moving forward, that he realized he was crying, tears streaming down his cheeks.

He had tried to scream her name but he had no voice and so he prayed that he would find her. He'd prayed over and over again. And then he'd hit her leg.

Struggling, he'd pulled Amina into his arms, half-carrying, half-dragging her lifeless body back in the direction he'd come from and then everything had gone black. As he'd fallen forward, his weight crashing down against his sister, her head had slammed harshly into the concrete steps. When he eventually came to, he was handcuffed to a hospital bed and his father was sitting by his side.

When Basil opened his eyes his father was still

staring at him intently. "I'm sorry, Father," he whispered, his voice barely audible.

Nasser's own tears pressed hot against his eyelids. "How could you, Basil? How could you do that to your sisters? To our family? Rasheeda trusted you to protect her. I trusted you. How could you betray us?"

Basil hung his head again, his gaze dropping back to the floor. He didn't have an answer, unable to find the words to explain how his own greed had put him there.

Nasser continued to berate him, his own anger all consuming. He couldn't remember ever being so angry with his son and his disappointment was telling. "You have broken my heart, Basil. I had faith in you. I believed you and you have done nothing but lie to me! You were supposed to protect your sisters and you put them in danger instead. That is not the man I raised you to be. You are not the man I'm proud to call my son!"

Tears rained over Basil's cheeks as he apologized over and over again. His father had always been stern and demanding but his love had been unconditional, the man wanting only the very best for them all. Basil had failed him and for the first time ever he was being made to face that fact.

A pregnant pause swelled between them. Basil's head hung low, unable to meet the intense stare his father was giving him. Before either man could say anything else the guard stepped forward, tapped him on the shoulder, and told him his time was up.

"I will come see you again as soon as they allow me," Nasser said.

Basil stole one last glance at his father. "Why would you do that for me?"

Nasser barely hesitated before he answered. "Because you are still my son and I love you."

Harper watched as Quentin put the final touches on one more wedding cake. This bride's colors were brilliant shades of orange and yellow and Quentin had captured them in the delicate flowers he'd molded from fondant, gum paste, and royal icing. She loved to watch her husband when he was in his zone. Quentin loved everything about his job and his skills were impressive. When he was feverish with joy doing what he loved, she found him sexy as hell. As if he had read her mind he lifted his gaze to meet hers. The seductive look he gave her was intoxicating.

Harper smiled brightly. "So, how long are you going to be?" she asked as she slowly played with the top buttons on the nightshirt she was wearing.

"Not much longer."

"Good. You wife could use a little attention."

"Then I am done," Quentin said as he raised his eyebrows.

Harper laughed as she moved to the counter, resting her elbows on top. She dropped her chin into her hands. Quentin winked an eye at her as he affixed the last flowers atop the cake.

"Did you talk to your brother tonight?"

Quentin nodded. "There's still no change."

"Did he tell you Rasheeda will be going home on Friday?"

"Yeah, he did."

"She looks great and she said she's feeling good. Rachel and I went to do her hair today. We gave her and Amina both manicures and pedicures, too."

"He told me. Bright red? Really?"

"Rachel picked the color. It was called Red Hot Mama."

"You can always leave it to Rachel to come up with some mess," he said, laughing heartily.

Harper smiled. "Rachel was able to convince Troy to go down to the cafeteria to get something to eat."

Quentin smiled. "I bet that didn't last long."

"No, he came back so fast I doubt he had time to chew."

Quentin shifted the cake into the cooler and began to clean up his workspace. "He won't admit it but he's having a really hard time. He's scared and I've never seen my big brother scared before."

"I was thinking the same thing. But I'm also wondering if he's just now mourning Pop's death, too. He never really grieved last year. Not like you and I did. Maybe the fear of losing Amina and the baby triggered something?"

Quentin shrugged. "Maybe. I think he just needs some time."

Harper tossed him a nervous look. She bit down against her bottom lip. "Can I ask you something, Quentin?"

He eyed her curiously. "Harper, you know you don't have to ask to talk to me about anything."

She took a deep breath. "Does it bother you that Troy and Amina got pregnant before we did?"

Quentin paused as he reflected on her question. He tossed dirty dishes into the dishwasher then moved around to his wife's side. He leaned with his back against the counter, his arms crossed over his chest. "I really hadn't given it any thought. I'm happy for them. But no, it doesn't bother me that they're having a baby before we are. I don't think we're ready to have a baby. How do you feel?"

"I was worried for you more than myself. If it was something that was important to you then I wanted us to consider it. But I agree. I don't think we're ready yet."

Quentin leaned to kiss her cheek. "Let's enjoy being godparents to Baby Joanna and an aunt and uncle to the new baby. When it's time for us, honey, we'll know." He reached for the tub of sugar, moving toward the pantry.

Harper nodded. She shifted forward and the nightshirt she was wearing rose up over the curve of her buttocks. She was wearing nothing beneath her top and when Quentin caught sight of her bare bottom, his hand stalled in midair, his focus suddenly lost. An erection hardened in his slacks.

"That is not fair," he said as he took a deep breath, gesturing with his eyes.

Harper laughed. "I told you I needed some attention." She reached for the empty bowl that had held the buttercream icing. Quentin watched as she ran her finger around the bowl's interior to collect the last remnants of sugary confection. She drew it slowly to her mouth and sucked it past her lips. First one finger and then another, licking each slowly.

Quentin shook his head, a wry smile pulling at his mouth. "You're a tease!"

She giggled as she moved toward the back stairs, her backside bumping from side to side. When she reached the door she unbuttoned her shirt completely, allowing it to drop to the floor.

Grinning, Quentin pulled off his apron and tossed it atop the counter as he raced behind her. "Can't have my baby needing attention."

23

The sun felt like gold across her face and it made her smile. Troy's voice was echoing in her heart and the rays of sunshine added to the joy. Amina slowly opened her eyes, allowing them to focus on the bright light throughout the room. She took a deep breath and then a second, wanting to fill her lungs with the gilded air that warmed the space.

Beside her, Troy was sleeping soundly. He sat in a chair by her bedside, his head resting against her side. One arm was tossed across her abdomen. Seeing his face brought tears to her eyes. She eased her hand over his head and gently caressed him. Troy jumped at her touch, lifting his head to stare up at her.

Amina smiled sweetly. "Hey, there!"

Troy's eyes widened, his own grin pulling at his mouth. "Hey yourself. Where've you been?"

"I was dreaming about you and it felt really good." Her gaze swept slowly around the room, taking in the beeping monitors by the bed and the line of IV fluids that was running into her arm. "How long have I been here?"

"Just over one week."

"No wonder I feel so well rested."

"I was really starting to worry."

She pressed a hand to the side of his face. "I'm sorry," she said, her consoling tone soothing to his spirit. She took another deep breath as she slowly acclimated herself to her surroundings.

"I should call your nurse," Troy said as he reached for her call button.

She shook her head. "Not yet. I want you all to myself for a little bit."

Troy kissed her hand as he entwined their fingers together. She suddenly sat upright, concern billowing over her face as her memories came flooding back to her. "Rasheeda?"

Troy shifted his body up against the bed as he wrapped his arms around her. "Rasheeda is doing fine. She's home and your father is taking very good care of her."

"What about Basil? And Kareem?"

"Basil's in jail. He's facing a host of charges including kidnapping, assault, fraud, and arson. They haven't been able to find Kareem."

She blew a deep sigh. "And my father is doing okay?"

"Your father officially withdrew from the election. He said that he needed to focus on healing his family and therefore couldn't fulfill the obligations of the office."

Amina paused to take all the information in. She blew another sigh as she lifted her eyes to stare at him. "And you're okay? What about your campaign?"

"I am now. I missed you."

"I missed you, too!"

Troy leaned to press a kiss to her cheek and then her lips, allowing his mouth to linger softly. "And I'm still in the campaign. Mike's been holding it down for me," he said when he finally pulled away.

"Good, because there's something I need to tell you," Amina said, her hand dropping to her tummy.

Troy smiled. "If it's a boy I'd like to name him Everett Donovan Elliott, after my pop."

Shades of happy flooded her face. "You know!"

Troy nodded excitedly.

"Is the baby okay?"

"The doctor says he's just fine. Now if it's a girl . . ."

She interrupted him. "It's not."

"How do you know?"

"I dreamed about our son, too."

For two weeks straight Troy waited on Amina hand and foot. He'd been treating her like she was porcelain, fragile and easy to break. She was past the point of being ready for them both to resume some level of normalcy in their lives. Although knowing she was right, he'd gone back to his daily responsibilities kicking and screaming.

Taking a quick glance at the large clock on the wall, Amina knew that Troy would be home at any moment and she wanted to be ready. She lifted the lid to the Dutch oven on the stovetop. The smothered chicken simmered nicely in a brown gravy she'd infused with mushrooms and onions. On her way home she'd picked up dessert from the bakery, a cherry tartlet with a chocolate and almond crust. Quentin had tossed in a half dozen yeast rolls fresh out of the oven. All she had left to do was to sauté the green snow peas with butter and garlic just before they were ready to eat their meal.

Moving from the kitchen to the bedroom, Amina slipped out of her T-shirt and jeans, changing into a form-fitting dress and heels. In the bathroom she checked her reflection in the mirror, pulling her fingers through the length of her curls. She heard Troy when he put his key in the door as he let himself inside, announcing his arrival. Taking one last look at her reflection in the mirror, she skipped back to the living space to greet him.

"Hi, honey!" she exclaimed as she pressed a kiss to his mouth.

"Hi! Don't you look pretty!"

"Thank you. I wanted to look nice for you."

"And you smell good too," he said as he nuzzled his face into her neck. "Like pot roast and gravy."

"I do not smell like pot roast," Amina laughed as she gave him a playful punch on the shoulder.

"No, you don't. I was just teasing. You smell heavenly. But dinner is smelling good too."

She reached for his suit jacket, pulling it over his shoulder and arms, then took it and his briefcase to the closet. "Would you like a drink before dinner?" she asked.

Troy smiled. "No. I'm good."

"So how was your day?" Amina asked as they moved into the kitchen.

Troy took a seat at the counter as Amina dropped a sauté pan onto the stove top. He watched as she began to prep the veggies for their meal. "Well, the Daughters of the American Revolution took me to task about certain elements of my platform. We agreed to disagree but I'm not sure they'll endorse me."

"You aren't going to make everybody happy. But I think you've impressed a number of people who'd initially written you off. I know you've earned my father's vote."

Troy smiled. "I still wish I could wrangle you for my campaign."

"Actually, Mike did. He asked me to appear at a parenting forum next week with the spouses of the other candidates and I agreed."

"Thank you. I appreciate that."

"Anything to get you elected, handsome!"

Troy shifted in his seat, lifting a leg onto the rail beneath the stool he was sitting on. "So, tell me about your day!"

"I spent the morning with Rasheeda and my father. Then I went to the office. There's a case that came across my desk that I'm interested in litigating."

"Really?"

"A staff sergeant in the army was home visiting his family. He went to a bar with his sister. He left the bar intoxicated. His sister took a taxi home. He fell asleep in the backseat of his car, in the parking lot, with the keys locked in the trunk of the vehicle. Local police woke him and charged him with a DUI. He was jailed for forty-eight hours before the family could make his bail. He's being deployed overseas next month and I plan to get the charges dropped. He did everything right and they're trying to make him out to be a criminal. When I'm done the city is not only going to compensate him for his legal expenses but they're going to publicly apologize to him and his family."

"So you plan to take on the Memphis police department?"

"Just preparing you, Mr. Mayor!"

Troy grinned.

When the food was plated Amina and Troy moved to the dining table. They continued talking through the meal and as he watched her grow excited about something that inspired her, he couldn't help but be mesmerized by her energy. Returning to the house every evening took on new meaning with Amina there, the space feeling like home was supposed to feel.

He pushed his plate away, sitting back in his seat. He blew a deep breath past his lips. "I'm full. This was delicious."

"I hope you're not too full. I have dessert."

Troy smiled, meeting the stare she was giving him. "Dessert?"

She nodded as she slowly licked her lips. "Uh-huh!"

The two sat staring at each other, a silent exchange passing between them. After a few minutes, Amina rose from her seat and moved in his direction. She extended her hand and pulled him to his feet. Leading the way she tossed him a lust-filled gaze over her shoulder. By the time they reached the bedroom door, Troy had eased her dress off her shoulders, his mouth just beginning to tease her flesh.

His loving was like morning mist on a warm summer day. Everything about Troy's touch was easy and gentle, his hand like a brush painting love over everything he laid hands on. Her pregnancy made him even more sensitive to her needs and she sometimes found herself having to be more assertive about what she wanted from him.

Amina was awed by his stamina, his ability to take her to endless heights with their lovemaking. Each kiss was as masterful as the first time he'd captured her lips with his own. She was learning every crease and dimple across his body, loving each blemish and scar.

She leaned on her elbow, staring down at him as he slept. He was sprawled out on his back, his naked body splayed open. One leg was bent at the knee, the other hanging slightly off the bed. Both arms were pulled above his head, one hand resting over his eyes. His breathing was heavy, a rhythmic inhalation and exhalation that she found comforting. She trailed a soft hand over his chest, teasing one nipple first and then the other. Her fingers stopped at his belly button, her pinky dipping into the small well. He didn't budge, still sleeping soundly, oblivious to her touch.

She shifted her body closer to his, continuing her exploration. Her fingers danced from his belly button to where the triangle of his pubic hair began. The hair curled tightly. The strands were tight and coarse, coiling in an intricate pattern. Amina found herself smiling as she teased her fingers through the wisps; smiling because with each pass his flaccid member twitched.

She eased a firmer touch against him, trailing the pads of her fingertips around the base of his organ. It awakened with a mind of its own and her eyes widened as it began to swell and grow. She placed a warm hand around it, handling it gently and when she did Troy shifted in his sleep, a low gust of air blowing out of his mouth. His legs opened a little wider, his bent knee extending outward.

Amina took a deep breath as she began to stroke him gently, a slow up-and-down glide against her palm. Troy was suddenly rock hard, the head of his cock glistening. Her hand continued to tease and taunt him and Troy moaned. It was a low whimper at first, intensifying with each stroke.

Leaning forward Amina blew a slow puff of breath across his skin. Troy suddenly gasped, his muscle quivering. His eyes opened and he lifted his torso ever so slightly, his eyes flitting open and closed as he stared down at her.

"Amina? Baby!" his voice came low and raspy, anticipation causing him to enunciate each word.

She smiled, her gaze locking with his as she shifted forward, rising slightly above his body. She licked her lips and then took him into her mouth, slowly sliding her tongue across his manhood. Troy gasped loudly and suddenly rocked his hips forward as his torso fell back against the mattress. "Ohhh, Amina," he moaned.

She continued with her ministrations. Her tongue bathed him as her lips and fingers gently massaged him. Up and down, over and over again. Amina knew he was close as he began to pulse against her tongue, the erotic sensation moving her heart to race. Troy's hips were bucking up and down as he thrust himself against her. His back suddenly arched and he shouted, her name spilling off the tip of his tongue. She tightened her grip, continuing to stroke him. Troy cried out again and his toes curled.

Amina's smile widened as she lifted her eyes back to his face. He was panting heavily as he rode the last waves of his orgasm, his own eyes rolled back in his head. As he came down from his high he lifted his torso back up to look at her.

"Wow," he said, still reeling as his nerve endings fired off their last impulses. "Where did that come from?"

Amina giggled as she lay back down beside him, snuggling her body against his. "I was trying to get extra credit for those lessons you've been giving me."

Troy laughed with her as he tightened his hold. "Extra credit? Baby, you just got promoted to the next grade!"

24

Amina, Rasheeda, and Harper were laughing hysterically as they left the cultural center after their self-defense class. Each time it seemed like the hysterics would end one would look at the other and the trio would burst out laughing all over again. The three had taken self-defense classes at Rachel's insistence, their sister-friend gifting the three of them their enrollment fees. "Dwayne's mother made me go," she said. "Every woman should know how to protect herself."

With a month of courses behind them, they only had another week left to perfect the lessons. After the evening's class, the instructor, a tall Chuck Norris look-alike, had wanted to praise Amina for her performance. She had demonstrated speed, strength, power, accuracy, and endurance and didn't allow her growing pregnancy to impede her efforts. He had moved behind her unexpectedly, dropping a hand to her shoulder. The touch had startled her and she'd reacted defensively, slamming him to the floor. Everyone in the lobby had stared in amazement.

Rasheeda had been the first to speak, a dry joke

breaking the ice. "Mr. Taylor, I don't think she did that right."

Harper had chimed in. "I think her technique was a little off. He landed a little soft to me."

They'd been laughing ever since.

"I cannot believe I just did that," Amina giggled.

"You can't? Mr. Taylor is the one who really got surprised!" Harper said.

Harper was driving, Amina riding shotgun, as Rasheeda sat in the backseat. She maneuvered the car through downtown, heading toward the bakery. "I already texted Quentin and told him we want chocolate cookies ready the minute we walk in the door."

"And cheesecake, too!" Amina added. "I really want cheesecake!"

"How are you not gaining a pound?" Rasheeda asked. "All you ever do is eat!"

Harper laughed. "You are eating a lot!"

"It's not me, it's Baby Everett. He's going to be the size of a linebacker when he finally makes an appearance."

"Keep telling yourself that. That baby is going to come here weighing six pounds and you're the one who's going to look like a football player," Rasheeda said with a deep laugh.

Amina cut her eye at her sister. "I still want cheesecake."

Harper shook her head. "So, Rasheeda, how are you doing? How are the wedding plans coming along?"

Amina's sister leaned forward in her seat. Her excitement gleamed from her eyes, everything about her body language screaming with joy. "Things are going really well. Father says I can have the wedding of my dreams. And Todd just found out that he'll be doing his internship in Atlanta! Mother says we can live with her so that I can go to school too!"

"I really like Todd," Amina said.

Rasheeda leaned back in her seat, a wide grin filling her face. "Daddy chose good!"

Amina and Harper both laughed.

"You're not wearing your face veil," Harper said. "Is that because you're engaged?"

Rasheeda shook her head. She ran her hand along the folds of her hijab. "I didn't want to anymore. Todd didn't have any problems with it and Father said it was my choice. I won't give up my hijab though."

"I really like the color of the one you're wearing," Amina said. "That shade of green is gorgeous on you."

"I think green is going to be one of my wedding colors."

"It is pretty," Harper added as she pulled behind the bakery into her parking space.

Rasheeda called the woman's name as she leaned even farther forward between the two. Harper met her gaze in her rearview mirror.

"Yes?"

"I want to ask if you'll be one of my bridesmaids?"

Harper tossed her hands up excitedly. "Of course! Yes!"

The three women squealed as Rasheeda kissed Harper's cheek. Exiting the car the trio entered through the rear door, their excitement leading the way. Quentin and Troy were in the kitchen, the two men chatting as Quentin pulled pans of pastry from the ovens. The women's animation stalled their conversation.

"Your wife is hungry," Harper said, nodding her head at Troy.

Troy laughed. "Cheesecake or cookies?"

Amina rolled her eyes.

"She wants both," Rasheeda interjected.

"She worked hard tonight," Harper said as the two women retold what had happened at class.

Troy shook his head. "You're becoming quite the rebel, woman!"

Amina eased her arms around his waist and kissed his lips. "Well, this rebel is tired and she needs to sit down," she said. She led the way through the bakery to one of the front tables.

Minutes later Quentin placed a platter of cookies and one slice of cake on the table. He slid the cake directly in front of Amina. The smell of freshly brewing coffee billowed through the room.

"Where's my cheesecake?" Troy asked.

His brother laughed. "Your wife is pregnant. I'm going to let her eating all the profits slide. You're not so lucky."

Troy tilted his head, his eyes meeting Harper's. His sister-in-law laughed heartily. "Am I not a joint owner of this business?" he asked. "Don't I own this property too?"

Amina's eyes suddenly widened. "Oh, my gosh! I completely forgot."

Harper busted out laughing, understanding shining in her eyes. The two women looked at each other and Amina started to shake.

Quentin shook his head. "Amina, I can understand you forgetting and we forgive you. Troy on the other hand doesn't have any excuse."

"What?" Troy said, looking confused.

Harper fanned a hand at him. "Technically, Amina owns the property."

Amina looked flustered, her head shaking from

side to side "No, no, no! Rachel redid the deeds. I just need to file them!"

Troy shook his head. He'd completely forgotten about the title transfer. He looked at Amina. "I should have known you were a gold digger!"

Tears suddenly misted Amina's eye. "No, no, no! Really, I would never do that!"

Harper reached out and grabbed her hand.

"Don't cry!" Rasheeda exclaimed. "They were just teasing you!"

"We were just teasing you," Quentin confirmed. "I'm sorry."

Troy wrapped his arms around his wife's shoulders. "Baby, it's okay. It was a joke!"

"It was a bad joke," Amina sniffled. "You all are my family and I wouldn't do that!"

Troy nodded. "We know that and we know you've had some things going on. Trust me, if it was a problem, Rachel would have schooled all of us!"

Amina swiped at her eyes, brushing away the tears that had fallen over her cheeks.

"I'm sorry," Harper mouthed, meeting Troy's look.

He nodded. "Hormones!" he mouthed back.

Amina reached for her cake, taking a bite. She savored the sweetness, everything feeling good again. "And don't be whispering about me, Troy Elliott. I am not hormonal!"

Troy tossed everyone a look, his eyebrows raised, and laughter rang warmly through the room.

The family spent another hour talking and laughing. Quentin was the first to check the time.

"I need to get back to work, family. I have two cakes to get done before morning."

"We need to run too," Troy said. "We need to get

Rasheeda home and Amina is about to be late for her curfew."

Amina laughed. "I'm good now. I've had cookies and cheesecake. My hormones are back in sync."

Harper laughed. "You are too funny!"

Hugs and kisses closed out the evening. As Troy led his two ladies to the car, opening the doors for them both, Rasheeda noticed the car parked down the street, something not feeling quite right about it. She would have sworn that she'd seen that car before, even thinking that it had been parked in the lot at the cultural center. She hesitated before getting into Troy's car, staring intently. Troy looked down the street toward where she stared.

"Is something wrong?" he asked.

Rasheeda shook her head. "No. I don't think so."

"Are you sure?"

She shrugged her shoulders. "It's probably nothing," she said as she eased herself into the backseat and Troy closed the door after her.

Nasser was waiting up for her when she came into the house. Rasheeda rounded her father's desk to give him a hug.

"Did you have a nice time?"

She nodded. "Class went really well and then we had cookies at the bakery. Troy and Amina brought me home."

"How is your sister doing?"

"She's good. She actually fell asleep on the ride home. Troy was going to wake her so she could come inside and say hello, but I told him to let her rest."

"I'll call and check on her tomorrow."

"You should go to her house to see her, Father. Amina would like that. She and Troy have a very nice home."

Nasser nodded. "Maybe we can go together?"

His daughter gave him a warm smile. "That would be fun!"

"I went to see your brother today," Nasser said.

Rasheeda's smile faded abruptly. She shook her head. "Good night, Father. I'm going up to bed." She moved quickly toward the door.

"Rasheeda!"

With a deep sigh, Rasheeda turned to stare at her father. She met the look he was giving her with one of her own. She had no interest in hearing about Basil. Rasheeda swore that if she never heard his name again it wouldn't bother her. She couldn't understand why her father had such a hard time accepting that.

"You need to forgive Basil, Rasheeda. He's your brother."

"You've already done that for all of us, Father."

"He's my son. And I have to acknowledge my responsibility in his wrongdoing."

"How are you responsible for Basil's bad behavior?"

Nasser took a deep breath, crossing his hands in front of his chest. "When you were all little children your mother tried to make me understand that I needed to allow you to express yourselves. To have a voice of your own. I was raised in a culture that said you did as you were told and nothing more. I was wrong to think that my way was the only way. I did you all a great disservice. I was also too focused on you never failing but I'm learning that if you don't fail it means you haven't tried. Basil was wrong, make no mistake about that, but he allowed his fear of disappointing me rule him."

"Which is what ended up happening anyway. He disappointed us all."

"He did, but even your brother is deserving of forgiveness. He has acknowledged his failings and has pledged to make amends. Love is redemptive, daughter, which is why Allah tells us to love."

"I don't know that I will ever forgive Basil for what he did to me. For what he allowed that man to do to me and Amina."

Nasser nodded. "I am so sorry for that. I should have known. I should have protected you. I failed you and Amina, and you both deserved better from me. One day I hope that you will find it in your heart to forgive me and your brother."

Rasheeda didn't bother to reply. There was an awkward silence shifting between them.

Nasser moved onto his feet, sauntering to her side. "I am going to miss you after you marry. I spoke to your mother and she is very excited about having you and Todd with her. He called this afternoon to check on you as well. I like him. He's a good man. And he loves you."

She smiled again, her head bobbing ever so slightly. "I'm glad that you and Mother are talking. It will make things easier when Amina has the baby. We can all be a family."

Nasser nodded his agreement. "Things will continue to get better. I promise you that."

Rasheeda took a deep breath. She turned to leave

the room but hesitated, turning back to meet his stare. "Father, do you ever regret that you let Mother go?"

Nasser paused momentarily to consider her question. Moving to her side he leaned to kiss her cheek. "I have many regrets, Daughter."

A little while later Rasheeda crawled into her bed. She reached for her electronic reader, turning on the device. As the unit powered on she couldn't help but think about her father and her sister and everything that had happened to them over the past few months. Change had been a good thing in more ways than she could have ever imagined.

She would miss her father, too. More than he would ever realize. Her father had always loved her and she had trusted that when she had no trust for anyone or anything else. Her father's love had guided her steps and affirmed many of her decisions. His approval had always been paramount, even when what he wanted might not have been what she wanted for herself. But she was learning that she could bring her own dreams to fruition and still have her father love her.

A light outside the window drew her attention. Rasheeda reached for the lamp beside her bed and flicked off the switch. Tossing back the covers she threw her legs off the side and moved to the window. Peering through the blinds she saw a car slowly turning in the cul-de-sac. Its headlights had shone in the window briefly as the driver made the circle and headed in the opposite direction. For just a brief moment Rasheeda thought it might be the car from earlier. When she was certain it wasn't she exhaled the breath that she'd been holding. Staring after the car, she watched until the lights disappeared from view, then headed back to her bed.

Troy cleared his throat as he called for everyone to listen. Quentin turned down the volume on the flat-screen televisions in the dining room. They were minutes away from the final election results and as the numbers continued to scroll across the bottom of the screen, there was very little doubt about the outcome.

He waved his hand, gesturing for everyone's attention as people pushed forward for a better view, no one wanting to miss a word he said. Amina stood behind him, a bright smile across her face. She rested her hands against the blossoming bulge of her pregnant belly.

Their day had started early, the couple meeting Quentin and Harper at the bakery. The family had traveled together to the polls to cast their votes. After, Troy and Amina had gone from poll site to poll site to solicit last-minute support. After lunch they'd gone to campaign headquarters where Mike was helping to coordinate rides for registered voters. A team of volunteers had wrangled family and friends to assist their last-minute efforts and then Troy had corralled everyone over to the bakery to wait for the results.

Troy stepped to the podium and microphone that had been set up in the room. A low hush fell over the crowd. Cameras flashed and tape rolled as the local media recorded the moment for posterity. He took a deep breath and held it, tears misting his eyes before he shook the sensation. Amina clutched her hands together over her chest as Quentin wrapped one arm around her shoulder and the other around his wife. The two women gave each other a look as Harper hugged her husband around the waist.

"Thank you, Memphis. I am honored and humbled to represent this great city as your new mayor. A few minutes ago I spoke with Mayor Pete and I want to publicly acknowledge his service to this city. He served with great passion and commitment and has earned a special place in our hearts and our history. Tonight, we thank him for a lifetime of service to his beloved city, and wish him and his dear wife, Peggy, all the best in the future.

"What makes this victory most gratifying is that every corner of the city was represented in the votes. It's a victory not only for myself but for all of you who believe that a common set of challenges must be met with common purpose. It's a victory for all those who know that we can overcome all things that have held Memphis back. Together, we will not allow our differences to become divisions.

"After five months of campaigning across this city I know that our greatness will be found in all of you. We will move forward together, as one city with one future, and it's all of you, who share a love for this city, and a determination to keep it strong, who will help me make this great city even greater.

"I want to thank all my opponents, and their supporters. Our goals were mutual, to make this city work for all its people. I look forward to drawing on their insights, energy, and experience in the years to come. I also want to reach out tonight to the members of the next City Council. We have the chance for a new partnership that will serve our city and its taxpayers well.

So thank you, Memphis, for this vote of confidence in our future.

"Many of you remember my father, Everett Donovan. It was Pop's love for his city that nurtured my own. I wish that he could be here tonight to share in this moment with me. I know that if it had not been for him I would not be the man who comes ready and able to serve you today.

"Lastly, I want to say to my wife, Amina, I love you and I could not do this without your love and support. Thank you, as well, to Mr. Mike Chamberlain and my campaign committee. You have all been a great source of strength. Let's continue our work together to make sure Memphis remains the greatest city on earth. Thank you."

The room erupted in applause. Turning, Troy opened his arms as Amina stepped into them. She reached to kiss his lips as he hugged her tightly. From his seat in the corner, Nasser nodded his approval. Rasheeda grinned widely as she reached for his hand, squeezing it gently.

People were coming and going most of the evening as they celebrated Troy's win. It was close to midnight when the crowd had thinned out enough for the family to finally sit down together. Troy, Amina, Harper, Quentin, Rachel, Dwayne, Miss Alice, and Baby Joanna all joined Nasser and Rasheeda at tables pulled together.

"Mayor Elliott!" Harper squealed excitedly.

"I am just so proud of you," Miss Alice chimed.

"Me too," Quentin added.

Troy nodded. "I couldn't have done this without all of you here supporting me," he said. "All of you." He met Nasser's gaze, giving the man a quick nod. His father-in-law smiled and nodded back.

"We have a lot to be thankful for," Miss Alice said. "You all have had some challenges but you stood by each other, loved each other, and you never forgot that you were family. You did what family does." Tears rained from her eyes.

Troy leaned to kiss her cheeks.

Miss Alice swiped at her eyes. "Mr. Salman," she said, tossing him a sly smile. "Would you do me a favor, please?"

Nasser smiled. "Yes, ma'am."

Her question was more a command. "Would you say a prayer for us? A prayer of thanks?" She gestured for them all to take hands and bow their heads.

Nasser smiled. "I'd be delighted."

25

Court lasted less than ten minutes. Their wait for Basil's case to be called took longer than the actual time he spent before the judge. Both the prosecutor and the defense attorney filed legal motions for the judge's consideration and a date for trial was set. Rasheeda and Amina had sat in a back row. Rasheeda had refused to sit in the seats behind the defense table, Basil being too close for her comfort.

As the judge called the next case Nasser hugged his son before the bailiff stepped in to separate them. Basil had stared in their direction, even venturing to toss his hand up to wave. Rasheeda only appraised him, her expression like ice. Amina tossed him a slight wave back. The two sisters eyed each other but neither bothered to comment. It would be another forty-five days before they would have to come back for the start of jury selection and Basil's trial getting under way.

In the parking lot of the courthouse Nasser thanked his daughters for coming. "Your brother asked me to tell you both how sorry he is for everything that has happened."

Amina cut an eye toward Rasheeda. Her baby sister's expression was blank. Forgiveness was not coming easily, if it was coming at all. Knowing how sensitive her father was about the situation, she was trying her best to help them each understand what the other was feeling. Their agreeing to disagree took on new meaning. She blew a deep sigh.

"Where are you two off to?" Nasser asked, looking from one to the other.

"I have a doctor's appointment. After that I have a legal brief that has to be written before the end of the day. So, I'll be headed to the office," Amina noted.

"I'm volunteering at the women's center today," Rasheeda said.

Nasser nodded as he pointed to his car. "Well, this is me. You both be safe and I will check on you later," he said. He leaned to kiss one and then the other.

Rasheeda shook her head as he pulled out of the space. "Does he understand that we aren't here to show Basil support?"

Amina shook her head. "He only knows that his family is together. He hopes the rest will work itself out."

"I don't know how to stop being angry at him, Amina. I'm so angry at Basil that I can't see straight sometimes."

Amina drew her hand across her sister's back. "I'll tell you like Troy told me. Pray on it."

Rasheeda nodded. "I do . . ." she started, her words cut off abruptly.

She saw him as he suddenly stepped from that familiar car, the dark sedan parked directly beside Amina's. The color drained from her face as he moved to Amina's side, sliding an arm around her sister's torso. His hand clutched her shoulder, his forearm resting just below her throat.

She called his name, the word muttered with a surprised breath. "Kareem."

He snarled, a harsh bend of his mouth that twisted his face. "So you haven't forgotten your husband-to-be."

"You were never going to be my husband," Rasheeda snapped.

Kareem's hand stroked the side of Amina's face. "I would have married you had you not been so defiant."

"Take your hands off me," Amina hissed.

Kareem grabbed her by the throat. Rasheeda took a step forward. "You don't want to do that," he said. His gaze was narrowed as he glared. "I would hate to see something happen to Amina and her baby." He tightened his grip. "Because I will snap her neck!" There seemed to be a standoff as he and Rasheeda glared at each other. He finally relaxed his grip and Amina gasped for air.

"What do you want?"

Kareem shot a quick glance around then. An officer from the sheriff's department stood off in the distance smoking a cigarette, and there was a young woman lost in conversation on the cell phone. No one was paying them an ounce of attention.

He turned back to stare at them both. He'd been watching them for days. First one, and then the other. Both had been oblivious to his presence, believing that he had disappeared in the wind. And he had. But instead of staying gone, he'd come back to claim what he believed was rightfully his. Where Basil had failed him, he planned to be successful. Rasheeda had been promised to him and he had every intention of claiming her. Amina would pay the penalty for having gotten in their way.

"We're going for a ride," he said. "I want you both to get in that car."

Amina shook her head. "We're not going anywhere with you."

"You'll do what I tell you."

"What happens if we go with you?" Rasheeda asked.

"I'm thinking the new mayor and his father-in-law will pay nicely to get Amina back. Her being with child, and all."

"No one's paying you any ransom," Amina chastised.

He hugged her closer to his body. "Too bad. You're not what I want anyway. I came back for Rasheeda. I came back for my wife."

"I am not your wife!" Rasheeda suddenly shouted.

Kareem's eyes widened. "You dare to talk back to me?" He suddenly released the grip he had on Amina, his hand raised as if he planned to strike her sister.

Muscle memory and instincts kicked in as the sisters both remembered their self-defense training. Kareem wasn't expecting the harsh slam to his midsection as Amina threw an elbow into his stomach before moving out of his reach, or Rasheeda suddenly crushing his nose with the heel of her palm. He was completely thrown off guard and in shock. He grabbed his face with both hands as blood gushed from his nostrils. He was still standing until one of the sisters slammed a booted heel into his kneecap and he lost his footing, hitting the ground with a loud thud.

Rasheeda tossed Amina a look of concern as she waved her hands above her head, shouting for attention. In seconds, law enforcement came running and

Kareem was surrounded by police. With their guns drawn they handcuffed the man, taking him into custody. Amina and Rasheeda stood clinging to each other as they struggled to calm their nerves. They were both relieved to know Kareem was finally headed to jail.

As two officers pulled him to his feet, Kareem eyed them both with contempt, his face twisted with rage. Rasheeda's gaze narrowed, her own anger still abundant. Before anyone could stop her she raised her hand and delivered a back-handed slap to the side of Kareem's cheek. She was ready to slap him a second time when Amina grabbed her arm and pulled her back.

"He deserved that," Rasheeda said, meeting her sister's stare.

Amina smiled, a soft chuckle easing past her lips. She nodded her head in agreement.

Amina lay across the bed, her body curled around an oversize pillow. Her muscles were tight, her joints sore. It had been a long day and she imagined it would be a longer night once Troy found his way home. Kareem's arrest had come with a host of questions, one police officer after another wanting to hear in detail what had happened in the parking lot. Every question was followed by the same answers, repeated over and over again. For a brief moment an eager sergeant had threatened to charge them both with assault for the minor bruises on Kareem's person. Rachel's timely arrival had put a quick end to the interrogation, both women finally permitted to go home.

Troy had been at the Governor's Mansion in Oak

Hill, attending the first of many political obligations. With his being four hours away, Amina had hoped to keep the news from him until he returned home. A scrupulous reporter hoping to land a scoop broke the news when he'd asked Troy for comment. For most of the afternoon it was a breaking story that played out on every local news channel and media outlet in the state of Tennessee.

They'd played phone tag for most of the afternoon and then Amina's phone battery had died. Amina knew he was probably beside himself with worry being unable to talk to her. She clutched the pillow closer and closed her eyes, needing to rest for just a quick moment before Troy found his way home.

It was close to eleven P.M. when Troy pushed his key into the door lock. He called Amina's name but there was no answer. The house was eerily quiet. Moving swiftly through the home, he found her sound asleep in the bedroom. She was snoring softly. One leg was thrown over the body pillow and she had kicked the blankets from around her body. Her bare legs peeked past an oversize T-shirt, the comfortable garment stretched over her growing girth. Looking down on her he breathed the only sigh of relief he'd had all day.

She was beautiful, a sense of peace painting her expression. She shifted ever so slightly and a low snort blew past her lips. Troy chuckled softly beneath his breath. Moving quietly, he took off his clothes, dropping them to the floor. He crawled into the bed, easing his body against hers. She was warm, her skin feeling like a warm blanket against his. He eased one arm beneath her head and the other around her tummy. A muscle quivered and the hint of new life beneath his palm awed him.

Amina snuggled her buttocks in the pocket of his crotch and he pressed a light kiss to the back of her neck. In the beginning there had been no one and nothing to distract him. He'd set a goal and accomplished it. Now he had Amina and soon a son, both the biggest distractions he could have ever imagined. For the first time he knew what his brother had felt when he'd known nothing could have kept him from Harper, not even the souls who had insisted they shouldn't be together.

And he understood the many lessons his beloved Pop had spent years teaching them. Family would always come first. Love would fix most challenges. Trust was imperative. And no matter what the meal, just desserts would easily soothe any soul.

Amina rolled into his arms. Her pregnant belly kissed the hard lines of his six-pack. She nuzzled her face in the soft cusp beneath his chin, kissing his flesh. "We missed you," she whispered as she snuggled against him.

"I missed you, too."

"I tried to wait up."

"I know."

"I love you, Troy."

"I love you, too!"

She suddenly smiled, rising up slightly. She reached for his hand and pulled it to her stomach.

"What's wrong?" Troy questioned, concern pulling at his eyes.

"There!" she exclaimed. "Did you feel it?"

Troy grinned, his smile wide. "He kicked!"

She nodded as she closed her eyes, sleep pulling her back as she whispered softly. "He wants a chocolate cookie!"

Don't miss the first book in the Just Desserts series,

The Sweetest Thing

Available now at your local bookstore!

1

Quentin Elliott suddenly grabbed the pastry dough he'd been kneading and flung it across the room, watching as it slammed harshly against the brick wall. On the other side of the space Troy Elliott paused, his own gaze moving from the wet dough sliding toward the polished concrete floor to his baby brother's face. Tears misted Quentin's eyes, stealing past his forest-thick lashes to roll down his cheeks.

"Do you feel better?" Troy asked casually.

Quentin shrugged his broad shoulders as he swiped at his eyes with his forearm. "Who is she? And why didn't Pop ever talk about her?"

Staring at his computer screen and the document he'd been working on, Troy paused momentarily before answering. "You know exactly what I know, Quentin. Maybe she'll be able to tell us why her father never told us anything about her."

"I just want to know why he'd leave her in control of the bakery. Didn't he trust us?"

"I don't think this has anything to do with trust, baby brother. Harper Donovan was his blood."

Quentin bristled. "But we were his family," he said defiantly, meeting his brother's intense stare. "Where was she when he was sick?"

Troy sighed deeply. "We may never know, Quentin. We can only hope and pray that everything works out when it's all said and done."

Quentin paused, his own stare moving back to the pastry that had puddled in a thick lump on the floor. "I miss him already," the man whispered loudly.

Troy nodded. "I miss Pop, too," he answered. "Now, clean up your mess and get back to work. Until she gets here we still have a business to run."

"He left you a sweatshop?"

Harper Donovan rolled her eyes skyward, meeting her best friend's gaze. Jasmine Holt's dubious expression almost made her laugh out loud. Almost. She shook her head and frowned instead. "A *sweet* shop!" Harper exclaimed. "*Sweet!* It's a pastry, bakery thing."

Jasmine's eyes widened with understanding. "Ohhh! Okay, that makes so much more sense." She paused for a split second. "So, what are you going to do with a *sweet* shop? And, one in Memphis, Tennessee, of all places?"

Harper shrugged her narrow shoulders, feigning indifference. "I don't want it. I don't want anything from him." She stared down at the certified letter that rested in her lap.

News of her father's death had come three days earlier, that letter detailing the date and time of his homegoing service. A telephone call from his attorney earlier that afternoon had confirmed her attendance and informed her of her inheritance. Since learning of her father's passing Harper hadn't been able to focus on much of anything. And now all she wanted was to ignore it all until it went away.

"You might not want it but you still have to deal with settling his estate," Jasmine reasoned, dropping down onto the sofa beside her.

Harper shook her head as she pulled her manicured fingers through the length of her short pixie haircut. "No, I don't. I really don't have to do anything I don't want to do. And right now I'm not interested in dealing with anything Everett Donovan had to do with."

The conversation was interrupted by Harper's maternal grandmother, the matriarch clearing her throat as she moved into the room and took a seat in her favorite chair. She tapped her cane harshly against the hardwood floor.

"You will not disrespect your father," the old woman admonished. "The man's dead and you owe him better than that."

"Mama Pearl, I'm not disrespecting him," Harper countered. "I didn't know him well enough to disrespect him."

"That wasn't all his fault," Pearl Townes answered. "Your mama had a lot to do with that."

"Maybe, but what was his excuse after my mama died?" Harper questioned.

The matriarch met her granddaughter's gaze. "Good question. It's one you need to ask yourself."

"You say that like it was my fault!"

"Harper, I imagine between your mama and all her evilness, and you just being ugly for no good reason, refusing to meet him halfway every time he reached out, that you two put that poor man through some things."

Harper rolled her eyes. "I didn't put him through anything," she said defiantly.

Mama Pearl scoffed. "Okay," she said, her head bobbing up and down.

"I didn't!" Harper insisted.

"Maybe not," Mama Pearl countered as she wagged her index finger in Harper's direction, "but I done told you time and time again that you and your mama both were wrong. When you had the chance to do better you should have. Now it's too late."

"I cannot believe you're blaming me!"

The old woman blew a deep sigh, her head waving from side to side. "No one is blaming anyone, Harper. I'm just saying that now is not the time to disrespect your daddy's memory with your foolishness."

Harper threw herself back against the sofa cushions, her lips pushed into a full pout. She crossed her arms over her chest.

Jasmine laughed softly. "So, when do you leave for Tennessee?"

Harper shrugged her shoulders a second time. "I don't know. I really don't want to go but . . ." She hesitated as she cut an eye in her grandmother's direction.

Mama Pearl interjected. "She's leaving tomorrow morning 'cause her daddy's funeral is on Thursday. And you will not miss your daddy's funeral," she said firmly, leaning forward in her seat to meet Harper's stare.

"But I don't want—" Harper started, her voice rising.

Mama Pearl cut her off midsentence. "You don't

get to say this time, Harper. *I'm* saying. You will honor your father by going to his funeral. Are we clear?"

Harper stared back, both women knowing just how much Harper hated the thought of attending any funeral. Something out of turn always happened when her family was sending off a dearly departed. If it wasn't some relative's bad behavior, it was a family secret being spilled because some cousin or uncle talked out of turn. Family weddings weren't much better.

At the last family gathering it was Harper's cousin Tuck whose tongue got to flapping around before anyone could stop him. The occasion had been Harper's mother's funeral where her aunt Bernice's third child found out Tyrone Taylor wasn't his daddy. Tyrone had only fathered Bernice's first two children, before Bernice had gotten into the bad habit of hopping from bed to bed across the great state of Louisiana. And although everyone knew Ullman James was the little boy's daddy, no one had ever dared to speak it out loud. No one until Tuck said something while they'd all been standing together in Hyco Zion Baptist Church's fellowship hall and Bernice's little boy just happened to be standing by her side. The ensuing drama still had family not talking to one another. Harper didn't want to begin to think about the secrets that might come out at her father's funeral.

"Tch!" The young woman sucked her teeth, her eyes spinning skyward as she threw her torso back against the couch for the second time.

"Girl, if you roll your eyes at me one more time," Mama Pearl admonished, shaking her cane in Harper's direction. "You will never be that grown!"

Her eyes wide with amusement, Jasmine repeated her question. "So, when will you be leaving?"

Harper sighed, blowing warm breath past her full lips. She looked over at her friend and tossed up her hands in frustration. "I guess I'm leaving tomorrow morning."